Seven for a Secret

Books by Mary Reed and Eric Mayer

Seven for a Secret

Mary Reed & Eric Mayer

Poisoned Pen Press

Poisoned
Pen
Press

Poisoned Pen Press
6962 E. First Ave., Ste. 103
Scottsdale, AZ 85251
www.poisonedpenpress.com
info@poisonedpenpress.com

Printed in the United States of America

For our parents

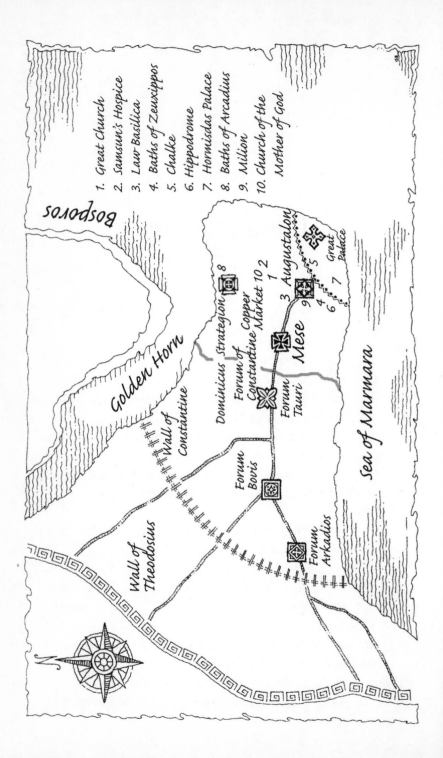

Bosporos

1. Great Church
2. Samsun's Hospice
3. Law Basilica
4. Baths of Zeuxippos
5. Chalke
6. Hippodrome
7. Hormisdas Palace
8. Baths of Arcadius
9. Milion
10. Church of the Mother of God

Golden Horn

Wall of Constantine

Wall of Theodosius

Dominicus strategion 8

Forum of Constantine

Copper Market 10 2

Augustalon

1

3 Mese

5 Great Palace

9 4

6 7

Forum Tauri

Forum Bovis

Forum Arkadios

Sea of Marmara

Chapter One

For once, the girl in the wall mosaic did not reply to the Lord Chamberlain's question.

"Why, Zoe?" John asked again.

Did her lips tighten?

No, it was only an effect of the unsteady light from the lamp that sputtered on the desk of his study.

Usually he could discern an answer to his questions, but not tonight.

He heard the creak of a footstep in the hall and glanced toward the doorway in time to see a retreating shadow.

Peter.

John's habit of talking to the mosaic girl distressed his elderly servant, though he did so often enough late at night.

But never before about an event like this.

Perhaps Peter had intended to refill the lamp or replenish the wine jug. Hearing his master's voice, he had discreetly returned to the kitchen.

John took a sip from his clay cup. "I overheard Peter discussing you with Cornelia. He called you a little demon, Zoe. Whoever you are, you aren't a demon, are you?"

If she were, it might explain what had happened that morning.

Zoe remained silent. She stared gravely from one corner of the busy bucolic scene on the study wall. She looked seven or eight. Her dark, polished eyes were older. They had seen much.

Had they seen into John's memories?

What she did not see—for her gaze never wavered—was the debauchery in the cut glass skies above her. The mosaic maker had angled the tesserae so that what appeared by daylight to be clouds were transformed by lamplight into riotous pagan deities.

John got up from his chair and carried his cup to the half opened window. From the barracks on the other side of the torch-lit square below came shouts and oaths, the greetings of military colleagues.

Familiar echoes from a former life.

John was a shade, a formless reflection in the diamond panes, looking out from a gray underworld at his own past.

Egyptian wine always brought the memories back for it was in Egypt he had first tasted its rawness. He swallowed another mouthful and felt the hot Alexandrian sun at the back of his throat.

He knew he should be cautious and recruit a few of those excubitors across the way to accompany him to his meeting.

He knew, also, he would not.

He sat down again in the uncomfortable wooden chair beside the simple desk. Nothing in the room's spartan furnishings marked it as a part of the dwelling of the Lord Chamberlain to Emperor Justinian. The all but unfurnished room was large enough to house several working families and the cunning mosaic must have cost the former occupant of the place—a long since deposed tax collector—more than a laborer could earn in years.

"You say nothing now, Zoe," John muttered, "but I expect you will explain it all to me eventually. Perhaps even that strange tattoo on your wrist."

In truth, while conversing with the mosaic girl, John often managed to explain puzzles to himself.

He glanced at the bowl of the water clock beside the door. Dawn was hours away. Although the heat of late summer lingered in the air, the hours of this particular night seemed as long as those of midwinter.

Earlier that day he had risen before dawn as usual, before Cornelia had awakened.

"I walked to the Mese. The air was chilly. The seasons are changing."

John spoke softly. He did not want to disturb Peter again. He described to Zoe, or perhaps to himself, how he had continued across the expanse of the Augustaion, all but deserted at that hour except for scavenging seabirds and the occasional heap of rags marking a sleeping beggar, past the Great Church whose dome glowed faintly from within against the lightening sky, and through the forum of the Law Basilica where the sellers and copiers of books clustered their shops.

Laggard carts rattled toward the city gates. He was up with the dogs. The gaunt beasts loped through the long shadows, nosed whatever refuse they could find in gutters and corners. When the sun had risen and carts were forbidden, the dogs could safely lie on the warm cobbles in the middle of the streets.

The cries of gulls, muted by distance, accentuated the emptiness. Mist rose from the pavements as if from a gray sea.

He could smell the sea.

His morning walks were longer since Cornelia had come to stay. He had never imagined they could be reunited and had grown used to his solitude. He was ever aware of her presence in his house.

He turned aside into the area known as the Copper Market. In the early morning light, lavender plumes of smoke from unseen furnaces rose above low brick buildings. From doorways and alleys there came acrid smells, unidentifiable to one who worked in ceremony and diplomacy rather than metal or glass.

During the past few weeks he had extended his morning walk to an unnamed square no different than scores of others in the city. Grates were still pulled down in front of its shops. A Christian holy man kept his endless vigil from a broad platform atop a pillar at one end of the open space.

The stylite stood motionless, gazing over flat rooftops in the direction of Mithra's rising sun. There was no one to observe the man, except for John and the gulls and the stray dogs. After a while a hooded acolyte emerged from the doorway in the base of the column and left the square, giving only a passing glance to the tall, thin man waiting nearby. No doubt it was not unusual for pilgrims to take up vigils near the pillar.

When the square was empty again John looked up toward the stylite but movement drew his gaze back to earth. His years as a mercenary were far in the past, but he retained the keen alertness of a guard on watch at the border of the empire.

A figure emerged from a doorway among the shops. Not the acolyte. The figure moved in John's direction.

It was no accident, John realized.

Although the Lord Chamberlain's plain indigo cloak, by its cut and fabric, marked him as a man who should not be on the street without a bodyguard, he had never been attacked. There was something in his bearing which convinced predators to wait for easier prey.

Or maybe, as his young friend Anatolius warned, it was only that Fortuna had smiled on him up until now, or else he had been spared by his old servant's God, as Peter insisted. He knew he did not have Mithra to thank, because Mithra was not the sort of deity who looked out for those who wouldn't look out for themselves.

His short blade was in his hand by the time he saw that the attacker was merely a woman. A street whore. Or so he thought, until she drew near enough for him to make out the shabby but once elegant robes and the purple shadow of the veil obscuring her face.

She spoke in a breathless, hasty whisper. "Come here tomorrow at the same hour. I have information. There's no time now."

She had looked around, as if panic stricken, and turned to leave.

John lifted the cup again. Not as far as his lips.

The lamp on the desk guttered and went out.

He could still see the mosaic girl. Her eyes glittered in the dim light from the window.

"Normally, I wouldn't have taken the encounter seriously, Zoe," he told her. "It was obviously some sort of mistake or a trick. But as she turned, I asked the woman who she was. She paused and pushed her veil aside just for an instant, long enough for me to confirm that what she said was the truth.

"Don't you recognize me, Lord Chamberlain? I am Zoe!"

Chapter Two

"If she really was the girl in the mosaic, John, it appears she's not going to get down off the wall this morning." Anatolius looked away from the square and squinted up in the direction of the stylite's column. John followed his gaze.

The sun sat above the cramped shelter into which the stylite had retired after performing his customary ablutions. John could discern the man's rigid form through a window cut into the planks.

"I see he's not one of those holy men who braves the elements day and night," Anatolius continued. "I thought suffering was part of the job. No wonder his column is in this out of the way corner."

The stylite's hooded acolyte had set baskets at the base of the pillar. No pilgrims had come by yet to drop offerings into them.

John and Anatolius had been waiting since before dawn. In the interim John had remained almost as still as the stylite, while Anatolius paced back and forth.

At first, John had been on edge. A ghostly swirl of mist or a shout carried from the docks on the early morning breeze made his heart race. Was it in anticipation of an ambush or simply of meeting Zoe and learning whatever it was she needed to tell him?

The woman who had so urgently requested an irregular audience with the Lord Chamberlain never appeared.

"I don't want to interfere with your work, Anatolius," John finally said. "Your clients will be waiting."

John's friend was a few years his junior, almost as slender, not quite as tall. He had a face Greek sculptors would have loved to model, and more than a few ladies of the imperial court who didn't know Polyclitus from Praxiteles shared their enthusiasm.

"I do have an appointment this morning," Anatolius admitted. "I'm finding people like the notion of hiring the emperor's former secretary to speak for them. The merchant I'm seeing today apparently thinks that if I could put a good face on Justinian's confiscatory proclamations—as he put it—I can surely turn the shipload of spoiled wine he sold into nectar. Spoiled, that is to say, according to the buyer. I don't like to leave you alone."

John scanned the square again. Merchants who dealt in quantities smaller than shiploads were opening their shops. An iron grating rose with an ear-splitting screech, letting loose the odor of yesterday's fish.

Nearer the palace the fragrances of spices or perfumes wafting from the doorways of better class emporiums alleviated the city's usual stench of decayed rubbish and animal droppings. In the Copper Market with its metal works, the other pervasive smell was that of acrid smoke.

A black dog slunk by and paused to sniff a cucumber crushed beneath a cart wheel.

At this point any sense of peril had been borne off with the mists by the light of day.

"I did not suppose I would be in danger in the first place, Anatolius. Besides, it's a lengthy walk back."

Anatolius gazed in the general direction of the Great Palace. "We'd have been better off if we waited at your doorway, in case Zoe came out! If you make these morning strolls any longer you'll find yourself neck deep in the Golden Horn!"

"You can be certain I'll stop a safe distance from the shore."

"A few weeks ago I would have been equally certain you'd never walk into a trap set by a stranger who approached on the street!"

"We have not been attacked."

"Of course not. The ruffians weren't prepared to deal with two men."

John pointed out that the woman might have returned if Anatolius had remained discreetly in the nearby alleyway as requested.

"I've already explained why I rushed out, John. I thought I saw something moving in your direction in the dark."

John's lips tightened into a thin smile. "I believe I could adequately defend myself against a three-legged cat. You should try not to become agitated so easily. It's a trait that won't serve you well before the magistrates."

"It seems to me you've been uncharacteristically agitated lately. How can you tell me you feel crowded in that enormous house with no one else there but Cornelia and a servant, anyway? I wish I hadn't suggested Europa and Thomas move to my Uncle Zeno's estate. Cornelia would probably be glad of their help. She told me she was planning to redecorate a few rooms."

John frowned. "I can arrange for any craftsmen needed, and frankly I'm happier with my daughter and her husband away from the palace. A Lord Chamberlain will always have enemies at court, and they'll use any weapon they can find."

Anatolius glanced around. "I suspect this square rarely bustles with activity, but there are people stirring now. Are you going to insist on staying longer? Your enemies won't necessarily confine themselves to harming your family, John."

John acknowledged the truth of this statement.

"Just because she used the name Zoe means nothing," Anatolius continued. "Everyone at court knows everyone else's business even if we don't come out and say so. Remember that poem I wrote about Theodora's days on the stage? I only showed it to a few close friends. I swear by Mithra that the court pages were repeating the last verse before the ink was dry."

"I saw the woman's face, Anatolius. She was Zoe."

"I admit the artisan made the child remarkably life-like but—"

"I've lived with that face for nearly ten years," John cut in. "Yesterday morning I met the original. Grown now, of course, but she was unmistakable."

"What about the tattoo? You said she had a tattoo on her wrist. You saw it when she pushed her veil aside. Now, you have to admit your mosaic Zoe doesn't have a tattoo."

John observed a child would not have a tattoo although a woman might, and that further he felt Anatolius was overreaching himself trying to find evidence against the possibility John had, in fact, by chance met the model for Zoe.

Anatolius shook his head. "If I didn't know better I'd say you were smitten with the woman. We should've arrived here with a contingent of excubitors ready to scour the streets, find the scoundrels who are behind this, and cart them off to the dungeons. Whatever their game is, I'd wager it's a crime, or would've been if—"

John held up a hand. "Wait, Anatolius."

A veiled woman in black robes moved toward them. She was only a few steps away. John cursed himself for allowing his attention to lapse.

When the woman reached the two men, she bowed slightly.

"Kindest excellencies! We are seeking to purchase a plaque for the Church of the Mother of God. It will be engraved with words to remind us of our beloved Empress Theodora's beneficence."

John produced several coins and dropped them into the woman's smooth hand.

She turned her head toward Anatolius. When he offered only a glare, she scurried away.

Anatolius stared after her in undisguised consternation. "What are you thinking about, John? That was nothing but a common street whore!"

"I could see that. It's not to say she doesn't need a few coins more than I do. Besides, how do you know she isn't one of Theodora's collection of reformed prostitutes? Your new profession is already turning you into a cynic, my friend!"

"That may be," Anatolius admitted. "But it's safer being a cynic. I'm not so sure all those prostitutes wanted to be reformed. They just wanted the free lodgings the empress was offering. Anyway, it's plain your mysterious woman isn't going to appear. Let's hope it was nothing more than a jest by some fool at court."

He looked around. "Yes, probably that's all it was. Someone in the palace playing a joke on the ever serious and imperturbable Lord Chamberlain. Doubtless, some rascals are sniggering about it right now. I have to be off. Don't waste much more time on this, John. There's nothing to it, but if you stand here long enough you're liable to attract trouble, especially after displaying a handful of coins."

Chapter Three

Anatolius paused at the mouth of the street and looked back into the square he had just left.

John remained standing at the base of the stylite's column.

Anatolius wondered if he should go back. He decided John would prefer to wait alone. Anatolius' client, on the other hand, would not appreciate waiting at all.

His way took him along a thoroughfare scarcely wide enough for two carts to pass each other. There were no colonnades and little shade. The second stories of the buildings projected outwards, almost meeting overhead in the narrower sections. Passing an archway, he walked through a sudden blast of heat emanating from the ovens of a baker or a glass maker's furnace.

He turned off onto another, narrower, way. Two men in grimy tunics brushed by him, staggering and trailing a miasma of smoke and wine. They were night laborers who'd stopped at a tavern on their way back to whatever place they called home.

Anatolius wasn't familiar with the area. He couldn't recall whether he had been on this particular street and John had not led him this way on their walk to the square. Nevertheless he headed unerringly and without hesitation in what he knew to be the direction of the Great Palace. Having always lived in

Constantinople, he was never lost. Perhaps it was something to do with the invisible map formed by the slope of the land, the direction of the breezes, the smell of the sea.

He had also learned to be ever alert.

Which is why the burly man about to step into a tavern did not escape his attention.

Anatolius noticed how the man turned his bearded face away quickly.

But not quickly enough.

"Felix!"

The bear-like head swung around slowly. "Anatolius! Must you announce my identity to the entire world?"

"If I'd wanted to do that I would have addressed you as Captain Felix." Anatolius managed an uneasy laugh.

Encountering Felix in front of a tavern was never lucky. It usually proved an evil omen, like a glimpse of a lone crow perched on a garden fountain. "It's more than likely the proprietor is already aware of your position at court, Felix," he continued, "not to mention boasting his patrons include the captain of Justinian's excubitors."

"If he didn't know before, he certainly knows now!"

At that early hour they had their choice of the few tables within the tavern. Felix sat with his back against a mosaic on the rear wall, a few strides from the door. The mosaic displayed a feast—assorted olives and cheeses, exotic fruits—an enticing pictorial menu of all that the establishment did not serve. The table could hardly accommodate both their wine cups at the same time, not that Felix bothered to put his down.

"You're in a bad humor today, Felix. Personal troubles? A lady?"

Felix frowned. "There's more to life than chasing women, difficult though you may find that to believe."

"My current mistress is the law. Haven't you heard?"

"Yes, of course. My apologies."

"So what is it that's troubling you, my friend?"

"Nothing. Nothing in particular, even though the plague carried off half my men and recruiting replacements is difficult to say the least. Men who like the feel of a weapon in their hands don't relish the prospect of standing idly next to imperial doorways waiting for a riot to break out."

"Now that the city's coming back to life, they might not have to wait for long. We'll be having enough riots again to suit their taste for action." Anatolius took a sip and grimaced. "Why, we can even expect decent wine to come on the market again soon."

Felix's mouth formed a slight smile, barely visible under his bushy mustache. "Whenever I drink swill like this it reminds me of when I was a young soldier. I made many a day's march on worse, I can tell you. But that was a long time ago. Justin was emperor. Now there was an emperor. A born soldier." He looked down into his cup. "The taste's enough to strangle the breath out of you," he concluded with grudging admiration.

"Like John's evil Egyptian stock. Maybe he likes it because it reminds him of when he was a young mercenary?"

"I haven't spoken to John for a while. Have you seen him lately? I heard he sent Thomas and Europa off to your uncle's estate."

Anatolius let his gaze wander over the flat fruit in the wall mosaic before speaking. He knew that John wouldn't thank him for alerting Felix to what Anatolius had already begin to think of as an embarrassing incident.

"It's true. Thomas is thriving as uncle's estate manager. He's actually very shrewd in his own way."

"But too naive in some ways. Constantinople's different than Bretania. It sounds like the best arrangement for everyone. The city's dangerous enough without having a family to worry about. Though the plague did thin the ranks of assassins along with my excubitors. It's been a long nightmare, but now we're waking up."

A shaft of light from the sunlit street had crept up the wall to illuminate an ornate bowl filled with bright orange and green striped melons of a sort Anatolius had never glimpsed, even on Justinian's banquet table.

"A nightmare," agreed Anatolius. "I'll never forget seeing grass growing in the streets, dwellings deserted, a smell all the perfume at the palace couldn't have conquered from the dead piled as high as if they'd stormed the Great Gate armed only with their teeth and nails."

"Give me a clean death, that's what I say," Felix muttered. "A soldier's death, not rotting from some vile disease. When I saw the plague ravaging the city I prayed to Mithra that I should not be carried away while lying in a soft bed, having accomplished nothing. Your words are eloquent! It sounds as if you're composing verse again."

"No, what I am composing is mostly wills. The plague reminded a great many people of the need for one."

"What an age we live in! Tragedy only inspires lawyers to scribble more documents. We have no Homers."

"Only those who fancy themselves Homers."

Felix grinned. "You're thinking of Crinagoras, aren't you? I hear at his latest reading a member of his unfortunate audience flung a cabbage at him. Hit a senator instead. Some passing beggar grabbed the cabbage before it had stopped rolling. Ran out of the place as if demons were after him. I suppose it became his evening meal. I don't blame him. I'd rather have a cabbage than a poem any day."

"Then you'd better avoid the baths this week. Crinagoras is planning another public appearance."

Felix stated it was a source of amazement to him that Crinagoras had not been set upon by disgruntled lovers of literature and carried off to be drowned in the tepidarium. Then he finished his wine and wiped his mouth with the back of his hand. "Do you know, wine always tastes better in a tavern than a well appointed atrium or an imperial reception hall? It was in taverns I learned to drink. Wasn't born to the palace. That's why I seek out places like this."

"I thought it might be to avoid anyone at the palace seeing you drinking, my friend, considering your history. Are you sure there isn't some woman troubling you?"

Felix grunted. "No. I am over that sort of thing. Like you. Don't worry about Bacchus and me either. We've made a truce. The line's been drawn. But you haven't told me what you're doing in this part of the city?"

Anatolius had set his empty cup down preparatory to leaving. He would have to hurry now to meet his client on time. He realized he was a bit lightheaded, the result of the raw wine, a lack of breakfast, too little sleep, and too much exercise so early in the morning. He thought of the two unsteady men he'd seen after leaving John.

Obscure squares in the Copper Market were hardly places for unguarded Lord Chamberlains. It did not matter if he had fallen victim to someone's idea of a jest, for the city was rife with real dangers.

A bunch of purple grapes stared at Anatolius over his companion's broad shoulder. He blinked and the face in the grapes went away. He could imagine a few more cups of wine and they might start speaking to him.

What if John insisted on pursuing the ridiculous matter further? Besides, Felix was bound to find out when the prankster began bragging—if indeed that's all it was.

Anatolius leaned forward and whispered, although they were alone in the tavern except for the proprietor. "Felix, I rely upon you to treat this as confidential, but who do you think John met the other day?"

"What do you mean? Some envoy perhaps? A Persian? A Goth?"

"No! I'm not talking about his job. It was Zoe from the mosaic in his study!"

"That's impossible!"

Anatolius nodded. "That's what I told him. And when we went to meet her again as arranged, she didn't appear."

Felix scratched his bearded chin. "John should consult a physician for a concoction to correct his humors. They must be unbalanced if he's starting to imagine things. What do you make of it? If John's in danger I should—"

"It's nothing but a prank. I'm certain of it." Anatolius immediately wished he'd said nothing. Mithra! He had as a bad a weakness for talking as Felix did for wine.

He recalled how he'd seen John last, waiting alone. He could imagine his reaction if a contingent of armed excubitors dispatched by Felix came rushing into the square.

"Forget I said anything, Felix. I can assure you, John's in no danger at all."

Chapter Four

John stepped away from the stylite's column to make room for a group of pilgrims.

The middle-aged men with peeling, sunburnt faces, their homely garments stiff with the dirt of a journey from the countryside, stared up toward the motionless holy man and put their fingertips to his granite pillar.

The sunlight felt hot. The finger-like shadow of the column fell across the square as if marking the hour. More passersby were in evidence. One or two beggars had stationed themselves near the pillar in order to take advantage of pious charity. The smell of fresh bread mingled with the acrid smoke that had begun to burn the back of John's throat, evidence of a bakery hidden amidst the forges and furnaces whose increasing clamor announced the beginning of a new day of labor.

The enticing odor reminded John that he had not eaten that morning. It was simply a fact to be noted. He was not a man who was driven by appetites.

Again he surveyed the square.

Perhaps Anatolius was right and Zoe was not going to appear.

The long watch was not difficult for John. During his years as a mercenary he had passed countless nights in Bretania, on guard in the chilly darkness at what had once been the edge of the empire. The nights had seemed countless at the time, but they were not, for now they were gone.

John's muscles remembered how to remain still but ready to respond immediately if attacked. He retained the trick of letting his mind doze while his eyes and ears remained alert.

He saw a woman, dressed in brocaded robes, step out of the canopied chair which her four Nubian slaves had set down in front of a goldsmith's workshop. A small army of retainers and guards accompanied her.

Not far off he heard an elderly man, who might have passed for Peter, haggling with a tired merchant over a bundle of limp greens.

"They weren't wilted when you started arguing about the price!" the merchant declared.

A hollow-eyed, dirty boy lingered nearby. Was he waiting for his opportunity to snatch one of the apples the disgruntled customer had already dismissed as worm-eaten?

No.

In fact, he was staring at John.

Steadily. Brazenly.

When he noticed John looking back, he turned and bolted.

John went after him.

Metal flashed in the sunlight as the guards posted at the door of the goldsmith's establishment drew their weapons. John was already past them, running out of the square and down a straight street without colonnades.

After an initial burst of speed, the boy slowed. As a young man John had been a runner. He knew how to pace himself and he made a point of regularly visiting the gymnasium at the Baths of Zeuxippos. Nevertheless, the boy was younger. As soon as John began to make up ground, his prey managed to pull away. John thought he could wear the boy down if they ran long enough and he kept his quarry in sight.

Laborers on their way to work and shoppers carrying baskets stepped aside in alarm. Later they would regale their friends and

families with the incongruous spectacle of a tall man in fine
robes in pursuit of a grubby street urchin, and not a few of the
theories advanced to explain the spectacle would be of a lewd,
not to say obscene, nature.

The boy veered sideways into an alley.

John followed.

It was possible he was being led into an ambush. He did not
think so. There was no doubt the pursuit had attracted attention,
which assassins would wish to avoid.

The alley turned at sharp angles, threading its narrow path
first one way and then another, its course defined by the surrounding buildings.

John leapt over a pile of rotting cabbages, his boots sinking
into a semi-liquescent puddle surrounding the remains of some
farmer's unsold wares, not yet found by the hungry. He slipped,
righted himself. His shoulder slammed into a brick wall an arm's
length to his right.

For a heartbeat he had taken his gaze from the boy, who had
vanished.

Impossibly, because John was at the entrance of a cul-de-sac.

A perfect spot to be waylaid, if attackers closed off its one
entrance.

Except there was no place for potential assassins to hide—or for
the boy to have gone. The buildings closing in the airless space were
devoid of doors or windows. The wall John had briefly touched
was hot. He guessed there was a furnace of some sort on the other
side. Later in the day, the narrow passage would be stifling.

Ahead, three long steps led up to what must have once been
a portico. Pale circles on the platform at the top of the flight
revealed where columns had stood. The wide door to the building it originally graced had been partly boarded over and secured
with a heavy rusted chain. It had obviously not been opened for
some time.

However, a corner of the board had been cut out and the
metal strapping bent aside, creating a gap large enough for a
boy, or a man as lean as John, to crawl through.

He ran up the steps and knelt by the opening. It appeared to have been gnawed by giant rats but was, no doubt, the work of beggars seeking shelter. Constantinople was too small for its populace. No space was allowed to go unused. Any place where rent was free attracted the homeless who scratched out a living, and often died, in dark corners and on the city streets.

A cool draught emanated from the building. John thought he could hear the fading sound of footsteps.

Then the boy was not lying in wait for him.

Others might be.

It would be folly for him to go in there.

He stilled his breathing and listened.

There was no sound.

He was certain no one was on the other side of the door. He had no sense of any other presence.

He took a handful of nummi from his coin pouch and flung them through the gap. The copper coins rang noisily against stone.

From within, there was no reaction. No intake of breath, no muffled sound of a weapon shifted, automatically, defensively. No scuffling for the coins.

John pulled his short blade from his belt, took a breath, and squeezed through the hole. A protruding nail ripped his robe from shoulder to waist, tearing a scrap of flesh with it.

He scrambled to his feet.

It was not entirely dark. Shafts of light, filtering through fissures in the derelict building above, criss-crossed a cavernous space interspersed with soaring columns. He was at the top of a flight of steps, matching in width those outside, but descending more steeply into darkness.

John's foot touched something heavy and unyielding.

As his eyes adjusted to the dimness, he realized it was one of several pieces of broken statuary—legs, a wing, and a horn such as the fabulous beasts described by Aristotle and Pliny might have displayed.

He started down the steps.

There was a movement in the darkness below.

Something pale. A mist. A phantom. It floated up toward him as he descended until it had resolved itself into a human form.

It was John's reflection in water.

He stopped abruptly at the edge of the gleaming surface. The water stretched back past the rows of columns, smooth as a black basalt floor in the Great Palace.

His heart had begun to race harder than when he had been pursuing the boy.

He was not surprised to find himself in a cistern. It was a common enough use for the basements of abandoned buildings.

However, he would have preferred to confront an armed man, or even more than one wielding weapons. He could never look upon deep water without remembering a freezing stream in Bretania and a familiar face staring up at him from beneath its surface, eyes fixed and unseeing.

John fought the urge to flee back up the stairway.

A sword in the back, a knife slashing one's throat—those were deaths he could face, but to drown was a horror past imagination.

Was that why he had been led here? To be overpowered and held under the water?

He would not go down to death without a struggle.

He looked around, gripping his blade tighter.

Little more than an arm's length away a figure rose from the water.

This time John recognized it as statuary immediately. It was a stern Greek goddess, sculpted from green porphyry.

A few steps and John could see another statue, this one of reddish stone, lying face down, barely submerged, at the feet of the goddess.

John shuddered.

He felt an urge to turn the statue over, to remove its face from the terrible water.

It was a remarkably life-like work. Even in the dim light, the subtlety of the musculature in the naked form was apparent. And the sculptor had chiseled every strand of hair.

Long, red hair which spread out and floated on the water's surface.

John bent and put his hand on the supine figure's shoulder.

He felt cool flesh.

Carefully, he turned the woman over.

The water was so shallow at the cistern's edge she might have escaped drowning, but she was dead nevertheless.

A welt circled her neck. John hoped she had in fact been strangled first, before her face was battered into an unrecognizable mask. The cheekbones had been smashed inwards, the nose crushed. The mouth was a gaping, twisted, toothless hole in the red stained ruin.

Yet she was not covered in blood.

Even had the woman been washed clean by immersion in the cistern, John knew, only too well, the color and smell of blood.

The woman had been dyed red from head to foot.

Why?

To conceal her identity?

The beating she had been given would have been more than sufficient to accomplish that.

John took hold of a delicate wrist and lifted it out of the water.

He saw what he had feared.

If he had not been looking for it, he would never have noticed because the dye had almost entirely concealed the tattoo. Only a faint shadow remained visible. Enough for John to recognize the scarab, overlain by a crude cross.

The same strange tattoo he had glimpsed the morning before, when she had raised her arm to push aside her veil.

The dead woman was Zoe.

Chapter Five

Grass and weeds obscured many of the graves in the tree-shaded cemetery which lay outside the inner wall of the city. The somnolent sound of insects overlaid by the cooing of doves resting in plump rows along the twisted boughs of ancient yews did nothing to disturb the slumbers of those buried beneath unmarked mounds or elaborate memorials.

John and Cornelia paced slowly along a narrow path to the outer side of the sacred space and came to a halt in a sun-dappled corner half hidden by a tangle of bushes. Several monuments were chiseled with pious sentiments and hopes for the departed.

"All is vanity," Cornelia read. "John Chrysostom wrote a homily on that. Peter once ventured to quote him at me."

"He's a favorite of Peter's. It's obvious from his writings he wasn't too fond of Lord Chamberlains."

"Ah yes. Eutropius. There was a Lord Chamberlain who would never have eaten his breakfast at the kitchen table. Unlike some."

They stood at the foot of a bare earthen mound. The anonymous woman buried there would not have been accorded even so modest a grave in a decent cemetery except that John had ordered it.

"It was kind of you to have her buried here when you don't even know who she was," Cornelia said after a time.

"I intend to find out both her identity and who murdered her," John replied.

An image of the red dyed corpse face down in the cistern floated to the surface of his thoughts, momentarily displacing the peaceful, sunlit surroundings.

Cornelia looked up at him, concern in her face. "Was she really the girl in the mosaic, the one you call Zoe?"

"She was the model for her. I'm convinced of it." He paused. "I know it worries Peter when he hears me talking to the mosaic, but Zoe and I have had many conversations. She knows more about my thoughts than anyone else."

"More than I do after our being apart so many years! Naturally you want to find out the truth of the matter."

"Beyond that, I suspect she was murdered because she spoke to me. And that means someone is concealing something which makes it even more important I discover the reason behind her death."

"Are you certain that's what's making it so important to you, John? How likely is it you'll be able to find out who she really was? Half the city is dead of the plague, and those left won't want to talk to a man from the palace. The only answer you get is liable to be a blade between the ribs one moonless night!"

"Ambushes take place everywhere in the city. Probably least of all on moonless nights when you're expecting them. In fact, I notice there's a pair of boots sticking out from behind those bushes."

Cornelia's eyes widened as she looked in the direction John indicated. "I see them and they're moving."

"Indeed they are," came a voice from the bushes. "And who dares to disturb the dead?"

At first glance, it might have appeared the man who stepped out from the vegetation was referring to himself. He was little more than a skeleton wrapped in rags. His eyes were milky and his skin pallid. He was however alive enough to wave a sword before thrusting its point into the middle of a patch of ivy wreathing the foot of a monument. "I don't get many people visiting this corner of the little kingdom I watch over. Who might you be? Family members?" His wheezing voice sounded suspicious.

"No—" John began.

The pale apparition hefted his weapon again. "Is that so? Couples think nobody sees what they're up to in the long grass." The man leered. John doubted the pale eyes could distinguish errant couples or anything beyond shadowy shapes.

"We were wondering about the person buried here," Cornelia said.

"Her?" The man spat on the bare mound. "Well, them that put her there said t'was by order of the Lord Chamberlain to the emperor."

He laughed, precipitating a fit of coughing that shook his gaunt frame. "Given what he is, it's much more likely she's some courtier's fancy woman. I'm already getting complaints from families whose relatives are buried here."

Cornelia gave the man an angry scowl and began to reply. John laid his hand on her arm and shook his head.

Oblivious, the cemetery caretaker continued. "They don't want their respectable dead anywhere near who knows what. Lord Chamberlain indeed! If the Lord Chamberlain arranged for the likes of her to be buried then Timothy the baker over here ruled Persia when he wasn't at his ovens."

He gave a hoarse laugh and patted the grave marker he stood beside. "I have my own troubles. Can't see too well, but mind now, I know every dip and bend of this cemetery. Them that try to dig up the dead find that out soon enough. I can make my way better in the dark than they can when the sun is high. Or rather I could before all them new graves appeared. Still, I'll soon learn my way around again."

John observed the recent visitation of the plague must have meant many more interments than in past years.

The other agreed. "I've had a busy time, keeping an eye on new burials. Fresh earth makes for easier digging, and there's less chance they've been robbed already."

"I'm sure you've kept a close watch on this grave," John said. "Has anyone visited?"

The caretaker emitted a wheezing snort. "Who'd visit such a one except you two? If that's really what you're up to. Or maybe her good friend the Lord Chamberlain? Do you know, in the course of my duties I once met a man who claimed he was the Lord Chamberlain. It's my belief he was a rogue intent on stealing bones to pass off as saints' relics."

He paused. "There's quite a brisk trade in relics. Every church in the city is filled with them and more than a few might have come from this cemetery if the truth be told, but not while I have kept watch. Anyhow, I was about to haul the fellow I was telling you about off to the authorities when a cat rescued him. Yes, it leapt right at me and that supposed Lord Chamberlain got away. Perhaps the cat was a demon. Perhaps they were both demons. Perhaps the real Lord Chamberlain is a demon. They do say the emperor is a demon and walks about the palace at nights with no face. Take care, my friends. Don't linger until night falls."

Chuckling to himself with a sound akin to a hoarse crow, the pale guardian of the dead turned and shuffled off without a word of farewell, dusty tunic flapping around spindly legs.

Cornelia stared at John.

John gave a thin smile. "Yes, I was the man he remembers. It was during the time I was investigating my friend Leukos' murder. I came to visit the grave."

They walked to Leukos' simple tomb, a vault which was in reality nothing more than a thin layer of plaster over a mound of dirt.

John felt the faint breath of a breeze against his face. He was aware of the almost imperceptible trembling of grass at his feet, forming a contrast to the stillness of the denizens of the cemetery he could see in his imagination, the stillness of his friend who had been gone for seven years already.

"So many things in the present point back to the past," John observed. "When we're young, everything leads to the future."

"It depends on what direction you turn your gaze, doesn't it?"

John laughed softly. "You prove my point. You've just reminded me of those nights in Egypt. Remember while the rest of the troupe slept, we'd lie in our tent and ponder Marcus Aurelius?"

"And wonder whether we were the only couple within a week's ride who were lying in their tent discussing Marcus Aurelius!"

"I'd wager we were the only couple consisting of a Greek mercenary and a bull leaper who discussed him."

"You never knew any other bull leapers?"

"No one else has recreated that ancient sport as far as I know. The skill was lost. To the past."

"How long had you been in Alexandria before we met?" Cornelia asked with an innocent look.

"Only a day or two," he replied, suppressing a smile. He added, in response to the unspoken question, "Not enough time to drink the dust out if my throat, much less warm a woman's bed."

Chapter Six

As they arrived home, John and Cornelia were greeted by the sound of Peter lustily singing a lewd marching song. His off key rendition continued to drift downstairs as they stood in the atrium, a sure sign the old servant was as deaf to their entrance as he was to the effect of his own painfully out-of-tune vocalization.

"It's livelier than that morbid old hymn written by Justinian," Cornelia remarked. She ran a hand through her dark hair. "I really must visit the baths. My hair feels like a gorse bush and I'm dustier than the belly of a cart ox."

"I'd be happy to escort you."

"Why, John? I'm perfectly used to going out and about by myself, you know that."

"It makes me uneasy," John admitted. "I've been contemplating engaging a bodyguard for you."

Cornelia put her hand on John's arm. "Better yet, you might consider having that private bath in the back of the house put back in working order."

"Would you like that?" He glanced up the wooden staircase in the direction of the singing, which had continued unabated. "Its mosaics scandalize Peter."

"Considering those lyrics he's been treating us to ever since we arrived, I doubt it! You wouldn't have to go to the Baths of

Zeuxippos every day if you had your own put in order. It would make a change, bathing with someone other than Anatolius and half the population of Constantinople."

John smiled. "True, although I would still attend to use the gymnasium regularly. I'll engage the necessary workmen."

"Thank you. And don't follow me at what you hope is a discreet distance, John."

Noting her expression, John ruefully agreed not to attempt the subterfuge.

After Cornelia had gone, John loped upstairs and paused at the kitchen door. Despite its open window, the room was warm, heated by a glowing brazier. The aroma of savory lamb and pine nuts hung in the air, drifting over the pungent smell of onions.

Peter looked up with a start from his chopping. His marching song turned miraculously into a hymn in mid-verse. Then he stopped singing. "Master, I didn't hear you. I should have attended the door."

His distress was evident. John suspected it had as much to do with the tacit admission of increasing deafness than any lack of attention to household duties.

"Do you wish me to bring wine to the study?"

"No, I can help myself. Continue with your cooking." John filled the cup that sat beside the jug on the scarred table at which Peter was working. "Peter, Cornelia tells me you refuse to accept her help in the kitchen."

"That is so, master. I feel it is not the place of the mistress to work as a servant. I have never proved incapable of carrying out my duties." The servant ducked his head to continue his work, but his hurt expression was not lost on John.

"Of course not," John replied. "But with another person in residence and Hypatia working elsewhere, there is more work for you to carry out."

John thought Peter looked uncommonly haggard. The lines in his leathery face appeared deeper and his wrists thinner. As he stepped away from the table to stir the pot bubbling on the brazier he looked unsteady. It would be difficult to persuade him to undertake fewer duties. It might be possible to arrange for Hypatia to return. Peter might be more amenable to accepting help from her. He would do whatever he was ordered to, but John did not wish to injure the old servant's pride.

"There's no need for you to try to do more than you can manage, Peter. As I've said before, you will always have a place here whether you can work or not."

Peter's lips tightened. He kept stirring. His spoon clanged against the side of the pot. "If I can't earn my keep, master, I will end my days in a monastery!"

"I could not allow that, Peter. You have been a loyal and excellent servant and deserve some time to rest in the sunlight when you grow old."

"You will forgive me saying so, master, but I am a free man, not a slave, and I may leave your employment if I wish."

John finished his wine and set down the cup. "We will discuss this some other time, Peter. Right now, there is something else I wish to talk to you about. I know you are always discreet and I appreciate that."

A smile added new wrinkles to Peter's face. "Thank you, master."

He left the brazier and resumed chopping.

John paused, seeking the best way to frame his question without casting aspersions on his servant's loyalty. "It concerns the mosaic in my study and the girl Zoe. As you know, I sometimes talk to her."

Peter hesitated. "I have heard you speaking out loud, if that's what you mean."

"This worries you," John went on.

"I would not question you, master. After all, I sing to myself."

"But I know that my speaking to Zoe distresses you."

A look of horror clouded Peter's face "Master! I wouldn't criticize you to anyone! Is that what you believe? I never talk about you or the mistress! What goes on in this house is nobody else's business. The court is a dangerous place and there are always those looking for information they might use for their own evil purposes."

Such as the fact the Christian emperor's Lord Chamberlain was a practicing Mithran, John thought. "I am sorry to have had to raise the matter," he replied. "My talking to myself, as you put it, is innocent enough, but I wondered if you had voiced your concern to anyone. I could understand it if you had."

"I assure you, master, I have done no such thing."

"I believe you. Yet the fact is somehow this habit of mine has become known to strangers."

Peter flushed with anger and flourished the knife he had been using. "They are talking about it on the public streets you mean? How dare they? But how could anyone know, master? Who would say anything?"

"It might have been a friend who let it slip," John mused.

Peter's expression brightened. "Ah. Well, if I may say so, master, young Anatolius can be indiscreet, and Captain Felix too, sometimes, well, after a cup too much wine. And then there are a number of courtiers who would be only too happy to make you a figure of fun."

Considering John employed one servant and entertained few visitors, it was difficult to think of more than a handful of people who might have overheard his conversations with the mosaic girl, let alone discovered the name by which he called her.

"They say the very walls of the palace have ears," Peter went on, as if reading his thoughts.

"They might," John replied, "but can they talk as well?"

Chapter Seven

"Of course I haven't mentioned Zoe to anyone! Furthermore, I'd be extremely annoyed if I didn't realize you had good reason to question me."

Anatolius gestured at his desk, piled with documents and scrolls. "With all the legal work brought about by the plague, I've hardly had time to speak to the servants let alone gad about the city gossiping about my friends behind their backs."

He picked up a scroll and waved it in John's direction. "I must get this summons delivered today. An old acquaintance of my father's has engaged me to bring a case against an estate. It involves the deceased children of deceased parents and competing guardians, some dead, not to mention grandchildren, several of whom might actually be alive. Or perhaps not. As you know, we have four months to conclude these cases one way or the other, before they are thrown out. It could take that long to find enough competent witnesses to swear to the pertinent documents. And, needless to say, our opponent will cry forgery in any event."

"Not as easy as going down to Avernus," John observed.

"No. More like trying to return." Anatolius gave a rueful laugh as he stared down into the jumble of documents. Following his gaze, John saw the image of a skull staring back from the tiled desk top.

Anatolius shoved a leather bound codex over the fleshless visage. "That was father's idea. He thought a man should surround himself with reminders of his mortality. What I say is mortality's perfectly happy to tap you on the shoulder and remind you when the time comes."

"The cupids at least bring a note of joy." John nodded toward the nearest wall, decorated with cavorting godlets playing musical instruments or driving chariots pulled by donkeys.

Anatolius smiled. "Yes. You'll recall this was my mother's reception room, and after she died father made it his study. I must admit I've noticed some of my clients looking askance."

"You hadn't thought of meeting them in another room?"

The suggestion appeared to surprise Anatolius. "I suppose I could move my study if I wished. You know, this place still feels as if it is my parents' house. Not mine. I expect it always will. Perhaps I should ask old Bony for his opinion."

"Who is he—or was he?"

"That's what I named the skull when I was a child. Do you imagine you're the only one who talks to inanimate representations? I used to have nightmares about old Bony. I'd hear a sound in the night and put my head under my coverlet. I imagined it was the skull, pulling itself up out of the tiles and rattling down the hallway after me. What kind of decoration would you choose for a lawyer's office, John?"

"Probably plain plaster. Are you certain you didn't mention Zoe to anyone? We all have a little too much to drink at times and some of us become garrulous."

Anatolius refused to be offended at the implication. "If intoxication's involved, the main suspect would be Felix. How long would I have lasted as Justinian's private secretary if I gave away secrets every time I drank?"

"A lover perhaps?" John persisted. "One's reserve often gets lost in the bedroom."

"I'm sure it's just what a woman wants to hear, John! Do you know, my little sparrow, you remind me of the girl on the Lord Chamberlain's wall. The one he talks to at night. Why, I can tell you the most amazing things about the Lord Chamberlain. He loves grilled swordfish and—"

"I concede the point, Anatolius! Setting aside the question of the name for now, then, first I want to find out the identity of the murdered woman. After that, I'll be able to work backward to those responsible."

"Maybe she died in a brawl with a client. That's a common enough end for some."

"Perhaps, but that's irrelevant to the matter in hand. You see, Anatolius, I've always been convinced that, because of its individuality, the girl in the mosaic was a portrait of an actual person, perhaps the artisan's daughter. If the mosaic maker is still alive, and I can find him, he might know who the model was."

Anatolius pondered the notion. "It's a long time since the mosaic was created. It was in the house when you acquired it, as I recall."

"That's right, a little less than ten years ago. The previous owner lost the place after the riots. He lost his head as well."

"Aside from so much time passing, those riots claimed a lot of lives and lately the plague has cut a swathe through the populace," Anatolius pointed out. "I wouldn't roll the knucklebones on your chance of finding the man you want to interview. I could ask one of the imperial clerks to consult the archives, given the house is on the palace grounds. There might be some record of payment for the work."

"Unless the previous occupant personally paid for the work. More importantly, I don't want to alert anyone at court to my investigation. It's purely a private matter."

"Yes, certainly. Very wise. But wouldn't it be even wiser to forget the whole thing?"

"That would be dangerous. The woman approached me for a reason. I am convinced she was killed because she was seen talking to me."

"Or it may have been a prank gone wrong, a mistake, a coincidence."

"Even so, I cannot be certain until I investigate."

"True enough, but that's not why you want to investigate, is it? John, the woman who was murdered, even if she served as the model, wasn't Zoe. She wasn't the girl you conjure up in your solitary conversations."

"Do you think I don't know that?"

"I believe you know it, but I'm afraid you don't feel it is so. We can't reason ourselves out of what we feel. Take it from a former poet."

John observed he had looked into the murders of friends before.

"But Zoe is family," Anatolius pointed out. "She's the daughter of your own imagination."

John shook his head. "You can't persuade me, my friend."

"I thought not. And now how do you intend to begin?"

"By making inquiries around the artisans' quarter. I will say I admire the man's work and want to engage him for another assignment."

Anatolius looked skeptical.

"It's quite true," John assured him with a thin smile. "Cornelia would like my bath repaired and its mosaic renovated. Its style and workmanship, not to mention its subject, are such that it was obviously the work of the same man."

"It's a pity mosaic makers don't sign their work. They must not have the egos of poets. Think how much easier your task would be!"

John agreed. "There's also the tattoo I've described to you. That will certainly narrow down the chase. Even though nobody claimed her body, someone is certain to know about a missing woman with such a distinctive marking."

Anatolius looked thoughtful. "The culprit must have feared she could be identified by the tattoo or he wouldn't have tried to conceal it with the dye. A scarab with a cross over it, you said. A peculiar combination."

"The cross was crudely done and somewhat blurred. From what remained, it might once have been an ankh. An Egyptian marking, like the scarab."

"Do the two together signify anything?"

John shrugged. "I spent a few years in Egypt. I was not preoccupied with studying the culture."

"One thing we do know, whatever the tattoo means, they are usually on women of the class employed by Isis, not to mention actresses and the like. I'd be happy to make appropriate inquiries among those ladies." Anatolius looked at his littered desk and sighed. "It'll make a change from winding up estates and trying to trace elusive heirs."

Chapter Eight

A burst of laughter greeted Anatolius as a girl clothed in rose-scented perfume and a wisp of silk admitted him into Isis' house. A gilded Eros beside the door announced the business of the establishment.

A niche by the entrance was piled higher than usual with the daggers and swords everyone in the city carried but which were not allowed inside. Most of their hilts were elaborately worked, some bejeweled. Anatolius added his own blade to the armory.

The sound of merriment emanated from a room opening off the hallway.

The girl noticed Anatolius' glance in its direction. "It's that Egyptian magician called Dedi, sir. Madam arranged for him to entertain a group of patrons." She half turned to look over her shoulder, obviously eager to get back to the performance. The silk mist she wore rose revealingly with the movement.

Anatolius was about to instruct her to take a message to Isis when the madam herself emerged into the hall. Isis was middle-aged and comfortably plump. She wore considerably more silk than her employee.

"Anatolius! What an unexpected pleasure! And how well you timed your visit! Do come and see the magick this diminutive ornament to the empire is performing. I'll wager the Patriarch would anathematize all of us, if he only knew what the fellow was doing!"

She placed a finger to her lips. "And he may well find out," she whispered in mock horror. "I recognized at least one deacon from the Great Church. No doubt he will claim he was here to gather information on the blasphemous goings-on taking place nightly in my house, although that's not what I hear from his favorite girl."

Isis grasped Anatolius' arm and pulled him toward the open doorway of a room decorated by a life-size statue of Bacchus in classical Greek style, attended by several marble satyrs engaged on various lewd pursuits. A crowd lounging on cushions strewn amidst the statues guffawed at the antics of an olive-skinned little man at the far end of the room.

Or, rather, Anatolius realized, at the talking skull on the table beside Dedi.

The skull was chattering about the Patriarch's private life and secret pleasures while Dedi's carp-like mouth did not move, except to pucker itself into an expression of outrage.

"Blasphemy!" Dedi suddenly shouted at the skull. "You wouldn't dare utter such scurrilous untruths if you were alive!"

He leaned forward toward the crowd and whispered loudly, "It's possessed by a demon!"

A murmur of confusion filled the room and the girl in silk, who had lingered beside Anatolius and Isis, emitted a squeak of dismay.

"Please, do not be alarmed," Dedi went on. He placed a ring of glowing charcoals from a nearby brazier around the skull and then produced a leather bag from which he poured what looked like irregular pebbles. "This is incense, blessed long ago by none other than Simeon the Stylite. A special gift to me from Empress Theodora, before whom I recently had the pleasure of performing."

"He's telling the truth," Anatolius said. "I happened to witness that performance."

The skull uttered dire imprecations as Dedi added the incense to the charcoal. Thick, pungent smoke roiled upwards. The skull emitted a keening groan as the dark cloud enveloped it. When Dedi fanned the smoke aside, the skull had vanished.

The crowd voiced its appreciation. Many sprang to their feet, craning to see better.

The loquacious skull was nowhere to be seen.

Anatolius noticed the prostitute beside him making the Christian holy sign and muttering thanks for the destruction of the evil thing.

"Isis, the entertainment is splendid, but I've come to make some inquiries," he said.

Isis waved a chubby, beringed hand. "Yes, yes. But first you must see this!"

Dedi had set upon the table a number of goblets, two jugs, and a large urn with a spout. He explained the urn contained wine and the jugs held water, inviting a man sitting nearby to approach and confirm this was the case.

After confirmation was received, Dedi drew wine from the urn, drank it, flourished the first water jug, and then poured its contents into the urn.

"This is an exceedingly peculiar vessel," he told his attentive watchers in a confidential tone. "I can't say whether it is magickal or accursed or just has humors of its own."

When he refilled his goblet from the spout, clear water streamed out, followed by a mixture of wine and water. Then, after more water was added, wine again.

Members of the audience crowded around to inspect the wonder.

"Isn't it amazing?" said Isis. "I'll wager Justinian would love to have an urn like that, if he weren't so abstemious."

Anatolius expressed doubt. "I'd expect the emperor to prefer to know that nothing will come out of an urn that didn't go into it."

"Spoken like a lawyer!"

Anatolius frowned. "Why does everyone insist on mentioning my new profession? It isn't as if I've changed. May we talk now in private?"

Isis led him away. A murmur of excited voices followed them down a corridor whose wall hangings told the story of Leda and the swan in a manner more graphic than tasteful.

Isis paused as she placed her hand on the swan-head latch of the door to her private chambers. "Do you know, Anatolius, these days there's as much money to be made in wonders as in sexual comfort? I have thought I will give up this establishment and take to selling gryphon's claws and salamander eggs and the mummified foreskins of saints. But then what would my girls do for a living?"

Anatolius helped himself to wine and tried to make himself comfortable on an overly stuffed couch while Isis went off to find further refreshments. Compared to the garish decor of the rest of the house, the room was simply furnished with a few finely wrought chairs and side tables and subtly patterned wall hangings which, he guessed, were, like Isis, of Egyptian origin. The polished sandalwood writing desk where she did her accounts was a reminder that she had long since ceased laboring in her profession and become an owner.

Isis returned with a silver bowl filled with nut-stuffed dates. "You're looking glum, Anatolius. You haven't suddenly developed religious scruples against my house, have you?"

"Certainly not! It's just that...well...I'm always of two minds when I come in here."

Isis daintily popped a date into her mouth and spoke around it. "Why, I'm surprised. I thought you'd had more than a few pleasurable adventures here."

Anatolius nodded. "I have. Only practically all of them have occurred when I've been...um...alone."

"And suffering from the pain of a broken heart? Tell me, will you be needing some solace today?"

"Not today. All I need is information."

"You have a mistress then?"

"Only the law. She keeps me busy."

"That explains why I haven't seen you much lately. Alas, all my friends at court have deserted me. Captain Felix hasn't crossed the threshold for a long while. I've missed seeing that bear of a man. Is he frequenting some other establishment? I recall when he swore he would marry one of my girls. Berta. Remember? But, needless to say, that didn't happen. Maybe he tired of searching for another Berta here and found her elsewhere."

"I don't think so, Isis. He knows better than to allow himself to become involved like that. Just as I've learned."

Isis sniffed. "Men never learn. Fortunately for me. Do you know, only yesterday I was pondering where I could find another doorkeeper now Thomas has left his post for the fresher air of the coast."

She tapped Anatolius on the knee. "Now tell me, you're a friend of his. Do you think Felix might be interested in the post? Though as captain of the excubitors he has power and wealth enough...and yet, the last time we spoke, he appeared to be very restless and not a little dissatisfied with his current duties."

Anatolius stared at Isis in astonishment, then realized she must be jesting. He laughed. "You're right! To hear Felix tell it, watching your door would engage his military skills to a greater extent than the tiresome duties Justinian expects of him. Which is to say, little in the actual fighting line."

"He hasn't been relegated to sharpening swords for the generals in the field?"

Anatolius laughed. "Hardly. He probably made it sound that way. Now and then these old soldiers get the urge to march all day and subsist on plain rations while fending off nocturnal attacks. I can't imagine why, but then I've never been a soldier. Anyway, Constantinople is more dangerous than any battlefield. Mithra knows there're backstabbers aplenty on the palace grounds, and all of them eager enough to insert a blade between someone's ribs if it would advance them even just the length of a reception hall. Speaking of rations, where did you obtain these excellent stuffed dates? I haven't seen dates on sale since before the plague arrived."

"I got them from a cook in the imperial kitchen," Isis admitted without a blush. "No knives were involved. He's taken a fancy to one of my girls so we came to an arrangement which benefited all of us, including my employee."

Dropping her voice, she looked at him appraisingly. "Speaking of which, I've engaged a couple of new girls since you were last here. One, in fact, met you at the door. Perhaps you might like to meet her behind another and more private door? The law is not nearly so warm or playful."

The thought of the prostitute reminded Anatolius of his reason for calling. "Do any of your new girls have tattoos?"

Isis stared back in consternation. "Tattoos? Is this a new fashion at court? I'm always interested in hearing about these things. I like to keep ahead of my competition. If you want a girl with tattoos—"

Anatolius grinned. "Let me tell you why I'm making inquiries, Isis. I'm here on John's behalf to consult you about tracing a woman with a tattoo on her wrist."

"It's been some little time since he visited too. Tell him I hope he'll come to see me soon, especially since he's not long returned from Alexandria," she grumbled. "Who else can I talk to about the old days?"

John had explained to Anatolius that although he and Isis had both spent time in Egypt they had never met there. Anatolius, as usual, did not bother to point out her error. She appeared to cherish the recollection. Her imagination? Or, perhaps, it was simply her own little joke.

"There's always that magician downstairs," Anatolius suggested. "It's only a couple of months since he was in Egypt."

"An excellent suggestion, but why is John seeking a woman with a tattoo? It seems a strange quest."

Anatolius explained the circumstances. "Personally, as I told John, I suspect the victim was a prostitute."

"I see. So as for the authorities…." She waved her hand dismissively. "We are nothing to them, except when they need a bit of bodily comfort or the next bribe is due. I wish I could assist, but the only tattoos under this roof decorate a couple of girls from Egypt, both of whom I saw this morning, and the tattoos are on their ankles." She glanced down at her feet. "Like mine."

"This is the third house I've visited this morning, and all to no avail. You'll keep an eye open though? The tattoo depicts a scarab with a rough cross on top of it. Does that mean anything?"

"The scarab is the sacred beetle. By cross you must mean the ankh? It signifies life. The gods carry them."

"John thought it might originally have been an ankh. If so, it's rather ironic under the circumstances, isn't it?"

Isis looked thoughtful. "If you don't discover anything useful for John, you may at least be able to help me. Let me know if any of the houses you visit are offering anything new to bring in more custom. Since the plague people seem more interested in miracles than in the natural joys of this life."

Anatolius agreed he would inform Isis if her competitors were providing any unusual services.

"I'll see that Leda does something special for you," Isis promised.

"Leda?"

"The girl who showed you into the house. Don't think I didn't catch your glance at her, but trying to give the impression you were looking elsewhere. Why, the first time you visited me as a lad, you pretended to be more interested in the wildlife in the floor mosaic than the wildlife surrounding you."

"I was scared out of my wits," Anatolius recalled with a smile. "You really remember that?"

"I have an excellent memory," Isis assured him, offering the bowl of dates again.

"Then you'll recall it wasn't that I came to that last place of yours of my own accord. I thought I was going to the market with one of father's servants and the man insisted he needed to stop there. He'd only be a few moments, he said, and left me in the atrium and...well...."

"You found more excitement than a basket full of fresh chives at a good price?"

Anatolius reddened. "It really was extremely negligent of—"

Isis made a shushing sound and put a finger to her lips. "You think so? Some fathers might become concerned that a son was spending too much time scribbling poetry. He might think it was time for him to become a man. Mothers think differently."

Anatolius thought that they would never know for certain if her surmise was correct.

"We can never know if what's in the past is a fact," Isis continued. "Still, it does keep springing surprises on us, even if it's supposed to be gone. If you don't wish to patronize Leda, choose whichever girl you desire." She gave an arch smile. "With or without a tattoo."

Chapter Nine

Despite a chilly drizzle which left the streets dark and damp under an overcast sky, a wave of heat washed over John as he stepped through a brick archway and into a wide courtyard. The heat emanated from a low, open-sided structure housing the circular hump of a brick-built kiln.

The workshop of the glassmaker Michri sprawled near the crest of the ridge overlooking the Golden Horn, at the edge of the Copper Market not far from the Great Church. John had been here before to commission glassware for imperial banquets and ceremonies.

Any other Lord Chamberlain would have delegated that part of his official duties, but John enjoyed inspecting glass goblets destined for imperial tables. These were things of substance. John missed the weight of a sword in his hand. The secrets of the court, measured advice, subtle political maneuverings, most of the matters he dealt with now, were insubstantial and the results of his efforts uncertain. It might be more satisfying to shape molten glass into a pleasing shape or turn up the soil of a field. In another life, he had envisioned himself retiring to a farm.

The maw of the kiln gaped momentarily red as a man, no doubt one of Michri's assistants, added wood to its glowing innards. Under the roof of the shelter the air steamed. The smell of wet stone and earth mingled with that of burning charcoal.

Michri stood at a long wooden bench and examined a translucent blue wine jug. When he noticed his visitor he put the jug down and stepped forward.

He was a hulking barrel-chested man upon whose massive shoulders was balanced a head as smooth and hairless as a blown glass egg. Whether the lack of so much as a shadow of an eyebrow was due to a lifetime's proximity to flames or whether the glassmaker shaved to avoid being singed while at work, John had never inquired.

"Salutations! A visit is always an honor, Lord Chamberlain."

John acknowledged the greeting. "I fear I have no commission for you, Michri, although it is not for lack of satisfaction in your work or artistry. The empress has in fact spoken most highly of your last contribution to the court."

"Ah, that was a challenge! Who but myself, Michri, could have carried out such a task, sir? To make copies of fruit and bread and fish, indeed every dish to be offered at the imperial banquet. They were such faithful reproductions our dear empress' guests could not tell until they touched them they were but artifices intended to delight and entertain?"

"Not even then. Senator Flaccus would have bitten down on one your apples if I hadn't noticed and solicited his opinion of the situation in Italy in the nick of time."

Michri laughed. "I'm sure Justinian appreciated the views of such an astute observer!"

"Theodora appeared to find them of interest." John did not mention that after the banquet the empress had ordered the glass food distributed to the hungry clustered at the gates of the Great Palace. Instead he pointed out that the tableware Michri had provided for the formal gathering had been much admired.

Michri dismissed the compliment with a wave of a hand. He scowled and his smooth forehead wrinkled where his eyebrows should have been. "Plates and wine cups! Beginner's work, Lord Chamberlain! But not everyone has the lung power to be able to manufacture a wine jug such as the example I just fashioned. Sufficient breath is not enough. The artisan must study for years to learn all he needs to know. It's not just poking a rod into molten glass and merrily puffing away, although to hear some talk any fool can do it."

As the artisan warmed to his topic his voice boomed. "No, there is much more involved. The worker in glass has to know how much fuel is needed to maintain the kiln at the correct temperatures and what type of wood to burn. Supposing he buys plain glass and wants to color it, he must have precise knowledge of the correct amount of copper or cobalt to add for the shade he needs. It's skill and knowledge hard won, you may be certain of that, Lord Chamberlain. The number of burns I've suffered in gaining them would make an icon weep."

He glared at his assistant, now busy stacking wood next to the kiln. Had there been friction between master and assistant? Had Michri's words, spoken more loudly than necessary for ordinary conversation, been intended as much for the ears of his assistant as for those of his visitor?

John glanced at the workshop bench. "I see there are several plates whose color matches the wine jug. A special task?"

"A new patron and a supporter of the Blue faction," came the reply, "hence the color of his glassware. He's anticipating a great victory for his team when chariot races run regularly again, and plans a celebratory gathering in due course. It was difficult finding sufficient copper for the tint with trade not yet back to normal, but I heard about a man in the quarter who'd received one of the last scrap shipments that arrived in the city before the plague. When I made further inquiries, I learned he had died before he could use it so I was able to purchase a sufficient amount inexpensively from his widow. I only hope my beautiful wares survive the celebrations."

In response to John's questioning look, he added, "You'd be surprised how many baskets of broken glass find their way out of the palace and back into my workshop. I can melt the shards down and reuse them. They're worth a few nummi to me, so a rich man's carelessness turns out to be small boon to the servant who has to clean up after him."

John gave a thin smile. "I'm certain that's the case. But I am not here to speak to you about your glassware. I want to question you about your trade in tesserae."

Michri looked surprised. "I will be happy to assist as best I can. Are there plans afoot for new mosaics at the palace? Or perhaps our beloved Justinian is contemplating construction of another church? Let me show you some excellent work." He retrieved a small basket from underneath the bench.

"I've some beautiful gold tesserae here," he went on. "My assistant has been practicing these past few weeks and has finally mastered the making of them. You see?"

He plucked up a few and handed them to John. "It took him some time and patience to learn not only how to put gold leaf on a cube but also the method of adding the final coating of glass to stop the gold tarnishing." He lowered his voice before continuing. "Even so, he grasped the technique a lot faster than I did as a beginner. I fear I am sometimes too harsh with him. It is because I have great hopes for his future."

John rolled the cubes around in his palm. They flashed and glittered, finding light even in the gloom.

Zoe was nothing more than a basketful of such glass.

No, that wasn't true. She was also all the conversations he'd had with her over the years and the hours he'd spent staring wordlessly at her, pondering over his wine cup.

And her model, the woman who had approached him in the square—the dead woman—was certainly special. Flesh and blood was worth more than glass, wasn't it?

It had begun to rain harder. He could hear it drumming on the roof. A gust of wind blew rain into the enclosure. Steam rose from the hot earth at the base of the kiln.

John expressed polite admiration for the tesserae and dropped them back into the basket.

"If it is to be a large job, I will need some time to prepare," Michri said. "And for certain colors, I can't be sure I can obtain the proper ingredients. On the other hand, I still have cakes of glass in certain hues ready to be cut."

"It would be a small undertaking. I understand you've supplied tesserae for years. Do you recall who created the mosaics in my house? It was about ten years ago. The tax collector Glykos owned the house at the time. I'd like to engage the same artisan for some repair work."

Michri's face wrinkled in thought and then he grinned. "I can assist you, Lord Chamberlain! I remember that job well, small as it was, because it required many of the tesserae to be prepared in a peculiar manner, oddly shaped and painted on one facet. When the mosaic maker insisted that such tesserae could be set into the mortar in such a way as to show different scenes according to the lighting, I was skeptical, but apparently his method works since I hear he's done several others since."

"It does indeed, Michri. The effect is startling. I will arrange for you to visit and see for yourself in the near future. Do you remember the man's name?"

"Certainly. He lives not far from here. His name is Figulus."

Chapter Ten

"Do I remember the mosaics I made for Glykos? I wish I could forget them." Figulus leaned forward on his stool to smooth the black curls of the smaller of two chubby infants who had crawled for cover under the table when John appeared in the doorway, shaking the rain off his cloak.

John's damp garments steamed in the warmth of the workshop. By keeping to the shelter of colonnades and second story overhangs, he had avoided being completely soaked by the downpour.

"So you are, indeed, the artisan responsible for the work in my private bath? I am happy to hear it. I wish you to carry out some repairs."

Figulus frowned and drew his hand away from the child. The mosaic maker was a paunchy, middle-aged man, unremarkable in appearance, except for his hands whose long fingers were as calloused as those of a bricklayer. "I regret that my next few months are quite full of assignments, excellency."

"The repair I have in mind involves the addition of apparel and altering the, shall we say, postures of certain figures. The previous owner's taste differed from mine and from that of my family."

"Ah, I see. Then as crowded as my schedule is, I'm certain I can find time to assist you."

The workshop was a spacious room with whitewashed walls. A youth in his twenties scooped handfuls of glass cubes from a row of barrels and sorted them into neat piles. Occasionally he glanced toward the other end of the table where John and Figulus sat.

The heaped tesserae glowed with color, as if the glass had trapped and accumulated the dim light seeping through the windows before reflecting it back in shades from red to deepest lapis lazuli. In a corner a younger boy created a design with colored marble pieces he pressed into a damp plaster bed held in a wooden frame.

"Perhaps it would be best to discuss the modifications at some other time, Figulus, considering the nature of the figures."

"Lord Chamberlain, as you see, like you I have a family. At the time of the commission I already had two sons, who are now my apprentices." Figulus waved a hand at the young men.

"When Glykos described what he wanted I was repelled," he went on. "The subject matter was unfit for a Christian household. But what could I do? I needed to feed my family. To refuse the wielder of such influence would have meant the end of my career. A good career, too. The empress has praised the decorations I made for the imperial residences. But then, didn't our Lord say we should give to Caesar what is Caesar's? What Glykos demanded was Caesar's, not a thing to which the Lord would lay claim. Naturally, I don't mean to impugn our current caesar who is a most godly man."

John said he understood. "What might be done about the mosaic in the study? The way it changes with the light reminds me of certain members of court. Ingenious workmanship I admit, but…."

"Offensive to any good Christian." Figulus finished the thought, then looked down at the infants under the table. They sucked their thumbs and stared up at John with wide eyes like a pair of owls. "All things of beauty come from the Lord. Don't you agree, Lord Chamberlain? What are the tesserae from which

I form my designs? In themselves, nothing, just dull bits of glass. They shine only when they reflect the light sent from above."

"Which requires some skillful intervention on the part of artisans such as yourself," John pointed out.

"That's true. In order for the finished mosaic to sparkle when it catches the light, the tesserae must be pressed into the wet plaster at varying angles. It isn't surprising that a mosaic can have a different aspect at one hour and quite another earlier or later."

"But not often so different an aspect as the mosaic in my study can present. Where did you learn the technique?"

"I discovered it for myself. I found that by cutting the facets at certain angles, and painting one side....but I must not waste your valuable time, Lord Chamberlain. Please believe me when I tell you while some of my patrons have asked me to put my skills to the most vile use yet I have had many worthy commissions. In one of the Patriarch's private chapels Lazarus opens his eyes when a lamp filled with holy oil is lit and set before it. If I may say so, I am particularly proud of that creation."

Figulus sat with his hands in his lap, long fingers intertwined as if he were ready to pray.

Those were the hands which had given birth to Zoe.

"I've spent hours admiring your work," John said. "During the daytime of course. Do you recall when you made those particular mosaics?"

"I remember exactly. It was in the sixth year of Justinian's reign. I finished the very day the Blues and Greens rioted against the emperor. Both factions poured out of the Hippodrome and fought in the streets. I feared for my life all the way home. It isn't something easily forgotten."

"You had already finished the mosaic in the bath at my house?"

"Yes, during the summer. When I heard what Glykos wanted for the study I delayed, hoping he'd change his mind. I became indisposed. I found several urgent commissions in other parts of the palace. Finally he refused to believe me when I explained that the winter was not the best season for that kind of work, that the plaster might not set correctly. He would not be swayed. So I began on a chilly day in January and finished the day the riots began. Or at least I thought I had finished."

John asked him what he meant.

Figulus glanced in the direction of his older sons, who continued their tasks. He looked down at his clasped hands uneasily. "I regret I will bore you with my reminiscences."

"Not at all, Figulus. I have always been fascinated by the mosaic in my study. Tell me what happened."

"Very well. As I said, I believed I had finished my repulsive commission from Glykos. As soon as I was back home, my wife and I knelt and thanked the Lord I didn't need to venture outside again. As the light faded we saw mobs surging through the street below our windows. When night fell it was worse for then of course we could see nothing. More than once the house door creaked and rattled as someone tried to get in."

"It was a dangerous time," John replied.

"It seemed to us that the gates of hell had opened. We were convinced the emperor must have died or fled, for otherwise he would have delivered us from the savages roaming the streets. For three days it went on. Then, before dawn, there came a terrible pounding at the door. My wife begged me not to open it, even when the frantic cries from outside told us who our callers were. But what else could I do? Glykos had sent two servants for me. He was not satisfied with the mosaic!"

"I am surprised the tax collector was concerned about a wall mosaic under the circumstances."

"He had lost his wits, Lord Chamberlain." Figulus shook his head. "Why, the servants he had sent were boys. They shook so badly they could hardly hold their spears. I remember looking back over my shoulder before we turned the corner. My wife was still standing in the doorway. I could barely see her though the swirling smoke that filled the street. I was certain I would never see her again."

"You managed to get through to the palace without harm?"

"Only by the grace of God. Armed men appeared out of the smoke and pounded past us. Some carried swords, others brandished short lengths of boards bristling with nails, or carried the hammers used by metalsmiths. They paid us no heed. Once I glimpsed a fierce melee down a side street. It was when we reached the Mese that the miracle occurred."

"Miracle?"

"Yes. A miracle. You can only understand the mosaic if you know about the miracle. My escorts and I had stepped through an archway and saw a torrent of flame rushing between the colonnades toward us, like water pouring though an aqueduct. As I leapt out into the street, the flames reached a lamp oil shop.

"I came to my senses on my knees, halfway across the Mese. I couldn't remember being propelled through the air or landing. The explosion had littered the cobbles with shattered bricks. I have thought about it often, and have come to believe the extreme heat made the oil boil and the pressure building up in the sealed amphorae caused them to explode. I started to stand up and couldn't. The edge of my cloak was caught beneath a column which had toppled over. The Lord had spared me being crushed. I gave silent thanks."

"You suppose you were spared so you could finish the mosaic?" John asked. "Now, what was it that Glykos wanted done?"

"I will explain, Lord Chamberlain. But first I must describe the miracle. It wasn't merely that I was allowed to live. You see, I had been carrying a quantity of tesserae in a wicker basket. As I got back to my feet I realized I no longer held the basket. It lay some distance away. Empty. And I knew there were none at the tax collector's house for, supposing I was finished, I had taken the unused tesserae away with me."

"The tesserae must have been scattered all over the street by the explosion?"

"That's right. Just as I was about to despair I noticed a glint on the pavement. Around my feet and stretching out on all sides constellations winked, reflecting light from the burning shops. I plucked up a dark red cube of glass. Then three blue cubes.

A curling line of green led to a handful of yellow. I scrambled around gathering what I could from the grimy stones. I managed to find a pitifully small portion of what I had brought. No matter, the servants urged me on."

The events Figulus had described struck John as lucky rather than miraculous but he did not say so. "Did you reach the palace without further incident?"

"Yes. Except there was an angry crowd outside the palace walls. Blues and Greens joined in thunderous imprecations against Justinian, interspersed with chants of 'Victory, Victory.' As I struggled to force my way forward, I heard shouts which sent a shiver through me. 'Glykos! The tax collector! Death to Glykos!'"

The doomed tax collector had arranged for Figulus to be admitted to the palace grounds. He was waiting in his study—John's study—staring out the window across the square below, Figulus said. John wondered if he had been watching for excubitors to emerge from the barracks opposite, waiting for the men who would escort him to his execution.

"If Glykos had not had the windows shut against the smoke, he might have heard the crowd crying for his head," Figulus said. "He held a cup of wine. The watery light of dawn had driven the pagan gods from the peaceful country scene on the wall behind him."

"And what was it he wanted you to do?" John asked. He had never noticed anything in the mosaic that had given the impression of being an afterthought or a repair.

Figulus, who had been speaking quietly, lowered his voice even further. "The foul man insisted I add a portrait of his daughter to the mosaic. I was horrified. You are familiar with the nature of the work. What man would place his daughter in a scene of such surpassing evil?"

John offered sympathy.

"Yet what could I do?" Figulus replied. "I am merely an artisan. Who am I to judge the whims of my employers? While I chipped away the corner of the mosaic and applied the setting bed, Glykos had the girl summoned. She was wide-eyed and silent. A grave little girl. I believe she was too young to know exactly what was about to befall her father but old enough to feel something was wrong. Now here is the strange thing. I had never attempted a likeness. How could I capture hers? And in a few brief winter hours, in a cold room that smelled of fear and ashes?"

Figulus lifted a hand and regarded his long, calloused fingers. "It wasn't my doing. These fingers were commanded by another power. What's more, the few tesserae I salvaged from the street were almost exactly enough, and the colors matched the girl's flesh and hair and the colors of her garment. How could that have happened without the Lord's intervention?"

John made no reply. He did not believe things happened because of the intervention of the Christians' god.

The mosaic maker seemed not to notice the Lord Chamberlain's silence. He made the sign of his religion and continued. "I secretly took one action to protect her innocence. I made certain she was looking straight out into the world, so that she would never catch a glimpse of the behavior of the pagan deities in her sky."

Why had Glykos wanted such a portrait? Given his reputation, he may have thought that thrusting a mosaic daughter into the care of blasphemous deities would taunt the god of the Christian emperor who was about to betray him. John asked Figulus whether the tax collector had revealed the reason for his request.

Figulus shook his head. "I have often wondered. Was it the result of a terrible upheaval of the humors? Perhaps at the very end, despite his wealth and power, Glykos realized his daughter was his true treasure. Being a worldly, grasping man, he expressed his love for her, as he did for material things, by asserting his ownership. By attaching her image to his wall. He was not altogether a villain. He paid me liberally in gold coins before I left."

John looked around the workshop. Figulus' older sons were still laboring assiduously with their tesserae. The infants had curled up and gone to sleep under the table like a couple of cats. Perhaps for a man who led a comfortable life it was easy and desirable to think the best of evil men.

"Everything you've told me has been interesting, Figulus. I know Glykos was beheaded and his body cast into the sea. As for his family...his daughter...I don't even know the girl's name. Did you learn that?"

"Agnes, Lord Chamberlain. That's what Glykos called her. I heard afterward that she and her mother were thrown out onto the street with nothing more than the clothes on their backs. It would have been more merciful to execute them both."

Chapter Eleven

"Being thrown on the streets isn't necessarily a death sentence," Anatolius pointed out. "Agnes probably turned to prostitution. If so, we were correct about the meaning of that tattoo on her body."

"I suspect Figulus would consider a woman's employment by Madam Isis or one of her colleagues to be worse than a death sentence," John replied.

He had arranged to meet with Anatolius at the Baths of Zeuxippos. They sat on curved benches beside the central fountain, under the gaze of the tight-lipped, bronze Demosthenes. The splash of falling water, amplified by the cavernous space, masked the echoing slap of sandals on tiles and the conversations of those passing by.

"I was careful not to make direct inquiries about the situation," John continued. "So far as Michri and Figulus are concerned I wished to commission repairs. I don't want word of these investigations reaching the wrong ears."

"Particularly since we don't know whose head sports the wrong ears. If nothing else, Cornelia will be pleased."

"It will please me, too. I'd prefer Cornelia didn't venture out alone."

"I'm glad I don't have a family to worry about," Anatolius observed. "Besides, if I did I might not be able to trot around to half the brothels in the city on your behalf. Not that I've had any luck tracking down that tattoo yet. I can continue to look, but now that we know the model for your mosaic belonged to court, it might be easier to check in those circles."

"Isis will keep an eye out for us too, now you've alerted her to the search."

"John, I was wondering…about Zoe…do you intend to call her by her real name now that you know it?"

"The girl in my mosaic has always been Zoe to me."

"I've often wondered how—"

"Anatolius! Lord Chamberlain! An attendant tells me you wanted to speak to me?" A short, muscular man approached. His black, cropped hair glistened wetly. His lumpy features might have belonged to a beggar, but not his green, pearl-embroidered robes.

Anatolius rose to greet his friend. "Francio! The Lord Chamberlain was asking about a courtier I had never met and I thought of you. After all, you know everyone at court, including those who have fallen from favor!"

Francio tapped the side of his nose, which had been horribly squashed in an accident—what sort varied with its owner's mood and his listener's credulity. "Let us keep that under the rose, Anatolius. But you flatter me even so. I don't know about everyone. Only those of importance. I don't have any gossip about the palace guards and servants and such, unless the servants are sleeping with someone important. Why, I could tell you…but perhaps I'd better not."

John mentioned the departed tax collector.

"Glykos? I seem to recall some mention of the name. You say this fellow died about ten years ago? I was only a youngster at the time."

"What about his family? I have reason to believe the mother and daughter remained in the city," John said.

Francio shook his head. "It's possible. Those who are banished from court might as well have sailed away across the seas."

John knew that many who fell into disfavor fled for their own safety. The lucky ones—landed aristocratics who were allowed to retain any of their holdings—retired to what remained of their country estates, or to the estates of relatives. But most at the palace owed their wealth and privilege to their positions and any palace official, even one as powerful as the Lord Chamberlain, held office at the whim of the emperor. With a few words, Justinian could turn a rich man into a beggar. Even the sentatorial class was not immune to having all they possessed confiscated.

Francio had screwed his face up in thought. "I do see some former courtiers at the Bathos of Zeuxippos from time to time," he said. "Anyone can get in for a copper coin or two. I suppose it's a way for them to enjoy the sort of surroundings they left behind, as well as an opportunity to talk to old friends."

"Or at least those who will still acknowledge acquaintance-ship," Anatolius put in.

"Perhaps one of these fallen courtiers would know something that would assist me?" John said.

"Indeed. And now that I think of it, I know exactly the man. His name's Menander. He was a silentiary. He fell from favor a long time ago so he's well connected to those who are no longer well connected. He knows everyone who used to be someone. What's more Fortuna has favored you, because I saw him right here not an hour ago."

"Where can we find him now?" John asked.

"He told me he was going to attend a poetry reading. He expected there would be plenty of wine, and his hearing isn't that good anyway. You know the poet, I believe. Crinagoras."

John suppressed a grimace. "Yes, he's a friend of Anatolius. Every time he visits my house the walls ring for days afterward."

Francio chuckled. "He does enjoy hearing his own verse. When I saw him this morning he was declaiming samples, to entice passersby to commission a work or two. His performances are always comical, even if it's not his aim. Last time he surpassed himself, because he recited at the very foot of Demosthenes there and mumbled even more than usual."

Anatolius remarked it was not surprising the orator's bronze brows were furrowed and his lips tight. "I suppose we'd better go and seek whatever lecture hall Crinagoras is using," he went on. "He's bound to chide me for abandoning my muse for the law."

"Crinagoras is going to entertain at my next banquet," Francio said. "I hope his presence won't stop you from attending. I'll be serving Arcadian dishes. Just simple country fare. Very unusual for my gatherings. John, you'll particularly enjoy the smoked cheese."

"Is the cheese by any chance produced on one of those farms your family owns?"

Francio frowned. "It could be, I suppose. I deal with city merchants. I don't know who supplies them."

"Francio is not a man of business," put in Anatolius.

"Certainly not," Francio agreed. "Particularly when the business would keep me out in the hills someplace. Why would I abandon the court to live amongst sheep and geese? Besides, the family is keen on horses. I remember when I was a child… well…." His voice trailed off as his hand moved for an instant to the side of his crushed nose.

"Is this man Menander from a landed family?" John asked.

"Not that I know of. He is, or was, a self-made man, which is to say a man made by the emperor. At some time he was of some value to Justinian. Only he and the emperor can say why. So he was granted a postion, income, a luxurious residence. Then he ceased to be of value and it was all taken away."

As he talked, Francio led John and Anatolius along a corridor where busts of emperors and philosophers on pedestals almost outnumbered the patrons. Doorways opened onto meeting rooms, libraries, and exercise areas. The only sign of the facilities themselves was a breath of humid air from an intersecting hallway leading further into the complex.

They found Crinagoras in a semicircular lecture area with a raised platform facing several benches. The benches were empty except for a long haired boy nibbling at a small wedge of cheese.

"Your audience is late in arriving?" Francio remarked.

"Oh, no," came the reply. "Indeed, there was an excellent turn out. My reading's finished. I've been writing shorter poems, to match my humble subject matter. No epics for onions!"

The poet was dressed in the voluminous old fashioned toga he always wore for his performances. John thought he looked pudgier than when he had last seen him. The ruddy features, framed by sandy curls, looked even softer and more child-like than John recalled, as if the man were aging backward.

Crinagoras gestured toward a table covered with empty earthenware dishes and jugs. "It all went exceedingly, wonderfully well, Anatolius. I provided just precisely the right amount of bucolic refreshment. Yes! The wine and cheese lasted exactly as long as the audience did."

"Was Menander here?" Francio asked. "We're looking for him."

"Menander?"

"A big old fellow. White hair. Gaunt. Stooped. Looks like the Olympian Zeus after a year in the emperor's dungeons."

Crinagoras frowned, setting his double chins in motion. "Well, let's see…I can't remember. I become caught up in the verse. I find myself transported into realms of imagination far removed from our tawdry, everyday surroundings. The audience might as well not be there."

"Menander was here," the boy on the bench piped up. He looked thirteen or fourteen. "I can tell you where he lives, if it's worth something to you."

Francio scowled at the youth. "And how would you know Menander?"

The boy shoved the remains of the cheese into his mouth before speaking around the bulge in his cheek. "I've had to help him home when he's drunk often enough."

Chapter Twelve

Home, to Menander, was a tenement behind the Church of the Mother of God. Francio remembered some urgent business and took his leave of John and Anatolius as soon as it became apparent that Crinagoras insisted on accompanying them.

The church and tenement were not far from the workshops of the artisans John had visited that morning. The rain had stopped and the lowering sun turned puddles and wet roofs red.

As the trio made their way through the russet light, the poet declaimed at Homeric length. "I need to stride the streets and fill my lungs with the same air as the simple folk."

He gesticulated so wildly his toga flapped and billowed like a sail. "Yes, those of us who make our living by our wits have yet much to learn from those humble souls who have nothing more than their stained and work-worn hands between themselves and an empty stomach."

He skirted the filthy, bare feet of a man sitting in a doorway, ignoring an outstretched, skeletal hand.

"Uncharitable bastards!" The croaking cry of the beggar followed them down the street. "May you rot!"

John swiveled on his boot heel and glared back. One look at the Lord Chamberlain's expression and the beggar found an urgent reason to leap up and scuttle away.

Anatolius gave John an inquiring glance.

"Perhaps I'm not in a charitable mood," John told him. "Besides, you're always telling me I shouldn't be filling every palm I see on the street."

Crinagoras looked pained. "I'm not so sure that I can find inspiration in a beggar. Certainly not from such a foul and insulting beggar. A ragged child, perhaps. For even the homeliest subject can become poetic in the hands of a master. Consider if you will Virgil's encomium to his salad. I intend to recite it at Francio's banquet since plain fare is the menu."

He paused and picked his way around dung lying in their path. "I have improved Virgil's work just a little," he went on, "in order that his archaic verse may fall more sweetly on today's ears. After that I shall recite one or two of my latest creations about life in the city, as it was before the plague arrived. These are darker times."

"And this is the dark alley down which we go, according to the boy at the reading." Anatolius plunged between two buildings leaning confidentially toward each other.

Crinagoras stopped and moaned. "Oh, but really, Anatolius, it will ruin my poor boots!"

The morning's rains had turned the passage into a swamp. Straw and half-decayed vegetable leaves littered the black surface of water broken by scattered islands of even less appealing ordure.

"Never mind your boots," Anatolius told him. "You can write a verse or two acclaiming their heroism."

"What an excellent idea! My friend, though entombed in the cold sepulcher of the law, your poetic soul still blazes like an eternal flame."

Crinagoras hitched up his long toga and tiptoed forward. He uttered a faint squeal as the water rose to his ankles. He took another cautious step and then flailed one hand at a swarm of huge green flies that had suddenly decided his face was more appetizing than an unidentifiable lump next to a wall.

The hem of the toga flopped into the mire. He grabbed at it. Slipped. Started to fall forward.

John's hand shot out, grasped Crinagoras' arm, and pulled him upright.

The grim smile he gave the poet was more appalling than the glare he'd directed at the beggar. "If I'm distracted any further by your eloquence, Crinagoras, I might not be able to catch you next time."

◇◇◇

The wood-framed tenement where Menander lived sagged toward the stolid brick back of the Church of the Mother of God as if in search of support. The entrance hall beyond the open doorway was unlit and its close air smelled of boiled onions.

In the dimness, the trio passed a woman seated at the bottom of the steep stairs. As they stepped around her, she raised her hand as if to beg, but instead drew a line on the plaster wall with a stub of charcoal.

The boy who claimed to have helped Menander home had given precise and accurate directions. At John's insistent knock, Menander threw open the splintered door of his third floor room.

He was, as Francio had described, an impressive figure, a stern looking man, broad shouldered, with bristling brows and white clouds of hair gathered around a craggy face. Though he was gaunt and bent, his flinty eyes were still level with John's.

Menander filled the narrow doorway. "If you are here about the money, you will have to come back next week. I am in the process of selling a few costly items and will pay you then." He spoke in carefully modulated tones.

"We're not here on such business," John replied. "I wish to ask you a few questions. I am—"

"Now I recognize you. John, the emperor's Lord Chamberlain, isn't it? My apologies. I was not expecting to see someone of your station in such a place." Menander stepped aside to allow his callers to enter.

John's first thought was that he had stepped back into one of the storage areas in which he had spent the days when he worked for the Keeper of the Plate. Menander's room, however, although it contained gold and silver, boasted a wider variety of precious objects. Glassware, furniture, statuary, wall hangings, and silks were piled in disarray. The congested space was bisected, floor to ceiling, by a loosely packed wall of treasures that sparkled and glinted like the iconostasis of a large church. John realized his filth-encrusted boots were defiling an expensive floor covering but Menander did not appear to notice.

"Please make yourselves comfortable," Menander said. "If you don't mind, we shall remain in my atrium." He glanced toward an irregular gap in the glittering wall. "My office, in the back there, is rather cluttered."

As far as John could tell, the nearest couch sat atop two others. The trio remained standing. Anatolius appeared bemused by the scene while Crinagoras gaped like a child.

Menander coughed. "As you see, I am blessed with many of the world's goods. Yet, for all that, I live simply."

John introduced his companions.

"Crinagoras I know," said Menander. "I found your poetry reading today most satisfying, young man. Your words will stay with me for some while. They provided food for thought."

Not to mention food for the stomach, John thought, noting a large wedge of cheese sitting on a silver plate.

"I'm certain Crinagoras is pleased you took something away from his reading," John said. "Do I understand correctly that you were, some years ago, removed from the emperor's court?"

Menander looked surprised at the sudden change in topic. "That is so, Lord Chamberlain. There is no point in hiding the reason why a former silentiary occupies such cramped quarters."

Anatolius murmured polite regrets.

"It is all too common, young man," Menander replied. "I was fortunate to escape with my head and this meager portion of my possessions. Not that I had more than a few cart-loads left, by the time I'd paid out enough bribes to get my treasures out of the palace. There was no truth in the charges. I do not blame our esteemed emperor, Lord Chamberlain. I am convinced Theodora's vile hand was in it." He smiled sadly. "I was very close to Emperor Justin. You'll recall that he opposed Theodora's marriage to Justinian for some time. After all, she was a former actress and hardly fit to wed his nephew, the future emperor. Theodora unfortunately has a long memory. Many of us who expressed admiration for Justin found ourselves exiled from the palace. Is there any foulness, any evil or crime in which she is not involved?"

Menander was a brave man to say this, or else intoxicated, John thought. Not to mention fortunate. Justinian was utterly unpredictable in his treatment of enemies. One might be summarily executed, the next merely stripped of titles and privilege and often welcomed back into the emperor's good graces within the year. Those with lives spared by the emperor's whims, along with families whose property had been confiscated either as punishment for misdeeds or for reasons known only to the imperial couple, comprised a shadowy, dissaffected army.

"How exquisite," exclaimed Crinagoras, plucking a small item from the marble curls of an ancient Greek bust. He held up a red, pressed glass icon, displaying the face of Christ no larger than a man's thumb.

Menander snatched the icon away. "Be careful! That's an hour of my life you held there! Perhaps two short hours of winter daylight, if I can get the right price."

"Whatever do you mean by that?" Crinagoras blurted out.

Menander pursed his lips in annoyance. "During my years at the palace I collected many things, some for their beauty, others because they fascinated me. Now I live by selling my treasures off to a dealer in such goods. I measure the time I have left by what remains to be sold."

"A melancholy calculation," observed John. He didn't add that by his reckoning the artifacts within sight would finance a large number of lifetimes, let alone the remaining years of a man Menander's age. Though, to be fair, there was no telling what sort of costly vices a former member of the court might have acquired.

"What is most melancholy," Menander said, "is considering which shall be the last cherished item sold."

Crinagoras beamed with excitement. "I'll find a few choice verses in your situation, Menander. It must be like living inside a water clock that's slowly emptying!"

"Isn't there a profession you could pursue?" Anatolius put in.

Menander's bushy eyebrows rose. "Work? At my age? Besides, I have a profession. I am a silentiary. Unfortunately for me, there is no call for my services at present."

It was true, John realized. There was only one emperor in the city employing men who could cut an impressive figure while standing beside a palace doorway.

"Don't you worry someone will steal these beautiful things?" Anatolius asked. "Treasures like these would normally be kept closely guarded. This building is hardly secure."

"There you are mistaken, young man. I chose this abode carefully. You must have noticed it abuts the church. Practically every tenant works for it, so I am surrounded by lectors and sub-deacons, by those who fill the church lamps, dust the icons, and polish the reliquaries. Weak though my physical fortifications may appear, my riches are protected by a mighty fortress of devout and honest Christians."

"Indeed," said John. "But those who are employed by the church do not share your palace background. Do you keep in touch with former friends? With others who have been banished? I've been told that you are well known among those who have lost their places at court."

Menander stiffened. "I have no complaint against Justinian whatsoever. If you are fishing for rumors and sordid gossip—"

"That's not my purpose. What makes you think so?"

The old silentiary stared at the red glass icon in his hand, set it on the plate next to the cheese, and sighed. "I am sorry, Lord Chamberlain. I spoke hastily, I admit. The last time someone began making inquiries about my acquaintances it soon became apparent he was far too interested in hearing scandalous tales about Theodora and grievances against the emperor. I'm not naive. I understand the ways of the court. When I realized what he was after and tried to put him off, he was not very civil."

John asked the name of the inquirer.

"He called himself Procopius. He accosted me at the Baths of Zeuxippos. He claimed to be writing a history and said he was employed by the general Belisarius."

"I believe Belisarius is currently in the city. He was recalled under a cloud."

"Let's hope he remains in disfavor then. No doubt the emperor can't wait to start some new, ruinously expensive military venture now that the plague is over. Perhaps we were luckier being ruled by the plague. At any rate, this Procopius was an unctuous and unpleasant little man."

Crinagoras sniffed. "I've heard of Procopius. I understood he was planning to pen some turgid prose about Justinian's architectural projects. The subject is as inspired as the typical legal document."

"I am not interested in rumors," John said. "I can hear as many as I wish at court. But I do seek information about a man named Glykos. What do you know about him?"

"Glykos? He was a tax collector, wasn't he?"

"Yes. He owned a house on the palace grounds, opposite the excubitor barracks, not far from—"

"I'm familiar with the house, Lord Chamberlain. By sight, that is. Glykos himself, however…."

"It's his wife and child in which I'm interested," John replied. "Glykos was one of those men the emperor had executed following the riots. His wife and daughter were spared, but thrown onto the street. The girl was named Agnes."

Menander shook his head. "I'm afraid I can't help you. I've never encountered anyone related to Glykos. The mother and daughter most probably turned to begging or prostitution. They could well be dead by now what with the rioting then and the plague just past. Or they might have departed from the city. If so, they could be anywhere."

"Is it possible they assumed another name?"

Menander's eyes narrowed and he pulled himself up straighter. For an instant John glimpsed the formidable demeanor that must have served the old silentiary well in the days when he presided over the great bronze doors leading into Justinian's reception hall.

"I assure you, I have never heard a word about the unfortunate mother and daughter, whatever name they might have chosen to go under, even if they are still alive."

Crinagoras gasped.

Glancing around, John saw the poet hastily put down a small, rectangular mosaic, an icon depicting a golden cross.

"What's the matter?" Anatolius asked.

Crinagoras eyed the icon warily. "It's been taken over by a demon," he stammered. "I…I…turned it toward the light and it changed from a cross to a…to…well…."

Menander laughed. "It serves you right, young man. Didn't I tell you not to disturb my belongings? May you have nightmares!"

"I have seen mosaics like that," John said. "Where did you obtain this one?"

"I don't remember, Lord Chamberlain. I've had it for years." He gestured around the treasure-packed room. "It's hard enough for me to keep track of the value of all this, let alone recall where every item came from."

Chapter Thirteen

John, Anatolius, and Crinagoras stood at the foot of the tenement stairs and contemplated walking back through the inky puddles of the alleyway, now barely visible in the deepening twilight beyond the doorway.

"I shall have to at least wrest some verse from this miserable excursion," muttered Crinagoras. "I'll call it A Paludial Passage. What could be more emblematic of the common life than slogging through muck and mire and—"

"I'm glad someone has found some inspiration here," Anatolius broke in. "John, you don't believe Menander knows nothing at all about Glykos' family, do you?"

"No. I would have expected him to have heard gossip or rumors if nothing else. It isn't surprising Menander would be uncooperative. A man who has been expelled from court isn't likely to have any great love of those who remain there, regardless of what he might say about Justinian to my face."

Anatolius looked down and scowled. "I'm in agreement with Crinagoras. I hate thinking I've got my boots soaked for no good reason. Perhaps Menander should be reminded of the consequences of misleading you?"

"I don't want to frighten him. There are plenty of others in his position and I wish to avoid spreading alarm about inquiries coming from men living in the palace."

John turned toward the woman they had seen sitting on the stairs on their way up to Menander's room and asked her where he could find the owner of the tenement.

The woman, who had been studiously ignoring the trio, looked away from contemplating the wall. "I hope there is nothing amiss, excellency?" Her tone was anxious. "I collect rents and keep watch and you can be sure I am ever alert. It's not everyone who will trust a woman with matters of business, but the owner of this fine dwelling is one."

The fading light fell against the wall beside her, illuminating a line of charcoal marks and smudges where a few had been rubbed away. The woman herself remained in shadow, a faceless figure with a rasping voice.

"Who is the owner?" John asked.

"The Church of the Mother of God," was the surprising answer. "All the tenants here work for the church in one way or another. Their lodgings are so close to it they don't mind paying a little extra for the privilege of not having far to walk."

She tapped the line of charcoal marks on the wall. "As you see, I keep track of them most carefully. I hope nobody is spreading bad things about any of them, excellency. Most are poor, but all of them are honest."

Anatolius complimented her upon the honesty of the tenants.

"The three of you are from court, aren't you? I am very observant, sir," she replied. "Menander isn't in trouble, is he? If he were, I would never try to conceal him from you. My job is to watch and collect rents. I work for the church, which instructs us to obey the emperor in all matters."

John did not observe that since they had just visited Menander, concealment would not have been possible. Instead, he asked the woman how long Menander had been a tenant.

"He's been here for years, excellency. Never been any bother. I will say. Very quiet, he is, even when he's imbibed too much. That's all I know. As I said, my job is to collect rents and keep watch. Also to make certain nobody lets half a room out behind my back. Not that I don't sympathize, for it's difficult to scratch out a living and getting more so every day."

She sighed. "But Menander…I cannot tell you much about Menander, I fear. A polite man, but not talkative. One who's lived at court—rubbed elbows with the imperial couple—why would he spend time gossiping with ordinary folk like me?"

"Are there any others from court here?"

"There's one other, excellency. Her name's Alba. She is from a famly that was once wealthy but she talks to us all and is kinder and more considerate than most. She cleans the church and gives most of what she earns to charity."

"Do Menander and Alba know each other?" John asked.

"I couldn't say, excellency. I've never seen them together. Alba is one who works each day laboring at the church or Samsun's hospice while Menander is in and out at strange times. I don't know how he occupies himself. Whatever he does, he often needs an escort to carry him upstairs afterward."

Alba occupied a small room on the top floor of the building, two floors above Menander. However, their informant advised them it was useless going back upstairs since Alba had been at the hospice all day.

As the trio stepped out into the gloomy alley and began to splash back to the street, the woman seated at the bottom of the stairs reached over and erased three marks on the wall.

Crinagoras looked back at her with evident curiosity. "The keeper of the gate," he muttered. "Like Cerberus, or—"

A scream interrupted his inspirational thought. A black, howling shape raced past them up the alleyway, and slid around the corner at the far end like a chariot rounding the turn in the Hippodrome. A hissing, brown terror followed, feet working wildly against the slippery ooze, sending up a shower of black water and filth.

"Mithra take those cats!" shouted Anatolius, wiping his spattered garments with his hands.

"Demons!" screamed Crinagoras, his voice hitting a higher pitch than the felines had managed.

His cry was as nothing compared to the wail of horror he emitted as he lost his balance and sat down, hard, in the muck.

John helped him to his feet. To his surprise, the poet seemed to compose himself almost immediately. In fact, even as he slapped ineffectually at the mud on his clothes, he smiled.

"An epic's come to me!" he blurted out. "Why, don't you see? The door to the underworld's in an alleyway in the Copper Market! Behind a church, no less! There's a moral there for all to learn! We see the keeper of the gate! We are attacked by demons! It will rival Homer! I am so sorry, Lord Chamberlain. I must return to my kalamos immediately before my muse deserts me. You will be able to proceed without me, won't you?"

Chapter Fourteen

The cavernous ward in Samsun's Hospice was chilly, the noisome air warmed by nothing but feverish bodies on close packed cots. Alba sat at the bedside of a shriveled creature whose sex could not be determined from a distance, alternately spooning nourishment between its withered lips and wiping the patient's chin and cheeks with a cloth.

Alba's back was to John. Her plain black linen tunic spread out on the straw around her stool, the long sleeves half covering her bone-white hands.

John waited for her to finish. He was in no hurry. He had set Anatolius the task of escorting Crinagoras home and of informing Cornelia that he would be late.

Alba spoke softly in the cultured tones of the court as she moved the spoon from bowl to mouth. That the utterly unresponsive person she addressed was capable of hearing had to be taken on faith.

The room echoed with a din of voices. Conversation mingled with the unintelligible sounds of suffering. John had learned to pick words out of the clamor at an imperial banquet or during races at the Hippodrome. He listened as Alba recounted the tale of a holy woman who had seen a glowing veil descend from a church ceiling. The veil swooped, circled, and then flew away like a white bird. The listener's brimming eyes glistened.

After a long time, Alba rose and turned. She wore the veil which covered her head and shoulders fastened at the neck in the manner of a cenobite. Framed by black, her colorless face shone like the moon on the dark water of the sea.

"Lord Chamberlain," she said. "Thank you for waiting. I know a place where we can talk."

◇◇◇

Alba lit a clay lamp and set it back down on the table beside an array of mortars and pestles, scales, and metallic instruments with uses John hesitated to guess. The flaring light revealed wooden shelves bowed under the weight of jars, jugs, and bottles filled with unguents and potions. Several crosses had been propped up on the shelves amid the medical supplies. There was no wall space for them.

Alba made no effort to sit on the stool in the corner. She remained standing in front of the lamp. Shadows obscured her pale face. John could not make out her age.

"I grew up at the court, Lord Chamberlain. I can feel when someone is gazing at my back. I remember you as a young man, when you worked for the Keeper of the Plate. I have only heard about your remarkable career since then. You haven't changed much."

A ghost of a smile formed on John's lips. "Some might say otherwise."

"The collector of rents told you I was here, didn't she?"

John nodded. "You do not sound very pleased I have found you, Alba."

"She is forever sending unfortunate souls to me, Lord Chamberlain. She implies that I can cure them. I suspect she collects a fee for her services."

"Can you heal?"

"Only the Lord can heal the sick, as any Christian could tell you. I try to offer comfort. But you aren't here to be healed or comforted."

"No. However, I do hope you can help me. Are you acquainted with Menander?"

She nodded. "He is a neighbor. He also used to be at court."

"Do you speak to him often?"

"I used to. Our families were banished a few months apart and we both came to live in the same building, which is how I made his acquaintance."

"I've just come from his room. He lives in a remarkable fashion."

"He refuses to accept the blessing the Lord has bestowed upon him." Her tone was even, but John detected a sudden coldness.

"What blessing do you mean? The treasure trove he was able to take with him?"

"Hardly, Lord Chamberlain. I mean the banishment itself. It was a blessing, since it is more difficult for a rich man to attain heaven."

Alba paused. "Yes, a blessing, for the Lord saw fit to clear away the obstacles along Menander's path to eternal life. He cannot see that. He is blinded by the gold piled up around him. What value has gold, except that assigned to it by men? Yet its glare obscures the light of the Holy Word as surely as the lights of this man-made city hide the blazing celestial fires overhead. I can tell you understand. You must be a man of religion. And yet, you are a rich man."

John did not deny it. He wondered what Alba would think of his spartan furnishings and lack of slaves. His simple tastes reflected his own nature. "Do you know anything about Menander?"

"We both received the same blessing. Now I care for the church, attend services, and offer my assistance to the poorest of the poor. He chose another path. I argued with him and prayed for his soul. That was a long time ago. I still pray for his soul."

"And what path, exactly, did Menander choose?"

"The same that most at the palace tread. Menander was always a man who indulged his passions. I believe he gambles and who can say what other vices he has acquired. He frequents the theater."

"He told you this?"

"Oh, yes. I've encountered him on the street from time to time. He's often arriving home as I leave to go about my work, and insists on describing to me what he has seen. Things no Christian woman should even hear about. He has begun to revel in wickedness. When I protest, he tells me it is all make believe, visions if you like. Well, I've had visions myself, of saints and angels, and I am prepared to state that saints and angels do not appear on the stage in Constantinople!"

She paused for a moment, staring at John in a fixed fashion. "Lord Chamberlain, do you ever have visions?"

"Never, Alba. I obtain my knowledge of things by my senses and by questioning. Which is why I have sought you out. You doubtless recall the house in which I live?"

John felt her penetrating stare drop away. "Glykos the tax collector lived there," she said.

"Did you know the family?"

"Only in passing. Comita was his wife's name. I heard they had a daughter. She was born after I began my new life."

"Did you see them after Glykos was executed?"

"Not very often. I had my own sorrows and we are always selfish about them, are we not? But I have occasionally run into Comita at the market. She looked very ill the last time we met. That was some years ago. She was trying to coax a farmer to part with a bunch of dried out beets for less than he was asking. He refused. You would have thought they were monstrous gems. Charity is often farther away from home than barbarous lands, I fear. I paid his asking price and we talked a little while. Comita told me she and her daughter were living with her late husband's brother, a man called Opilio. A sausage maker. Forgive me, if I have said too much," she murmured. "Why should someone from the palace express an interest after all these years? Has Justinian perhaps decided on a pardon?"

"No, Alba."

He felt her stare on him again. "Are you certain you have not had visions, Lord Chamberlain?"

"I assure you I have not."

"Visions are not always of saints and angels. Did you know I scrub the floors of the church? When I first knelt on the freezing tiles to begin the bitter labor to which I had been reduced—for so I considered it at the time—my knees were still smooth and unbruised and my hands uncalloused. The sun had not yet risen high enough to light the windows. Alone, in the dark, I pictured my friends at the palace, asleep at that hour in their soft, warm beds, as I should have been. I could have washed the floor with my tears...

"Then, I heard a voice. A whisper. By the time I realized I was hearing it, there was only the memory. What I remembered it said was this. 'Rejoice for all is the Lord's will....'

"I jumped up. My first thought was one of the workers who fill the lamps was mocking me. I saw shadows, the gray windows, the dim shapes of pillars....

"Then I noticed a faint gleam on the wall near where I had been working. A ray of lamplight slanted across a small icon of Elisabeth the Wonderworker. Oh, I did not know her at the time, but I made inquiries, as you can imagine....

"She was born of wealthy parents. When they died she gave away all her possessions and traveled to Constantinople to take up a monastic life and minister to the poor and the sick. How fortunate I was. Elisabeth had to choose to give up worldly things herself. My choice was made for me. It was Elisabeth who had spoken to me."

Alba had turned slightly. Now the light illuminated her features in a soft mist. She was no youth, but her face appeared as unlined as that of a child.

"Perhaps, Alba, you were speaking to yourself?" John said in a gentle voice.

"No, Lord Chamberlain. It was Elisabeth. And how fitting it was. For at the end of her life, an icon of a saint on a church gate spoke and instructed her to prepare for her journey to heaven....

"For years I have looked to Elisabeth's icon in the Church of the Mother of God and waited for her to speak again. I look forward to that day, because I believe the mosaic icon will speak when it is time for me to ascend to take my own place in heaven."

She paused for a heartbeat. Her gaze did not waver from him. "Do you think me foolish, Lord Chamberlain, to expect a mosaic to talk? No, I can sense you do not."

Chapter Fifteen

"Visions?"

"Visions!" John confirmed, taking off his boots.

Cornelia combed her hair. She was gazing toward the diamond panes of the window, in which John could make out her faint reflection as well as his own. Whether she was looking at herself or him in the dark glass he could not say.

Her thin linen tunica left her arms bare. John could see the movement of their firm muscles. She was as lithe as he remembered on their first meeting over twenty years earlier. Now there were sparkles of gray in her hair.

"And do you have visions, John?"

"Nightmares sometimes."

"I don't wonder. You need a better bed. You'd sleep more soundly."

John lay down on the cotton-filled mattress. The bed frame creaked under his weight. It was the same bed he had used since he moved into the house. He had never given it any thought before. Now that Cornelia had mentioned it, he could feel the lumpy cotton pressing uncomfortably against his bony frame.

He didn't think his nightmares had anything to do with the bed.

"I wish you'd let go of this matter of the mosaic girl, John. From what you say, the poor dead woman must have been a common prostitute. It's the sort of crime the City Prefect will solve, if it can be solved, and if it's even considered worth pursuing. Life is cheap here. Look at the state of those boots! You've been venturing into places a Lord Chamberlain shouldn't be going without a bodyguard."

"Anatolius and Crinagoras accompanied me for part of the time," John protested.

"Ha! It would've been you protecting them if it came to blade work." Cornelia laid her ivory comb on the wooden chest below the window. "No matter how long I live in this city, I will never get used to it. So bright when seen from the sea, but full of darkness even at noon."

"That's true, and it's something that I wish to address. Apart from this matter of the mosaic girl as you call it."

"You know, when you were younger you wouldn't be talking about girls, mosaic or otherwise, when we were alone in a room with a bed."

John laughed. "Well, I may surprise you yet. But I am concerned for your safety, Cornelia. As you just pointed out, it isn't wise to be walking the streets alone."

"I'm only out during the day and I keep to well frequented places. I don't wander down muddy alleyways. Or did you find some foul swamp to wade through?" She wrinkled her nose.

"I should have left my boots downstairs," John admitted.

"Yes. Peter will be upset. But don't worry about my safety. I've taken care of myself in Alexandria and—"

"Yes, but in all the other places you lived, you weren't a member of the Lord Chamberlain's household, as I have said before. Men in my position have enemies. Many enemies."

Cornelia sat down on the bed beside him. John was aware of her perfume, faint as a memory of their days in Egypt, and the warmth where her hip touched his.

"I know you have enemies, John, but I find it hard to understand. It's not as if you're an ambitious man."

John laughed. Odd as it sounded, she was right. "What further ambition could I possibly have?"

"You could crave still more power and more wealth. The empire isn't enough for Justinian. He wants Italy back. He never has enough churches either. He keeps building more. Everyone has ambitions. And consider Anatolius. He aspires to write poetry for future generations."

"That's Crinagoras. Anatolius has turned his thoughts entirely toward the law."

"You don't believe that, do you? And consider Captain Felix. As high as his position is, wouldn't he prefer to be leading an army on the battlefield?"

"Probably. When he joined the excubitors they were led by Justinian's uncle Justin, a military man. Felix has always admired Justin. It's true, though, my office came to me, rather than my seeking it out. However, whether I am ambitious or not, there are those who fear my power, or resent it, and have reason to do so."

John patted the mattress beside him. "May I invite you to lie down?"

Cornelia settled into the curve of his arm. "No doubt," he went on, "I am a threat to many at court. It's no good looking at me like that. In serving the emperor I have harmed people, sometimes without realizing it. Others may believe I have deliberately harmed them, or might simply resent me for reasons known only to themselves. And any of these people might try to hurt me by hurting my family. Which is why you should have a guard when you go out. I will have to look into finding one."

"But John, I was the one chiding you just now for going about unguarded. You see, we think alike. Who wants a guard underfoot all the time? As I was saying the other day, I'd like to see your private bath restored. Then I wouldn't have to go out so often, would I?"

John smiled. "As it happens, I've traced the artisan responsible for the mosaics. Considering how lewd they are, they may require some modification in addition to repair."

"I think not. They're finely crafted and nothing is shown that would embarrass either of us. Peter could be instructed to avoid the room if it is offensive to him. I can clean it myself. And the hypocaust doesn't function any more, except as a good place for rats to nest."

"I will engage for someone to look at that also." John brushed an errant gray hair away from Cornelia's face. "Is there anything else you'd like?"

Chapter Sixteen

John wished to talk to Opilio, the sausage maker Alba had mentioned, but he decided to talk to Figulus first.

Although he had spoken with the mosaic maker about the repairs he desired, he had not made final arrangements and it seemed to John that investigations would be better served by giving Cornelia something pleasant to contemplate, rather than brooding on the possible dangers posed to him by looking into a murder. Then too, he supposed the refurbishment might serve as an apology to Cornelia for the obvious distress his investigations were causing her.

A servant asked John to wait in the doorway of the workshop. After a while Figulus' wife appeared. John had not seen her during his initial visit. She was stout and her prematurely gray hair made her look too old to be carrying a red-faced whimpering infant under each arm. She was also exceedingly short, shorter than Figulus' older boys, who were ostensibly poring over tesserae scattered across a work table but casting sidelong glances at the visitor.

John stated his business above the mewling of the squirming infants. The mosaic maker's wife looked displeased. John couldn't tell whether it was with him or the infants or both.

"I am afraid it is not possible to speak with Figulus right now," the woman said. "He's out on a job. Is it some...special...work you're interested in?"

"Yes, I suppose you would call it that."

The woman looked John up and down. Mostly up, given her stature. "I thought you might be one of...those customers." She glanced over her shoulder and glared meaningfully at the boys, who complied with their mother's unspoken order as slowly as they dared and slunk out of the workshop. "If you want to see some examples of the special work, it would be best to return during the evening, sir. We keep them locked up, because of the children."

One of the infants swiped at John with a pudgy hand, fell far short, and reached out again. The other seemed more interested in trying to grab his mother's hair.

"I've seen examples of the work," John said. "In fact, they cover the walls of my bath. I've spoken to your husband about repairs. I merely need to make arrangements for it to be carried out."

"I see...well...." Figulus' wife slapped lightly at the fists of the reaching infant and then pushed the hands of the other away from her head. "You can find him right across the street from the law courts. He has an important commission there."

◇◇◇

"Yes, Lord Chamberlain, by the time I've finished this will be a lavatory fit for any magistrate or even the City Prefect himself."

Figulus stepped down from the marble bench that ran the length of the long, narrow room. The openings in the bench had been covered with boards. Several workmen were busy in a far corner, making a blue sky, or perhaps a sea, out of tesserae. The smell of wet plaster almost masked the usual odors.

"I am to do the more detailed work," Figulus explained. "The magistrate who hired me specified that in particular."

"Will these pictures change their character with the light?" John asked.

"Oh, no. The magistrate simply wanted a more attractive place for lawyers to deliberate. You know how uninspiring these public lavatories can be."

John did not mention he avoided such facilities whenever possible.

He saw that the work was half completed. The theme was classical. There was Hercules cleaning the stables. Next to him Sisyphus rolled his stone up the mountain.

The mosaics were an improvement on the graffiti scratched into the unfinished walls. No doubt many of the witticisms involved lawyers and magistrates or Theodora, or all three. Presumably the glass tesserae would be more difficult to deface.

"Most impressive," John remarked politely.

Figulus beamed. "Thank you, excellency. I am hoping that citizens will feel an urgency as they pass by at the very thought of what awaits them in here."

"Doubtless more than a few citizens on their way to the courts will feel the need to stop and admire your workmanship, Figulus. Now, I trust you will have time to for those repairs I asked about?"

"I can spare a few days and one or two workers right away and meantime I have some experienced men I can trust to carry on creating the clouds and mountains here."

"Your business appears to be thriving."

"The Lord has been generous to me," the mosaic maker said with a smile.

"Your wife seemed to think I was a customer of another sort."

Figulus stopped smiling. "What do you mean?"

"She thought I had come to look at some special work of yours. I suspect the sort akin to that on my walls. Do you have much call for that sort of work?"

"Only as is necessary, Lord Chamberlain. It pays well and I have expenses. My understanding was that you were not interested in work of that nature?"

"I am not. Simply curious."

Figulus' smile returned, but it did not appear very convincing. "Very well then. When would you like me to start on your bath?"

◇◇◇

Opilio's shop was not far from the courts. John bent his head to avoid the sign that graphically declared the wares for sale within. Cut into the shape of a giant sausage, it jutted far out into the colonnade, almost certainly in contravention of the ordinances. It looked as if the sign maker had repainted something intended for a brothel. Or perhaps it merely appeared that way to John thanks to a sleepless night. He could not shrug off such nights as easily as when he was younger.

At least he had managed to convince Cornelia that his morning's destination, on a broad, busy thoroughfare just west of the Augustaion, posed minimal danger to unguarded Lord Chamberlains.

Not that it was far from where he had been the day before. He could see the timbered roof of the Church of the Mother of God, rising over the surrounding buildings, a few streets, and innumerable dank alleys, away.

The interior of the shop smelled of savory and cumin. A stout old man, bent and balding, with massive forearms, put down his funnel and gave a twist to the casing he'd been stuffing.

"You're the man from the palace," he said. "I've been expecting you! I'm surprised you're alone." He dropped his half completed sausage into the pile of empty intestines heaped on the counter, some dangling onto the floor.

"You say you were expecting me?"

"Don't worry. The sausages are ready. Do you intend to carry them back by yourself?"

"You seem to have mistaken me for someone else. Are you Opilio, the owner of this shop?"

"That's me. And you work for the emperor, don't you?"

"True enough."

Opilio came out from behind the counter, brushing his hands on his greasy tunic. He was short, his lack of height entirely due to bowed legs which appeared to be half the length one might have expected judging by his torso. "The sausages are in my storeroom. I shall get them right away. They are of finest Lucanian variety, the sort they make in southern Italy. The same kind Augustus enjoyed. Yes, I hear Justinian's entertaining a Persian high-up and wants to remind the foreigner of Rome's great traditions."

He chuckled. "It'll remind him how Justinian's taking back Italy from the barbarians too. Once he's done with Italy, he'll get after Persia. I hope I live to see it. Nothing says Glory of Rome like a succulent Lucanian sausage."

"I'm afraid I haven't come for sausages, Opilio. While it is true I work for the emperor, I'm not a servant."

The other gaped at John and then asked him what in fact he did.

"I am Justinian's Lord Chamberlain."

Opilio guffawed. "And I'm the famous eunuch general Narses! I like a fellow who has a sense of humor. Would you lift your boot?" He bent over in awkward fashion. "You're standing on a casing."

The sausage maker must have noticed the fine workmanship of John's boots or possibly the subtle gold thread worked along the hem of John's cloak, because when he straightened up, one end of the errant intestine in hand, his formerly ruddy face had turned as white as if someone had cut his throat and hung him up to drain his blood.

"I apologize, excellency. An honest mistake. I would never wish to insult our great emperor. I am the staunchest of supporters."

"No matter, Opilio. I can see the humor in being mistaken for a servant when I venture into the streets."

The color began to return to Opilio's face. "Well, then, how can I assist? I have it! You are here to purchase sausages for yourself. Why, the empress herself praised my wares! Or so I hear. I have not spoken to her personally, although perhaps it is an everyday occurrence for you, excellency? Perhaps that is where you heard of me?"

John smiled. Anatolius had once got into trouble for including both the empress and sausages in the same verse. That information he kept to himself. "I am often summoned to her presence, Opilio, but not daily. She has not mentioned your sausages to me."

Opilio looked disappointed.

"I wish to talk to you about a young woman named Agnes," John continued.

Opilio frowned. "Agnes?"

"I understand she was your brother's daughter?"

Opilio slapped the length of intestine he was holding down on the counter. "It's true, Lord Chamberlain, but I haven't seen her for a long time. She was always an ungrateful child. She refused to help with my work. Wouldn't deign to do even the simplest of the jobs. Clean the entrails? Oh no, far too nasty. She was used to a life of wealth and privilege. Girls like her don't dirty their fingers on the nasty insides of pigs, although they're happy enough to have those insides on their dinner plates. Agnes was always willful, but she grew worse after her mother died."

"Comita is dead?"

"Yes. She went to the Lord almost three years ago."

The sorrow in his tone was unmistakable. "I can tell you were fond of her," John observed. "My condolences."

The sausage maker looked away. "I don't want you to think I am concealing anything from you, excellency. We were to be married. She used to say the family of a sausage maker would never starve. But she left me for my brother. He was a clerk at the palace at the time. Ruthless, greedy, and underhanded. It was obvious he would do well for himself and so he did. And after all, living on the palace grounds is not the same as occupying a few rooms near the Copper Market with the smell of smoke and worse always in the air. As she said, making sausages is such a low occupation."

From the way Opilio said the final words it was apparent that they were as fresh in his memory as if they had been spoken an hour before, even if he had repeated them in his thoughts ten thousand times.

"Yet you took mother and child in, so I am told."

Opilio shrugged. "They were my brother's family. And to be fair, Glykos had sent much custom my way. We used to joke that those at the palace felt safe eating my sausages since the tax collector's brother wouldn't be inclined to poison them. Particularly since their demise would have resulted in a decrease in tax revenues. As it turned out, I now own a perfectly respectable home, although hardly a mansion. I might have had a mansion too, if my brother hadn't fallen out of favor. I was about to be given a contract to provision the army. Yes, Lord Chamberlain, there can be gold in entrails, if a man is not too dainty to seek it."

John observed that the loss of the contract must have been distressing.

"What is a mansion worth? What was my brother's house worth to him in the end? I'd prefer to live with pigs and eat from their trough in a world where Comita still lived." Opilio dabbed at a watery eye. Then his lips tightened. "It's as well she died. She never had to see what Agnes became. An actress, which is to say a whore. I did my best, but when her mother died, I couldn't control her. Who was I but the poor, rejected, younger brother of her father?"

He sighed. "Why should she heed my advice or respect my commands? Before long she was going about in the lowest places with the lowest personages. She was seen at theaters—or what she called theaters—and in the company of so called actors and actresses. Then she suddenly seemed to have money. I confronted her. She denied earning it in the common way, but had no other explanation. A man in trade must be careful of his reputation, excellency. Wagging tongues have ruined many a business. Seeing she could support herself, by whatever vile artifice, I turned her out."

John said he understood. "And you have not seen her for some time?"

"No, excellency. It's been months now. Nor do I ever care to see her again. She has my brother's blood in her."

What would Opilio think if John told her his errant niece was dead? Would he be pleased? More likely he would immediately regret all he had just said. John decided not to tell him yet. The fewer who knew Agnes had been murdered the fewer would be alerted to his investigation.

He questioned Opilio further but the sausage maker had nothing of consequence to add. He said that Agnes had rarely mentioned the names of her disreputable acquaintances.

"Did she mention a man named Menander? I am told he was a patron of the theaters."

Opilio shook his head. "I've already told you, excellency, she said little to me about her acquaintances. I made it plain to her I did not want to know. As for the theaters where she claimed to perform, they were usually nothing more than some public or private area taken over temporarily, as far as I could gather. You will understand I had no desire to seek them out."

"I may return in a few days," John said. "Meantime, try to think if there's anything else you can tell me. Before I go, there's one more thing."

"But I've told you everything. My old head is as empty as these poor casings awaiting my funnel."

"I don't want to question you further, Opilio. I've decided I'd like to purchase some sausages after all."

Chapter Seventeen

Although Opilio at first insisted that he had not wanted to know about the unwholesome places Agnes frequented, John's interest in his wares, especially at the exorbitant price quoted, assisted the sausage maker's memory.

Thus he learned Agnes had let slip a location where reprobates of her sort often congregated to put on what they were pleased to call performances.

Following Opilio's directions, John soon found himself on the long narrow street leading to the square where Agnes had approached him.

A strident cry caused him to look up. A raven rose from the top of the wooden cross on a nearby roof. Then another raven appeared and another. John counted them. Seven.

Their wings beat furiously. For an instant they hung over him, their shadows hovering beside his boots. Then the birds gained height and soared off.

John looked away, back to earth, to an archway from which issued a breath of warm air both acrid and appetizing. Stepping under it, he discovered among the businesses, opening off the packed dirt courtyard beyond, were a public bakery, a dye house, and a coppersmith's workshop.

The city felt limitless to those confined to its maze of streets and alleyways, amidst the crowds and clamor and stench, where every new turn opened upon a new world—a forum, a church, tenements, warehouses, a line of shops, a monument to a dead emperor. There was no limit to what might be found in the capital. The ravens in the sky would have seen that despite all that it contained, Constantinople was a small place. No location was far from any other. From the southern harbors on the Marmara to the northern shore along the bay of the Golden Horn was an easy walk, even for earthbound creatures, made difficult only by the necessity of ascending and descending the steep ridge that formed the backbone of the peninsula upon which the city sat.

John's investigations had thus far not taken him beyond the Copper Market to the north and west of where the Mese ended at the Augustaion. He wished he could ascend like the ravens and peer down into the brick and marble tangle of the city.

He remembered the old rhyme, common in Bretania, which foretold the future by counting black birds. Seven was for a secret. If he could join those ravens would the secret he sought be easily seen? Or, as the rhyme went, was it a secret never to be told?

As John entered the courtyard, he heard raised voices. People bustled about under the columned roof of a semicircular exedra, reached from the far end of the enclosure by three long, low steps.

The structure resembled a smaller version of the front of Isis' establishment. Its curved wall contained a number of doors. Most, however, were boarded up. Two obese gilded Cupids, wings encrusted with soot, looked as if they'd have a hard time climbing out of their wall niches, let alone soaring with the ravens, in the case of the Cupids not to scavenge for scraps but to search for the lovelorn.

John hailed a youngster hauling a basket of loaves out of the bakery toward what was clearly the make-shift stage Opilio had mentioned disparagingly. At the mention of Agnes, the boy's eyes narrowed, but he raced off, and as John mounted the stairs, a woman emerged from one of the functioning doorways and came toward him.

"My name's Petronia." The speaker was dressed in an thread-bare yellow tunic. Her finely chiseled features, set off by black hair fashionably coiled at either side, were as perfect and white as those of an ancient Greek sculpture from which time has worn the last vestige of pigment. She was no longer young, but John was old enough to appreciate stubborn, aging beauty more than the careless, unchallenged, and common prettiness of youth.

In this case, the beauty was somewhat diminished by the monstrous phallus the woman wore.

She cocked her head to one side reprovingly. "What right do you have to stare like that, coming in here with your sausage in your hand?"

John looked down at the offending articles hanging loosely in his grasp for want of a basket.

"Save that lot for the wife," Petronia cackled, swaying her hips in order to waggle the stuffed, leather protuberance jutting from beneath her garment. "Oh, I'm sorry, sir," she continued with a simper. "Did I offend you? We are all Christians here."

"It wasn't that." John's tone was sharp.

The playful expression left her face. "I overheard you asking about Agnes."

"Do you know her? Daughter of the tax collector, Glykos?"

"We share a room, off and on," the woman replied. "I haven't seen her for a few days. What do you want with her? A private performance? Are you looking for Agnes in particular or might I be of assistance?"

"I wish to question her," John replied.

Petronia was suddenly wary. "And who are you to come questioning me?"

"I am Lord Chamberlain to Justinian."

Petronia opened her eyes wide in feigned surprise. "Of course you are! That explains why you carry sausages about in your hand. Well, it's makes no difference to me who you are. All our best patrons are pretending to be something they aren't, or at least aren't any more. It's hard to say on what side of the stage the best actors reside."

"Many of your patrons used to be at court?"

"That's right! This quarter suits those who want to stay in the city, or have no place left to go. It's not the most desirable area, what with all the smoke and furnaces and smells and such, so the rents are reasonable. Yet it's near enough to the palace and the Baths of Zeuxippos where they might run into old friends for a chat. Or at least old friends still willing to recognize them."

A number of people John took to be Petronia's fellow thespians strolled about, talked, and gesticulated. They didn't seem curious about the tall, thin stranger in their midst. Just another patron. There were as many women and dwarves as men.

"You offer those who once enjoyed the privileges of the palace something of the culture they miss," John said. "I imagine you are well patronized?"

"Indeed. We're one of the few troupes to stage the classics. We're doing a new version of Lysistrata."

"That explains your unusual adornment."

"What did you think? Old Aristophanes didn't take full advantage of the comic situation. We've eliminated all the boring dialog and debate. We offer something friskier. You're lucky to find us here. We don't rehearse every day. As it happens we like to stage our performances during the afternoons when they're holding one of those religious processions. There are always pilgrims waiting for the procession to begin, so we do well enough."

"Doubtless some would say you're taking coins that the pilgrims would otherwise offer to the church."

"Oh, I expect we do the church a good deed," came the airy reply. "There are bound to be pilgrims who feel guilty about having come here and seen…what they saw, and so give more to the church than they intended in the first place."

John glanced around. "Do you employ this place regularly?"

"We call it our theater. It's been deserted for years."

"I don't know if I've ever heard of a failed brothel before," he replied, inclining his head toward the Cupids.

"It didn't fail. Theodora had the girls rounded up to help populate that convent of hers across the Marmara. Not that these girls wanted to be saved, but a job's a job and it wasn't that hard to be a reformed sinner. Rumor is that the empress paid the madam to talk them all into moving, with the madam taking on the new duties of abbess."

"Who owns it now?"

"No one knows who this ruin belongs to. I believe whoever it is doesn't care to come forward. It's not much good for anything. The cubicles would all have to be torn down and the whole inside repaired, so it stands here ignored and perfect for our uses. That is to say, this part serves for a stage and we store our props in the back."

"And there are plenty of rooms left over for getting in and out of costume?"

"Indeed. Our patrons sometimes…assist with that."

Petronia's demeanor suggested she hadn't heard about Agnes' death.

John told her.

The powder on Petronia's face could not have turned any whiter. Her eyes, however, plainly registered shock and she put a hand to her mouth, muffling a gasp of horror.

For a moment she tottered, as if about to collapse. She walked unsteadily to a wall niche and sat at the foot of a Cupid. She wiped away the tears before they could ruin her makeup, blinked, and attempted to compose herself.

Her sitting position thrust the leather phallus up in front of her face. She pushed it aside, and then fumbled with the strap holding it around her waist. The phallus fell off and she kicked it away.

"There, and I'm glad to be done with the nasty thing. They do get in the way. And that's a small one compared to some we've used on stage. How vexing they must be."

She covered her face, burying her failed smile. When she finally looked up her pale makeup was half gone, showing fine wrinkles at the corners of reddened eyes.

"What is it you want to know? I haven't seen Agnes for days, as I told you. And now, now I will never see her again. I'll miss her." She paused. "But before you ask, I know little about her private life. Women like us are always busy. Even when sharing a room we don't see much of one another and we don't share our woes. They're all the same anyhow. When that bastard Opilio kicked her out I offered her shelter. If you got those sausages from him, I'd have a servant taste them for you before you eat them."

"Did she have other friends, Petronia? I'm not here to cause anyone trouble. I'm trying to find out who murdered her."

"You really are from the palace, aren't you? Who do you think killed her? Who's usually responsible when an…an…actress is murdered?"

"I realize it is a dangerous profession. I have reason to think this might not be related to her work. Did she ever mention a man named Menander?"

"Didn't have to. We all know about Menander. He's one of our most generous benefactors."

"Could there have been a closer relationship between her and Menander?"

A sound between a laugh and a sob escaped Petronia's lips. "What would Agnes see in an old man like Menander? What would Menander do with an actress? But I understand what you mean. I might as well tell you. I don't want you to think I'm holding anything back. Talk to Troilus."

She got to her feet, supporting herself with a hand on the pudgy thigh of the gilded Cupid. "Yes, Troilus might know more than I do. He's a handsome young man. Youth seeks out youth, doesn't it? His shop is just in the back there. He sells all manner of curiosities."

She pointed toward a doorway on the end of the exedra, then, seemingly overcome by emotion, swayed, and fainted.

Chapter Eighteen

ohn caught Petronia as she collapsed and lowered her to the ground. Several of her fellow actors rushed over and before long had her head propped up, pressing her discarded phallus into service as a pillow. Petronia made unintelligible moaning sounds and her eyelids twitched without opening.

"I brought her some very bad news," John told a dwarf who glared at him. The dwarf held three wooden balls of the sort used by jugglers, and looked ready to hurl them in outrage. "A friend of hers, a girl named Agnes, was found murdered."

The statement sent the troupe into uproar.

John decided it would be futile to seek further information from them, and went to the door Petronia had pointed out.

Troilus, the young shopkeeper who knew Agnes, had not bothered to erect a sign advertising his business.

Inside the building, doors appeared at intervals along a short hallway scarcely illuminated by light entering from the entrance. Beneath the dust coating the plaster walls John could distinguish faded paintings depicting the delights once for sale on the premises.

The artist had possessed more imagination than skill.

John pushed open one of the doors and glanced in. The bare, cobwebbed cell was filled almost entirely by a bench large enough to hold a mattress. Were the cells in Theodora's foundation for former prostitutes much different?

The hallway ended at another corridor running across it at right angles. At the juncture, part of the wall had been knocked out and a crude plank frame inserted in the exposed brickwork.

John peered through the opening, recalling the flight of steps that had led him down to the cistern where he had discovered Agnes' corpse. There were four steps here, formed by worn blocks that might well have once served as bases for statues. By the flickering light of some torch beyond his range of vision, John saw the area at the bottom of the makeshift flight of steps was dry.

The subterranean room was little more than a dim empty space from which shadowy archways led into darker spaces. No doubt this was the basement of the building abutting the structure of which the exedra formed a part, or else had belonged to a building that no longer existed.

Underneath the streets of Constantinople lay a bewildering geography of basements, vaults, sub-basements, cisterns, and ruined foundations, buried and forgotten as new structures succeeded the old, a continual rebuilding necessitated by the forces of fire, earthquake, riots, imperial power, and commerce.

John did not have to puzzle over which direction to take. On a crate in front of him lay a stained and cracked marble arm. It might have broken off of a statue of a Greek philosopher. The forefinger was raised, but now, instead of emphasizing some profound truth, it pointed toward one of the archways.

To John's disappointment, the wide corridor beyond slanted down to a closed iron grating set in the wall. He bent over and tested the chain attached to the grating. It was locked to a bolt in the concrete floor.

He put his face near to the bars. A dark abyss on the other side of the grating swallowed up the weak light from the corridor. He could make out nothing. A chill draught touched his face bringing with it the smell of dampness and mold.

He gave the bars of the grating a tug. They didn't even rattle.

"Not the first philosopher to point to a dead end," John muttered to himself.

Then again, the marble arm might have belonged to an orator or an emperor. It was impossible to be certain with nothing more than an arm to go by.

"If you're looking for Troilus, he's out."

The voice had the pitch of a rusty hinge. The pallid face from whose thin, colorless lips the words issued poked out from a dark gap in the wall on one side of the grating.

"To whom am I speaking?" John asked.

"My name is Helias, sir, and I am a maker of sundials."

The speaker was nearly as short as the thespian dwarves John had left tending Petronia. "I can tell you are a man whose business requires punctuality," Helias continued. "A man without an hour to spare. This is why you are vexed at Troilus being unavailable. You would find one of my portable sundials invaluable."

"A portable sundial?"

Helias' small head, barely reaching John's chin, bobbed up and down. "A most excellent device. Please, allow me to demonstrate."

John followed the little man into his shop. He had long since learned that the surest way to secure information from a merchant was to show an interest in his wares.

Two clay lamps on a work table provided Helias' workshop with light. After two paces the masonry floor gave way to dirt. The sound of dripping water filled the air, not a result of moisture running down damp walls, John realized, but from assorted water clocks strewn everywhere.

"Some of my time keepers are in need of repair or adjustment," Helias said. "The bowls are all sound. My water clocks are guaranteed to make no more noise than sunlight sliding across a smooth marble dial. I do not want my customers to count the hours they are kept awake by their clocks, although they would be able to do so most accurately, sir." Helias gave a creaking laugh.

John stepped over a shallow bowl whose interior featured a mosaic of the night sky, avoiding a copper clock decorated with an etched Poseidon emerging from the descending water to indicate the passage of time.

When he reached the work table Helias held up a silver sunburst, by appearances an ornamental medallion of the sort used to fasten a cloak at the shoulder.

"You see, sir, it opens like a jewel box," Helias demonstrated. "But inside, rather than jewels, you have the time." With his thumb he pushed up the hinged gnomon in the center of the miniature dial. "Each sundial has an inscription, chosen by the client. This one was commissioned by a silversmith, and will be inscribed 'All my silver will not purchase an extra hour.' A thought we might all ponder. Yes, indeed we may."

John remarked that it was certainly a clever device. "But why do you choose to work down here in the gloom, Helias?"

The sundial maker heaved a sigh. "Many of my clients have asked that question, sir. They think it most peculiar a purveyor of artifacts which require light to function should keep his establishment in a place where sunshine can never venture. The fact is, I dislike strong sunlight and avoid it as much as possible. Is that so odd? Do you suppose the tanner cares to spend his time wading through urine simply because he needs to use it on his hides? When I am out in the sunlight I cannot stop calculating the hour by the position of my shadow."

John observed he could appreciate Helias' difficulty. "I calculate time in a similar manner, by observing the position of the sun over the rooftops, which is why I do not need one of your sundials. I shall, however, mention them at court." He noted that Helias' shoulders slumped.

"That would be most kind, sir. I hope you do not think I am enamored of wealth. We must all find a way to live. Sometimes I wish I had found another way, that I had never heard of sundials, so that I could enjoy the glorious sun the Lord has given

us, like any other man. I would be much happier if I could stop
the sun, like Joshua, for then there would be but the one fixed
hour. That would mean I would be unable to continue with my
work since there would be no purchasers of sundials. As it is, I
spend most of my time down here or in church."

"But you also make water clocks."

"Water doesn't follow one around like the sun, sir. But as
it happens, I am also working on a portable water clock to be
carried during the night or on cloudy days. It might appeal also
to others who would prefer to keep the sun out of their affairs.
And now, how may I help you?"

"I was told your neighbor, Troilus, sells curiosities. Does he
sell these portable clocks of yours?"

Helias snapped the miniature sundial shut. "I should think
not! I would not permit it! You should be thankful that grating is decently lowered and locked, sir. Most of the wares that
young man sells were better destroyed than displayed for all to
see. Lewd pagan statues, sir, obscene lamps shaped like, well, let
me just say they wouldn't be out of place in houses godly men
never visit. You can deduce the sort of clients he encourages to
call on him. It's reflecting poorly upon my own business, being
next to his dreadful shop. And that's not the worst of it, sir! Why,
the other evening he insulted me in a gross fashion!"

John held up his hand, stemming the flow of words. "I am sorry
to hear it, Helias. I fear that time is urging me to make haste. You
understand, I'm sure. Do you know when Troilus will return?"

"It's difficult to say. He runs his business in a very irregular
fashion. He often vanishes for a few days. Gone to purchase
stock, or so he claims." Helias narrowed his eyes and his mouth
tightened. "Are you seeking to make a purchase? Not everything
he sells is blasphemous or obscene. Perhaps you are seeking a
religious relic? For display at some church? In that case, I would
be willing to convey a message to him when he reappears."

"It isn't merchandise I seek, but a young woman."

Helias' scowled. "I don't see many young women here, sir.
Very careless about time, they are."

"This woman is an actress. She's with the troupe that has its theater up above. You've probably seen her now and then."

"I try to keep my eyes averted from the unholy things that go on at that theater of theirs, sir. But what does she look like? Painted like the whore of Babylon, no doubt! How would I pick her out from all the rest?"

John hesitated. What in fact had Agnes looked like? Her corpse, with its battered face, told him nothing. He had glimpsed her living face for an instant when she approached him in the square and lifted her veil. What had he seen? That she was Zoe, just as she had told him. Nothing more.

How had he known she was Zoe?

"Her eyes are striking, exceptionally large and dark. And she has a tattoo on her wrist," John said.

"I don't look at women's wrists, sir, and I imagine more than one actress has tattoos."

"She was a friend of Troilus."

Helias frowned. "I have seen a young woman in his company. An actress. Whether her eyes were dark, I can't say. She visits him regularly. As a faithful church man, sir, I have spoken to Troilus more than once about consorting with such low women, but all I receive in return is abuse. Yet I say it again, I would rather cross the Mese than have to pass close by this actress friend of his, and here I am, trying to earn an honest living right next door. I am not certain what he is to her, but you can rest assured it isn't what even the most charitable of us might think."

"She will not be visiting again, Helias, for I fear she was murdered. It happened exactly a week ago."

Helias stared in amazement. "A week ago, you say?"

"Yes. Why? Did you see her that day?"

"Not exactly, sir, but as sure as the sun will rise tomorrow, I can tell you who killed her. It was Troilus."

For a moment John was speechless. In the silence he was aware of the clocks' relentless dripping. He had spent days following a trail that led from one person to the next, with no end in sight. Had he reached his goal with such shocking abruptness?

"That is a grave charge, Helias. Are you sure it isn't just your disdain for the man speaking? What proof do you have?"

Helias' piercing voice rose to an even higher note. "I saw him drag the body in, sir. Of course, I didn't know it at the time. But what else could it have been?"

John ordered him to explain.

"A week ago I was working here late at night when I heard a scraping noise outside. Naturally, I peeked out. One needs to keep an eye on what is going on, especially after dark."

He paused. "There was Troilus, dragging a big sack, sir! It was just after midnight. I know because I was inspecting some of the water clocks and they all showed the same hour. It wasn't so odd that he would be bringing stock in at such a time, because, as I told you, he keeps a peculiar schedule. But I did wonder why he had not enlisted some assistance. Whatever was in the sack must have been more than he could lift comfortably by himself. I didn't think any more about it, sir, until you mentioned the murder. The sack was exactly the right size for a body."

Chapter Nineteen

Anatolius wiped away tears with the sleeve of his tunic, blinked, and squinted around Francio's steamy kitchen. Almost immediately the garlic-saturated air started his eyes watering again.

"Mithra!" he muttered.

Francio was nowhere to be seen. A small army of servants rushed about carrying bowls and brandishing knives, somehow avoiding fatal collisions. The clank of pots violently stirred or pushed around the long brazier running along one side of the room reverberated from the sooty walls and low ceiling.

He would have left immediately, except that he had come here on serious business.

To investigate a murder.

Since parting with John outside Menander's tenement, Anatolius had not been able to put the murder out of his thoughts.

This morning he had arrived at the steps of the law library with the gulls but couldn't concentrate on research. Instead he kept wondering how a common prostitute could have known the name by which John addressed the mosaic girl on the wall of his private study.

Francio might be of assistance. He was familiar with every rumor, true or false, at the palace. He would know who, if anyone, might be aware of John's solitary conversations.

He had shoved the Digest and its dusty old jurists aside and left for Francio's house. However, the nearer he got, the more wary he became of revealing too much to his gregarious friend. Curiosity had carried him from the atrium to the back of the house and into the kitchen.

As he tried to decide whether to leave, a basket was suddenly thrust under his nose. It was filled with what looked like wilted weeds.

"Here's them herbs you wanted, sir." The basket holder's garments were too ragged for a servant. "I even located some of that rue, and nasty stuff it is."

If there was any odor of herbs, Anatolius couldn't distinguish it beneath the reek of garlic. "You're probably looking for the master of the house," he said, just as the man they both sought strode out of the chaos toward them.

Francio's elaborate clothing looked out of place in a kitchen, even if it was thematically appropriate. Rondels embroidered with parsnips, lettuce, and radishes sprouted from his earthy brown dalmatic. He exchanged a few words with his herb supplier, shooed the man off toward the far end of the room, and turned his attention to Anatolius.

"Merchants have been in and out all day. They're wonderfully obliging. As well they should be. There's not a better customer in the city, except perhaps the imperial couple. Justinian and Theodora's banquets rival mine in size if not imagination. But why have you dared to venture onto my culinary battlefield, my friend?"

"Battlefield? I'd have described it as a riot. I'm surprised your place isn't burnt to the ground every time you decide to entertain."

 . Francio laughed. "It looks like a riot because you are not schooled in the strategy of the kitchen. This is merely a skirmish in a carefully planned campaign. My soldiers need the experience. When the day arrives for that rustic banquet I mentioned, they will not cower in the face of a cheese and garlic paste."

Anatolius remarked he was surprised to find Francio in the kitchen.

"A leader rides out at the head of his army surely?"

"Justinian doesn't!"

"He must stay here to lead on the theological front," Francio chuckled. He made his way through the hubbub and bent over a bubbling copper pot until his flattened nose came perilously close to the turbulent liquid within. When he straightened up, his lumpy face was bright red from the heat of rising steam.

"Excellent!" he remarked. "Just the right amount of coriander. Another hard fought victory is at hand!"

"Your cooks have boiled, grilled, or roasted every creature that lives. I'd have thought it would be easy for them to prepare a simple peasant dish."

"They aren't used to simple dishes. And when there are so few ingredients, mistakes cannot be disguised, not even with a sauce."

"You've enough garlic in here to disguise a shipload of spoiled fish." Anatolius ran a hand over his eyes but the stinging miasma seemed to have settled onto his fingers. His eyes burned still more fiercely.

"I apologize for your distress, but all this is not the finished art. No one enjoys the smoke from the glassmaker's furnace or the sweat from the poet's brow, do they? Do lovers of verse stroll into your study unannounced and complain about your efforts? I'm certain you haven't barged in on me without good reason. There must be some urgent business?"

Anatolius decided he might be able to learn something without giving too much away. "I need to call on your expertise again. It's about a private matter. Not exactly scandalous, but potentially embarrassing."

Francio tapped the side of his nose. "Sounds fascinating! Am I about to learn something?"

"No. I was just wondering how such stories spread?"

"By mouth. How else?"

"But, let's say, a person at the palace had an unusual habit…."

"Let's say there was anyone at the palace who didn't. Now that would be interesting. What sort of person is this? A servant? A senator? Man or woman?"

"Hypothetically, an official."

"You lawyers are a circumspect bunch. This habit, does it involve, shall we say, an unnatural practice?"

Anatolius frowned. "I don't think I'd go that far."

"I can tell by your expression that whatever you are talking about is extremely unnatural. You will need to control your expressions better in front of the magistrates, my friend. I don't grasp what you think I can tell you. Rumors and gossip have a thousand roads but only a single destination, which is to say the entire city."

"I can't believe everything becomes general knowledge," Anatolius observed. "I'm not speaking about an indiscretion at the Hippodrome or in a brothel."

"Where then? Come now! You want to know who might have whispered scandal into someone's ear? How can I tell you if I don't know what it is? Don't worry about revealing the details. As you know, I am the soul of discretion."

"You wouldn't dare to say that on oath!"

Francio looked hurt. "I only parcel out what I know as seems absolutely necessary. How do you suppose I maintain my popularity?"

"By your golden tongue?"

Francio grinned. "Flattery is a good tool. It usually works, no matter how clumsily one employs it. Now, you say this mysterious behavior which is not scandalous, but which I deduce is quite unnatural, occurred not in public but in a private place. Such as…?"

"A place similar to, for instance, a study."

"Oh yes. You're referring to the Lord Chamberlain's habit of talking to the mosaic on his wall, are you not?"

Anatolius might as well have been hit in the stomach. He couldn't seem to draw breath to reply.

"Yes, this is fairly well known," Francio went on. "It isn't a very popular story. The Lord Chamberlain is considered so eccentric, all in all, his speaking to bits of colored glass hardly raises an eyebrow. And before you ask how the story could have got out…well, he has a few friends who have visited the house, not to mention servants, and has even had some unwanted visitors over the years, I'd wager."

"I'm positive I didn't mention it to anyone."

"Not even to some lady? I daresay we will all reveal anything under the appropriate circumstances."

"That's what Justinian's torturers claim too. You're right. Yet I truly don't believe I've ever breathed a word about it. As for his servants, Peter wouldn't disclose his master's secrets, even to the imperial torturers."

"Ah yes, Peter. John doesn't have many servants, does he? The paucity of servants strikes people as far more peculiar than him talking to mosaics when he'd had too much wine. You might not know any of this. Since you are one of the Lord Chamberlain's closest friends and he is a powerful man, many are doubtless reticent about sharing such opinions with you."

"Indeed. This is the first time you have shared this information with me, Francio."

"You never asked, my friend. Unfortunately, I can't tell you how John's little secret got out. It's spread too far from its source."

Francio peered again into one of the pots on the brazier, grasped the protruding handle of the ladle, and gave a lusty stir. A few drops of liquid splashed out and evaporated on the coals in a hiss of steam.

Anatolius decided he should get back to the library. "I was interested in who might know about Zoe," he said. "But it sounds as if there's nothing to be learned."

Francio dropped the ladle back against the side of the pot. "Zoe. That's what John calls the mosaic girl, isn't it? Now that I only learned a few weeks ago."

"Then the name isn't common knowledge?"

"I just told you I didn't know about it until recently."

"I see your point, Francio. Who was it who told you?"

"Crinagoras. I can't remember precisely when it was. I spend so much time here on the battlefield and the scene is always just like this. You'll recall I invited him to compose some verse for my banquet? His original idea was to recite odes to the various rooms of the wealthy and powerful to form a poignant contrast to the humble fare on the table, as he put it. Well, he came here and started declaiming samples of what he intended to write. The poem about the decorations in a certain senator's residence was scurrilous enough to give me second thoughts. When he started describing John's mournful conversations with Zoe I made him put the whole lot in the brazier. I thought he'd plucked the name Zoe out of his imagination. I should have known better. He hasn't got much imagination."

Anatolius couldn't hide his disappointment. "Mithra! Then I've wasted my time. I thought you might be able to narrow it down for me, but if Crinagoras wrote a poem about Zoe, you can be sure her name was all over the city before the ink was dry."

Chapter Twenty

A corpse covered in wet dye would be difficult to handle without leaving some trace, even if it were secreted in a sack.

John hadn't noticed any sign of staining in the corridor leading to Troilus' shop.

He considered possibilities as he stood in the sunlight outside the entrance to the subterranean realm where Helios and Troilus conducted business. On the other side of the courtyard, the man John deduced was a dyer sat on a stool by the doorway to his business in the shade of a rainbow covered awning.

No one would have arrived with a body and asked that it be dyed.

However, dye might be obtained at such a place.

The dyer appeared to be enjoying the rehearsal, which had reached a point where actors were busy knocking each other over with their leather phalluses.

John couldn't see the humor in it.

The stricken Petronia was nowhere in sight. John walked over to the man, who immediately sprang to his feet.

"Good day, sir! Welcome to the shop of Jabesh! I can supply every color under the sun and some the sun has never seen."

Jabesh was an angular little man with glittering black eyes and a beard that was little more than a dark stain. He flapped the baggy sleeves of his tunic, upon which were sewn colored squares of every imaginable hue, apparently samples of his work, making him a walking advertisement for his craft.

There were several shades of red, but how a dye applied to white linen might compare with the same used on livid flesh, John could not say.

"I see you are authorized to work for the palace, Jabesh," he remarked.

The dyer looked down at his hands, stained a telltale purple. "Like my father and his father before him. Though I am but a humble laborer I wear the imperial purple today. I was preparing silk on commission this morning. Are you here on court business?"

He stretched out his arm to display a multicolored sleeve. "You see here only some of the colors I offer," he went on. "My family is descended from the very dyers who created Joseph's many-colored coat."

"Have you sold dye to anyone recently?"

Jabesh lowered his gaudily decorated arm. "I am a craftsman, not a merchant. If it's dyes that are wanted, I suggest consulting an apothecary."

"I understand it isn't your usual line of business, but perhaps you have sold dye in special cases?"

Jabesh's hands clenched into purple fists. "Has Troilus sent you? If you're one of his friends, you can tell him I won't sell purple to anyone at any price. It's illegal. It could cost me my livelihood and my life."

"Troilus has tried to purchase purple dye?"

"That's right, sir."

"Did he say why?"

"No, but it was easy to guess. He wanted it on account of that woman of his. He came around wheedling me after I refused to sell it to her."

"You mean Agnes?"

"I don't know. I'm not interested in the names of actresses."

"Yet you're not averse to enjoying their performances," John observed with a slight smile.

From the direction of the stage drifted the dull, repetitive thump of simulated gladiatorial combat with obscene leather weapons.

"I like a little culture now and then," Jabesh admitted. "Many of the actors are men, as is proper. As for the so called actresses, you can dye a beggar purple but it won't make him emperor."

John kept to himself the thought that dyeing a whore purple might very well make her empress. "When did this woman approach you?"

"She's cajoled me more than once. A few weeks ago she started to try to persuade me and I believe she would have given me what men pay her for, if I had been so stupid as to take the risks I mentioned. Finally, it would be a week ago, Troilus tried to talk me into agreeing. No one except a craftsman authorized by the emperor would have such dye. You can't buy purple from an apothecary any more than you can pay to have your robes dyed purple."

John asked if any reason had been given for the couple's interest in an illegal dye.

"No, sir. My guess is she wanted to play act."

"With the troupe? It would be just as illegal and more dangerous in public to appear in such garments even onstage."

"Not all performances are public. She often brings costumes in, you see. The troupe uses the same old rags over and over and they have me dye them occasionally so the audience thinks it's seeing something new. There's more color than fabric to those costumes now. The actors might as well parade in here naked and jump into my vats before they perform."

John wondered if, in fact, the body he'd seen had been submerged in one of Jabesh's vats before being left in the cistern.

"Your workshop is secure?"

"Certainly."

"You do a lot of work for the troupe?"

"Nothing beyond coloring and recoloring their rags. Every color but that reserved for the emperor. When a play requires it, I come as close to the imperial hue as the laws allow. Not very close, but close enough so that when an actor says, 'Ah, what a lovely purple tunic you are wearing, Theodora,' the audience grasps the idea."

"The troupe has performed plays about Theodora?"

Jabesh glanced around and lowered his voice. "Only at private functions, sir. Not that I've seen any, or care to. They are vile, or so I've heard. Not that I know any details. I believe they call one production A Secret Account. I suspect it's Troilus' painted woman who pretends to be Theodora. She behaves as if she is the empress even when she isn't on stage."

"Why is that?" John could not imagine the dark eyed, sorrowful little girl he knew pretending to be an empress. He had to remind himself that Agnes was not Zoe.

Not really.

"She puts on the airs. There are more than a few ladies in the neighborhood who used to be members of the court and come by their airs naturally, as you might say, but none of them can match her. In any event, she has no right to pretensions. You can tell. The common sort of woman always overdoes the act. It's not just the mincing about pretending to be better than she is. There's the way she soaks herself in perfume." Jabesh waved a purple hand as if to disperse a foul odor. "Do you know, it just occurred to me. Maybe she wants the dye for herself. I wouldn't be surprised if there are men who would pay well to spend the night with a woman in purple."

"You may be right, Jabesh. What about this scurrilous play? Do you have any idea where the troupe performs it?"

"No, sir, but I don't want to make it out to be more than it is. It's nothing but a bit of fun. Or rather, some peoples' idea of a bit of fun."

"The actors are your customers after all."

"Yes. That's right. Like all of us, they need to serve their customers. Look at this." He grabbed his sleeve, bunched it and displayed a square of garish orange next to an overpowering green. "Have you ever seen a more hideous combination? Yet an excellent patron of mine will insist on sending these barbaric colors to wear on his finest robes, not to mention his wife's garments and wall hangings."

"I can believe there is an audience for performances that do not show the empress in the best light."

"Especially around here, sir. People who have been cast out of the palace—and there are many of them—do not think kindly of Justinian and Theodora. Some like to plot revenge."

"Is that so?"

"It's the same as the play. Nothing, really. Something to pass the hours. You can see how they would enjoy a play that mocks their enemies. Then they go out drinking and continue acting themselves. As soon as the tavern closes they'll storm the palace walls. But needless to say the uprising is always put off to a more auspicious time."

"How do you know this?"

"Customers grumble in front of me. What do I matter?"

"And you say that Troilus' friend was involved in this…play acting?"

Jabesh looked distressed. "Yes. As I said, they don't mean it seriously. Perhaps I should have said nothing."

"No. I appreciate your honesty. Someone I spoke with earlier was not so forthcoming. He will soon regret it."

Chapter Twenty-One

"Lord Chamberlain! I am honored to have a second visit so soon!"

Opilio stood on a stool, draping a garland of links over the doorway to his shop. Glancing down, he must have taken note of John's stern expression because the smile on his ruddy face faded.

"There's nothing wrong with the sausages, is there? Were they not to your liking?"

"I haven't tried them." John's tone was curt. "You will provide me with more information since you appear to have neglected to tell me everything you knew."

The stout sausage maker climbed down, nearly lost his balance, and reached a hand out to steady himself against the wall.

"I've been doing my best to recall the smallest detail that might be of use," he protested. "But I fear my poor brain is as empty—"

"—as one of your casings," John cut in. "Just as it was a few hours ago."

"That's it, alas."

"I find it hard to believe you would recall your niece associating with actors and actresses but her spending time with malcontents plotting against the emperor would entirely escape your mind."

The color drained from Opilio's face. "Plotting against... no...no...of course not. She's a common little prostitute, that's true enough, or at least she was when last I saw her. But a prostitute...that's one thing...to plot against the emperor...that's another thing entirely...."

"Indeed. After all, it is not treasonous to harbor a prostitute under one's roof."

"Treason?" Opilio looked stricken. "Why would anyone suspect me of treason? There's no one in Constantinople more loyal to Justinian than I am. Why, I would kiss the ground our glorious emperor walks upon. I mean, if I ever found myself anywhere near such ground. Not that I would try put myself in the vicinity of the emperor."

John was silent.

"I...I...but...Agnes...I turned her out!" Opilio stuttered. "If I'd known she was plotting against the emperor, I wouldn't have turned her out, I would have turned her over to the Prefect immediately, even though she was my niece."

John remained silent.

"I wouldn't harbor a traitor if she were my own dear mother, excellency," Opilio continued, near to tears. "In fact, I would hunt her down and strangle her with my own hands."

"Justinian would be gratified to hear that."

"And I'm not ashamed to say it. What is a relative's blood as compared to the wellbeing of the empire? We are all mortal. The empire lives forever."

The sausage maker stood to attention, with all the gravity of a silentiary at the entrance to Justinian's reception hall, albeit a short, bent, bow-legged silentiary in a tunic streaked by bits of offal.

Was he truly worried about being charged with treason, or was he afraid the high official who was displeased might put an end to his business dealings with the palace?

"You understand if there is anything you are not telling me this time, you will regret it. Do you know a man by the name of Troilus? He sells curiosities."

"The name isn't familiar."

"He is acquainted with your niece."

"Agnes knows far too many men!"

"Then she never brought him to your home when she lived with you? It is possible he went by another name."

"I did not allow Agnes to carry on her filthy business in my home, excellency. None of her acquaintances—men or women— were welcome, because they were all of the same sort."

"Then you did not know Agnes had a taste for purple and that she comported with plotters?"

"As I've already told you, excellency, I know nothing of that. I can believe Agnes might have a taste for purple but as for seeking to bring down the emperor...." Opilio shook his head. "She's a foolish girl. All she cared about when she lived here were baubles and vanities. I doubt she's changed. On the other hand, a woman in her profession does not necessarily know the plans of those she entertains."

"Are you sure of that?"

Opilio clasped his hands together as if on the verge of wringing them or praying. "I must be honest, talk about plots is often in the air, like smoke from the foundries," he replied. "Every week there's talk of such things, yet what is it? Just talk. That's why I said nothing. After a while one doesn't even take note of it. If any of these plans were serious, no one would be prattling about them in public, would they?"

He paused and contemplated the linked sausages framing his door. "Yes, excellency, you can depend upon it. It's all just idle talk. I suppose those who once basked in the presence of the emperor must find it boring to live in this quarter. That's why they hold all these meetings, at out of the way places, to liven their drab existences up a bit."

"Exactly what out of the way places are you referring to? Don't lie to me, Opilio. I am anxious to attend one of these meetings."

Chapter Twenty-Two

A handful of men had clustered near the base of a porphyry column in the far corner of the spacious court between the Baths of Arcadius and the water. Morning sun spilled a silver wash across the court's polished stone. John and Anatolius observed the men from a distance.

"A peculiar place to congregate if you're planning to depose the emperor," remarked Anatolius with a grin. "Or perhaps they don't realize they're conspiring at Theodora's feet? I can't say I see much resemblance."

John admitted that the painted statue, which he knew was meant to represent the empress, did not much resemble her. "She may well have looked like that in her youth," he concluded.

"If she had been the Christian's Mother of God in her youth rather than a prostitute."

John agreed that the empress had never worn such a beatific expression during any of his encounters with her, but then Theodora had long hated him. Why it was he had never discovered, although he suspected it was in part due to his high position at court, allowing him constant access to and possible influence upon Justinian.

Her statue gazed away from the city, as if it was looking away from the sinful world in the direction of the convent she had established on the other side of the water. John doubted she would be one of those powerful personages who in due course would retire to a life of contemplation.

"Remember, Anatolius, we only have Opilio's word that he overheard Agnes saying this was a favorite meeting spot for her disaffected friends."

At this hour there was no one else at the seaside court aside from solitary strollers. The sun had been rising as John and Anatolius made their way down a steep street that ran out of the Copper Market and ended at the Strategion, not far from the court in the northeastern corner of the city. Agnes seemed to have had a predilection for the hours before crowds flooded streets and squares.

John could appreciate that.

"Isn't that Menander?" Anatolius pointed out the broad shouldered old man conversing in the middle of the group. In the sunlight the man's white hair formed a nimbus above his craggy features. "Very suspicious, don't you think? He certainly carries a grievance."

"They could be discussing anything. The fine weather. The excellent statuary. The mosaic girl in my study."

"Yes…well…I'm sorry about Crinagoras' indiscretion."

"I am not concerned with common gossip but, as you said, since Crinagoras wrote a verse referring to Zoe anybody in the city could know it as a result. I had hoped if I could find out how Agnes learned the name it might give me an idea of what and with whom she was involved and why she was murdered."

"I'm sure Crinagoras would be apologetic if he realized what he'd done," Anatolius offered.

"I'd appreciate your not bringing him to my house again. Everything he sees or hears is liable to be spread far and wide in bad verse. I particularly do not care for people eavesdropping on my conversations."

"You must be fair, John. As I explained, Peter said you were in the garden. I left Crinagoras beside the door to go and look.

When you and Cornelia walked into the atrium arguing about a woman—someone called Zoe—he could hardly fail to notice."

"So he imagined Cornelia and I were arguing about Zoe? A most welcome sort of visitor!"

"I told him it wasn't what he thought."

"And explained who Zoe was?"

"Well…yes…I suppose I shouldn't have. But what was I supposed to say? That she was a real woman you and Cornelia were arguing over? Crinagoras means well, John. I've known him since he was a boy and it's true he now spends time communing with his muse…."

"But I talk to a wall mosaic. Is that what you mean?" John's lips tightened. "Cornelia was distressed at my muttering to the wall, as she said in Crinagoras' hearing. It is my way of clarifying my thoughts. People will murmur as they read. It keeps one's thoughts from racing away out of control."

Anatolius looked at his feet.

"When I was a boy I memorized Homer by reciting to myself while I walked," John went on. "However, I'm not likely to write a poem titled Crinagoras Bores His Muse. As I said, I do not wish to have him in my house. It's not just my own privacy I have to worry about now, as you know."

Anatolius said he understood. "When I confronted Crinagoras about it, he assured me that he had raced over to Francio's with the verse. Flew as if he had Mercury's wings on his feet is how he put it. The ink dried as he ran. He swore he had only the copy that Francio made him burn. He never recited the poem to anyone else. In fact, he never had time to memorize it. His poems write themselves, or perhaps his muse does. He tried to explain it all to me."

"I do appreciate you looking into the matter, Anatolius. It narrows my field of inquiry." John kept his gaze on the men standing at the base of Theodora's statue.

The group was still in conversation. A stiff breeze carried laughter and an occasional word wrapped in the smell of the sea to the two watchers.

"I believe I can wander close enough to get some sense of what they're discussing," Anatolius said. "Best if you stayed here, John. If they see the Lord Chamberlain coming they'll scatter like gulls."

John watched his friend cross the dazzle of the square. The younger man passed in and out of the long shadows cast by the statues and decorative columns that jutted up, a sparse forest of stone and metal.

If Agnes had become involved with plotters, or moved among them, she might have intended to give John a warning. That would have been reason enough for her murder.

Ever since he had begun looking into her death John had moved through an eerie calm. He had encountered no hint of danger, no sign of an adversary.

Those who could best conceal their intentions were the most dangerous.

A shout drew his attention.

A man standing at a distance from the group had called out to a small ship which glided by nearly on a level with the court. The creak of the rigging was audible.

John squeezed his eyes shut for a moment. The image of sunlight flashing on the dark sea swells lingered. When he opened them again he thought he could make out the woods on the opposite shore and what may have been meadowland. It reminded him of the bucolic scene on the wall of his study.

He had sat alone with a jug of wine late into the night. Peter had been wise enough not to pause by the doorway. Cornelia had given him over to his humors.

He stared at Zoe and tried to see Agnes in the glass visage. Not the grotesque face of the drowned woman or the living face he had glimpsed in the square. Was there truly a resemblance? Could the mosaic maker have captured a likeness in tesserae?

How could the solemn little girl have grown up to be an actress or a prostitute?

Not that John considered Zoe a child. Her dark eyes had seen too much.

She had the form of a child. What was she really?

Would he know, if he discovered who Agnes was and what had happened to her?

Did he want to know Agnes?

"John!"

Anatolius approached, trailed closely by a man John recalled seeing at more than one official function at the palace.

Procopius was of average height and build, remarkable only for his immaculate dress and grooming. Above a high forehead, his perfectly trimmed hair lay as unmoved by the sea breeze as the hair on a sculpted bust. The stripe along the hem of his unwrinkled robe and at the ends of his sleeves—not too wide, not quite purple—matched the purplish stone in the silver clasp that pinned his cloak at the shoulder.

"Lord Chamberlain. I am deeply honored. I have explained to your companion that I am not seeking the emperor's head."

Procopius may have been smiling. It was hard to say. He had the impossibly smooth skin of a girl. His dark gaze fixed on John with the glittering eyes of a snake.

"I spoke to Menander," Anatolius put in. "He told me that some friends like to meet here to take the air. It's a reasonable distance from the palace. A sensible spot for those who are still in Justinian's good graces and might prefer not to be seen with old acquaintances who have fallen out of favor."

"And are you one of these old friends, Procopius, or were you asking Menander for more scandalous tales about Justinian?"

"I was questioning Menander, Lord Chamberlain, as you so astutely observe. And what a wealth of tales these people have. What glorious grievances. Indeed, if one could pay an architect with grievances there would rise halfway to heaven a temple dedicated to the condemnation of our noble emperor that would put the Great Church to shame. Alas, you cannot buy pretty churches with grievances. You can't even eat grievances, though you can live by them. And just as well because grievances are all they have left, thanks to the evil emperor's rapacity and vile treachery. He has robbed each and every one of them. These are their words, not mine. But then I do not have to explain that to a man of such perspicacity as yourself."

"How do they suppose they've been robbed?" John asked.

"Why, let me see, every way under the sun, and many ways known only to the dark. False accusations are a specialty." Procopius began to tick off the ways on perfectly manicured finger. "He has accused some of polytheism, others of heresy. One is accused of being an Arian. See there, gathered at Theodora's feet, you have pederasts and defilers of nuns. Some of those men spoke treasonously or sided with the Greens. And one poor fellow arrived at the law courts to discover his dear father had named Justinian as his sole heir and done so in handwriting more like a court scribe's that of the departed."

"Justinian never assigned me such a task when I was his secretary," Anatolius said. "I knew all the scribes. I'd have heard about anything like that."

"Certainly such villainy would never have got past you. It's all sheer fantasy. The flowers of bitterness taken root in idleness. But how very fascinating these tales are!"

John thought Procopius sounded a bit too interested in such slanders and said as much.

"I can see how it might puzzle you, Lord Chamberlain. In fact, I am composing an encomium to our matchless ruler. But consider, one cannot look into the sun." He raised his hand slightly to gesture at the bright orb which had risen well above the sea. "To gaze at such glory is to be blinded. Even its reflection on the water hurts the eyes. But you can look at the shadows it casts. A great man's enemies are his shadows and in their grievances against him you can see his virtues."

"I have no doubt the words you eventually compose will please the emperor, Procopius. Have you heard of any restiveness which might be taken seriously?"

"Every angry word I hear is taken seriously by the broken man who utters it. But, no, I have not encountered a single person who contemplates attacking the emperor with anything other than false bravado and threats whispered in secret. Indeed

I believe this court is a popular meeting place due to the public latrines located so conveniently behind the baths. The moment these brave souls announce their opposition to the emperor, they need to rush off to relieve themselves."

"If you haven't heard of plots, have you heard anything about a woman named Agnes, or Troilus, a dealer in antiquities?"

Procopius pursed his lips and appeared to consider the question. "The names don't sound familiar, but I hear so many names. I may have written something down. You might want to visit me when I have had a chance to consult my notes. I am sure that as Lord Chamberlain you have many interesting stories to tell."

"The stories I might be inclined to tell are probably not the ones you are interested in hearing. Still, I would appreciate the opportunity to speak with you again."

Anatolius wanted to question Procopius about the architectural book he was reportedly writing.

John excused himself and walked in the direction of the sea. He stopped well short of the edge of the courtyard from where it was only a step down to the dark waves. The sea appeared to slope upward in the distance. John had the uncomfortable impression that the water might come rushing down at any moment.

On further consideration, he wondered what could be gained from speaking further with Procopius. It was Troilus he needed to question. The antiquities dealer had arrived at his shop with a large sack the very night Agnes was murdered. He had known Agnes. He could have stolen the dye that had been used on the body from Jabesh's establishment, so near to his own.

Had Troilus fled? It seemed possible. Though he had no reason to think so given his single visit to the closed shop.

Knowing the identity of the murderer would not tell him all he wanted to know about Agnes.

About Zoe.

Or would it?

He thought again of the strange calm which enveloped his investigations. A deceptive calm. A calm like that of the sea gently lapping the stones, yet much too close.

He needed to know more. Not merely for his own curiosity, or even to avenge Agnes. Knowledge of some plot would explain her death. Anyone who sought to topple the emperor had already wagered his life on a desperate bet.

He would not stop at one killing.

Chapter Twenty-Three

"Mistress, the gentleman has arrived!"

Cornelia turned and saw Peter peering through the doorway to the bath.

She had decided to look in on the workmen who had arrived earlier to begin repairing the neglected room. Two of them were up to their ankles in green gruel at the bottom of the circular marble pool which occupied most of the space, seeking to unplug the drain with a heavy metal rod. The third, a paunchy, middle-aged man who had introduced himself as the mosaic maker Figulus, stood on the edge of the basin, next to the marble Aphrodite, scowling up at the cracks in the domed ceiling.

"The gentleman? What do you mean, Peter?"

"I was in the garden and heard footsteps, and caught a glimpse of someone going upstairs. A stranger."

"You didn't confront him?"

Peter looked surprised. "I thought you must be expecting a visitor."

"No. I'm not expecting anyone." Cornelia could feel her breath coming faster. She chided herself. The city made her nervous, as did John's investigations.

The visitor could be anyone. A friend of John's. Someone on business. A palace messenger. She made an effort to control her breathing. "Figulus, are there just the three of you?"

He had been prodding at some loose tesserae in the wall mosaic and pretending not to listen to the conversation. "Yes, lady. Just three. The Lord Chamberlain said he wanted these mosaics...um...altered, rendered more fitting. Do you have any idea exactly what he has in mind?" He shuffled his feet.

Cornelia saw Peter's lips tighten as he glanced at the mosaics which so discomfited Figulus. They depicted in a detailed, earthy manner what the goddess Aphrodite symbolized.

Perhaps the mosaic maker had misheard John's instructions.

"No, I don't want any alterations," Cornelia replied. "They are to be repaired. I like them."

She went into the hallway, which was cluttered with tools, bags, and barrels of tesserae and plaster.

"Let's find out who our visitor is," she said to Peter. She couldn't entirely keep anxiety out of her voice.

As she started back down the hall, she heard one of the workmen, his voice amplified in the empty, marble room, laugh. "A lady like that likes pictures like these. Wish I was his excellency!"

"Not me!" came the reply. "You don't know anything about the Lord Chamberlain, do you, you fool?"

The atrium was deserted. The front door stood open, a cart piled with building materials visible on the cobbles beyond.

"Do you have a weapon, Peter?"

"Yes, Mistress, but it's in my room upstairs."

"Never mind then." Cornelia started up the stairway.

"Mistress, you shouldn't go up alone!" Peter protested, following her.

How ill advised to leave the door open, Cornelia thought. It had probably never occurred to the workmen that a Lord Chamberlain wouldn't have swarms of servants close at hand instead of one elderly man.

No one to shut doors and guard them against intruders.

The wooden steps creaked under her feet.

There was no one in the hallway upstairs. She went into the kitchen and picked up the poker beside the brazier.

"Take one of the knives, Peter. We'll risk appearing very inhospitable if it turns out to be a senator or someone sent by the emperor."

The weight of the iron poker in her hand made her breath come more easily as she stepped out into the hallway again, half expecting someone to burst forth from one of the rooms.

She lowered her voice before speaking to Peter. "The footsteps you heard? Was it just one person or more?"

"Only one."

Of course, Peter's hearing was not very reliable. Cornelia took a few steps. She set her jaw and exhaled slowly. When she'd traveled with the troupe, she had specialized in leaping bulls in a recreation of the old Cretan tradition.

There always came that time, as the bull charged, when it was necessary to take the decision and leap, to bridge the chasm between thought and action despite fear.

A hulking assassin might have lain in wait. Or she and Peter might find themselves facing a band of armed ruffians.

She raised the poker and stepped into John's study.

A slender young man, his hair prematurely silver, lounged at John's desk and stared pensively at the mosaic on the wall.

He barely turned his head at her entrance, but merely put down John's wine cup. "Ah, there is someone alive in this place after all. I was beginning to think that cunning child on the wall was the sole inhabitant of the house."

The man was dressed like a merchant in a well cut blue tunic and a short, dark blue cloak. He did not appear to have a weapon.

"Who are you and what is your business?" Cornelia demanded.

The man stood, without any display of urgency. "Have I disturbed you? I'm most sorry. I was given to understand the Lord Chamberlain wished to speak with me. I thought I'd save him the trouble of seeking me out again. As a courtesy, you understand."

"Do you consider it a courtesy to simply walk into people's homes and wander around unannounced and drink their wine?"

"When I arrived, there were fellows hauling things in so I just followed them," the visitor protested. "There was nobody at the door and the furnishings are so sparse, I thought the Lord Chamberlain must have moved out while the work was under way."

"And you are…?" Cornelia demanded.

"My name is Troilus. I am a dealer in antiquities and curiosities, which is why this mosaic so intrigues me. I only wish I owned such a wonderful piece of art."

"The Lord Chamberlain is not here."

Peter lifted the knife he used to chop onions. "Shall I see the villain out, mistress?"

"No, we'll both escort him out. I will tell the Lord Chamberlain you called, Troilus. I'm sure you will be hearing from him very soon."

Chapter Twenty-Four

"You entered my house uninvited. I will have an explanation."

At the sound of John's voice, Troilus looked up from the bench in front of his shop upon which he was arranging a display of glassware. His face went as white as his hair. "Lord Chamberlain!"

"You seem startled, yet I am told you didn't appear concerned when you were discovered trespassing."

"I didn't hear you. You walk very quietly. Naturally I was startled when you addressed me."

The ensuing silence was broken by the hollow drip of water.

When John arrived, the grating in the corridor wall next to the sundial maker's shop was open. A torch by the entrance partially illuminated the sub-basement beyond. In the middle of the cavernous space sat Troilus' establishment, a rambling, ramshackle conglomeration of planks, bricks, and canvas.

The sub-basement had once been used as a cistern, judging from the dark water stains rising to shoulder level on the widely spaced granite columns that vanished overhead into a smoky fog of darkness. Fallen columns, mostly shattered, were strewn across the puddled concrete floor.

"Lord Chamberlain, I presented myself at your house because my neighboring merchant told me you wished to interview me, and naturally I thought it would be permissible to—"

"If you think it acceptable to enter a dwelling without authority, why do you keep this business locked up when you are away?"

"But there were workmen going in and out," the other protested. "I meant no harm."

"Those in the house had no way of knowing that. I could have you prosecuted, particularly since you invited yourself to sample my wine."

"Your wine? I mistook it for a jug one of your servants had forgotten."

"After you had sampled it."

"Not at all. The aroma of that kind of Egyptian wine is quite distinctive to those who are familiar with it."

The color had returned to Troilus' face, along with the arrogant demeanor Cornelia had described. He was not, as she had thought, old. His hair had grayed early and he had the prematurely lined skin of a hermit newly arrived from the desert.

"Then you would steal from the servant but not from the master?"

Troilus set the molar-shaped flask he had been holding on the bench displaying his wares, next to a trio of hexagonal green glass jugs decorated with flowers in wheel cut lozenges. "I should think a servant owns nothing in his master's house, Lord Chamberlain. Perhaps I could interest you in some of my glassware? Take anything you want as payment for the wine. You could use another wine cup perhaps?"

"I could, if the cup can explain to me why you were dragging a large sack in here late one night last week."

Troilus shrugged. "I'm a merchant. I deal in goods. I'm often to be seen dragging sacks. My task is easier than that set Sisyphus since it's all downhill to my shop. My customers drag their purchases back up into the light."

If Troilus had expected a smile from John, he didn't get it.

"Have you been robbed, Lord Chamberlain? I assure you I never deal in stolen goods. Not knowingly. I purchase my wares from respectable people and sell them to the same."

"This sack was about as long as I am tall. You were seen with it eight days ago, around midnight. What did it contain?"

Troilus laughed. "Now I understand! Helias has been spying on me again. Isn't that right? It's on account of my antiquities. Not everyone admires glorification of the human form or understands pagan beliefs. I'll wager he told you I was dragging a corpse. Do you think he invented that tale on the spot? It's a favorite slander of his. He even brought the City Prefect here once. Nothing came of it."

John requested details.

"It was years ago. He's harassed me for that long. I'd move rather than put up with it, but what other place could suit me so well? As you see, I have room to expand down here. We're standing in what's left of Lausos' palace after it burnt down sixty or so years back. After I moved in, I came across some excellent pieces from that famous classical collection of his and they gave me a good start on my business venture."

"Indeed. And I suppose you aren't paying anyone rent either. However, I haven't come to inquire about your business. I would advise you to think carefully, because if you can't answer my questions you might have time to reflect on it in a much darker place than this. Now, about the sack Helias described. What was in it?"

"How could I forget that purchase? Step inside and I'll show you."

John ducked to avoid the lintel of the crooked doorway. Inside, a miasma of smoke glowed in the light from lamps scattered amidst haphazard piles of goods. It was akin to standing in the cargo hold of a wrecked ship or for that matter in Menander's cluttered room. In fact, many of the items on display might well have been purchased from Menander. Hadn't the actress, Petronia, told him that Menander was well known to the troupe which worked practically on Troilus' subterranean doorstep?

"I needed a roof over my merchandise," Troilus explained. "The vaults are in disrepair, and when it rains, it's like a waterfall down here. If you'll excuse me, I'll retrieve the object that inflamed Helias. I shall not be long."

Troilus vanished into a back room.

John looked around. A dozen amphorae of varying sizes, most notably one suitable for transporting the wine supply for a Dionysian banquet, sat against one slanting wall. A plain wooden stool nearby displayed an ivory triptych with a Biblical scene. Perched beside it—and John suspected it was not by accident—was a bronze candlestick in the form of a naked Aphrodite, hands above her head, standing in a frozen froth of wavelettes.

Other offerings on sale included clay lamps of lewd design encrusted with representations of male organs. On a low table decorated with insets of ebony and mother of pearl sat bronze combs, cooking pots, and statues of pagan deities. A tray of jewelry invited the eye to untangle its carelessly heaped contents—finger rings, some displaying enamel bezels, a gold chain necklace threaded with garnets, silver wire earrings with pearl pendants, and a child's green glass bracelet.

Had all this merchandise been legally obtained, as Troilus claimed, or had his stock been stolen from homes abandoned when their owners fled the recent plague?

An item John would not have expected to see in any business caught his attention.

The large skeleton stood in a cobwebbed corner. The back end had belonged to a horse, but grafted to the front were the bones of a man. Closer inspection did not immediately reveal the means by which the parts had been fastened to each other. However, the man's thigh bones could be discerned, welded in some manner to the larger equine bones. The human bones, especially the legs, appeared deformed and eaten away in spots, whether in the course of their marriage to the remains of the horse or from disease John could not venture to guess.

"I see you admire my centaur." Troilus had returned, hauling a sack of the size Helias had described. "Might you be interested in purchasing such a rare and unusual curiosity? It would cause much comment if you displayed it in your atrium."

John declined the offer. He could imagine Peter's horror at having such a monstrosity in the house, even though it had obviously been manufactured.

"Here I have an exceedingly rare artifact, Lord Chamberlain. The owner didn't want to part with it, but his wine supplier was pressing him for payment. It's one of the items which offend Helias. There's another."

He gestured toward a shadowy alcove.

John felt his skin prickle.

A soldier peered out at them.

"That's Saint Sergius," Troilus said. "He's an automaton. Sadly, he no longer works although I've thought of having him restored. He could scare off thieves. Do you think a saint would object to guarding a shop? After all, the saints are supposed to look after us, aren't they?"

He smiled. "I was told that after appropriate preparations, when set in motion red liquid bubbles from his shoes. It represents the blood shed when the martyr was forced to run for miles in footwear with nails inside. Even as that dreadful sight unfolds, the saint raises his hands to heaven, holding the palm branch of martyrdom. Thus may we all overcome pain and sorrow and receive our reward."

Was the piety in his tone exaggerated?

"The frond was missing when I purchased him," Troilus continued. "It appears that during a particularly lively social gathering, poor Sergius suffered at the hand of an intoxicated guest, whereupon his companions thrashed the careless man with the palm branch. It had come loose, but that broke it entirely."

"These unusual goods of yours must be extremely expensive. I'm surprised you can find buyers in a spot like this," John observed.

"Buyers find me, Lord Chamberlain. They have to find me. No one else sells what I sell. Do you know what financed me when I first set up shop? It was the nose of Zeus from Olympus. It was from a statue in that collection of Lausos I mentioned. Who knows what else might still be down here? I've scarcely begun to explore all the corridors and basements and cisterns."

He seemed unconcerned about being confronted by Justinian's Lord Chamberlain. Nor did he appear in any particular haste to reply to the question of what he was doing in John's house. "What I'm interested in, Troilus, are the contents of that sack. I do not intend to wait further. Speak."

"My apologies. Here, I'll show you."

Troilus bent down and turned the lip of the sack back, revealing the shiny head of the largest leather phallus John had ever seen. It was the length of an entire man.

"There's Helias' so-called body," Troilus smirked. "It would probably distress the pious hypocrite more than a corpse. I've nicknamed it Polyphemus. I wager some wealthy brothel owner will pay me a tidy sum to put him on display. Or perhaps I could interest the troupe. I do a lot of business with them, scrounging up various odd items needed for their performances." He pulled the sacking back over the obscene artifact.

"Do you know an actress from the troupe? A woman named Agnes?"

"Oh, yes indeed. She likes to try on the jewelry I have for sale, although she never buys any."

"Perhaps you have given her some baubles?"

"What do you mean, Lord Chamberlain?"

"That she is more than a customer. That was the impression I had from Petronia."

"You've been talking to Petronia? I see. For a man of your position, you do spend a lot of time in places less salubrious than the palace. If I owned that fine house of yours, I'd stay there. Well, Petronia sees things from her own perspective, but, yes, you could say that Agnes and I are friends."

There was nothing in Troilus' tone to indicate that he had learned about Agnes' death, from Petronia or in any other manner. John thought it best not to say anything.

"And how familiar are you with the company Agnes keeps?"

"Not very. Except when they come to me in search of a trinket or a bit of the past."

"Did Agnes say anything about dissatisfaction with the emperor?"

Troilus laughed. "Who outside the palace doesn't grumble about the emperor? Or inside the palace, I imagine. You would know better than I."

"I understand that concocting intrigues against Justinian is a popular sport? Did Agnes mention such scheming?"

"We don't talk about politics much, Lord Chamberlain." Troilus stared at the sack at his feet. "People like to fantasize but these dreams they cultivate of returning to the palace have as much to do with reality as Polyphemus there. The last time I saw Agnes she was recounting those rumors about Theodora's bastard son and imagining how he might be used against Justinian."

"One variation or another of that rumor makes the rounds every year. It's nearly as popular as accounts of Theodora's escapades with the geese during her acting days."

"Exactly. So you agree with me it's all nonsense, Lord Chamberlain? I do a considerable amount of business with former courtiers. They love to spread such scandalous reports."

"People like Menander?"

"Yes, like Menander. You do know everyone, don't you? Now he's a man who's always selling and never buying. As I was saying, these people will dwell on rumors. I suppose it adds some excitement to their lives and what else can they do being now as powerless as beggars in the streets? I say if it makes them feel better to talk about a long lost son enlisting the excubitors to depose Justinian with the blessing of the empress, well, perhaps they'll feel like purchasing a few more valuables from me in anticipation of celebrating the great day. Particularly since the day will be a long time coming."

"Indeed. And when did you last glimpse Agnes?"

Troilus paused for thought. A draught stirred the smoky haze in the shop as a guttering lamp threw animated shadows across the walls.

"It was the very night I hauled in Polyphemus," he finally replied. "I hadn't seen Agnes for a few days and wondered what had become of her. So early the next morning I went over to Petronia's room, where she often stays. To my relief, Agnes was there. However, she rushed out not long after I arrived and I haven't seen her since."

Chapter Twenty-Five

Actresses apparently earned more than John would have guessed.

Petronia was well enough off to live outside the smoke and fumes of the Copper Market, on the edge of the ridge overlooking the Golden Horn, almost within sight of Michri's glassworks where John had begun his investigations. From the windows of her third floor room it was possible to see the narrow inlet to the north as well as the wave-rippled waters to the east.

The actress invited John to sit upon an oversized wooden chair, painted in a manner which made it resemble a gem encrusted throne from a distance.

John remained standing beside a bed against the wall. Pieces of statuary—busts of philosophers and small gods and goddesses on pedestals—were perched on a table and on the floor by the brazier. They were used on stage, John supposed.

Petronia pulled shut the heavy curtain that divided the room and concealed from view the second bed John had glimpsed as he entered. The curtain must have been a discarded stage backdrop. Amid its folds could be discerned an assortment of Greek temples.

"I haven't been back to the theater since you brought me the terrible news," she said in answer to his question. Her face was as pale and perfect as it had been the day before. The thin tunic she wore hung loosely from her shoulders, revealing the clear demarcation where the white make-up ended at the base of her slender neck.

"Someone else will have to tell Troilus if he doesn't already know. I couldn't bear to see his reaction when he hears…." she faltered.

John asked her gently how well the pair had known each other.

"I fear I don't pry into my friends' affairs, Lord Chamberlain, although I know it's the common belief that actresses have no discretion or shame."

"Some may think that, Petronia. I can understand that you are upset by the death of your friend. Is that why you neglected to tell me that Troilus visited you here the morning of the day Agnes died?"

"Troilus? Visited me?"

"It was early in the morning, he said."

Petronia turned toward the window facing the sea. John could not see her expression. "Oh, yes. I see. What I meant was that he wasn't visiting me. A young fellow like that…why would he? It was Agnes he came to see."

"Did he often visit her?"

"No. He was concerned about her, he said. He hadn't seen her for a while, which explains why he arrived before dawn. Can I offer you some wine, Lord Chamberlain?"

Petronia took a cup and blue glass flask from a niche beside the brazier. "No?"

She poured herself wine, sat down on the edge of the bed, and gestured toward the large painted chair. "Please, please. Ascend the throne. You're close enough to it, after all. It's one we use on stage. We used it last in Agamemnon. Our version is always popular. Uproarious, you know."

John declined. He fixed the actress in his gaze. She had leaned forward so that her tunic fell open, revealing an expanse of tawny skin below the white powder covering her neck. "It would be best for you to tell me everything that happened. I can see you may have wanted to protect Troilus but I can assure you, if he is responsible for the murder neither you, nor anyone else, will be able to save him from justice."

Petronia emptied her cup, refilled it, and gave John a bleak smile. Her eyes glistened. "Troilus murder Agnes? I can't imagine such a thing, Lord Chamberlain. They were…well…he would never have harmed her." Her lower lip trembled as she raised the cup to her mouth again.

"You said Troilus arrived here before dawn?"

"I can't say exactly when but it was still dark when Agnes left. The sky was beginning to lighten. I don't know what they talked about. She has her own place." Petronia nodded toward the painted backdrop partitioning the room. "I've trained myself not to hear what I'm not meant to hear."

"Praiseworthy, indeed, but you must have heard something of their conversation since they exchanged angry words."

Petronia stared at John in horror. "Who said so?"

"It was obvious, since you seemed so reluctant to tell me."

Petronia shook her head. "How foolish I am. An old actress trying to deceive the Lord Chamberlain. But you are correct, for they did indeed argue. I didn't hear precisely what was said but I could tell from their tone."

"And then Agnes left?"

"Yes, although it was not on account of the argument. Agnes and I were already up when Troilus came pounding on the door. Agnes had to meet someone, you see. That wasn't so unusual. She often had early appointments but she would never say what they were or who was involved."

"And Troilus?"

Petronia dabbed at her eyes with her sleeve. She looked at John pensively. Her jaw clenched. She was silent for what seemed like a long time and then her chest moved as she took a breath.

"Troilus stayed here afterward. He needed someone to talk to. He thought Agnes had an assignation."

John nodded his understanding.

"She did," Petronia continued, "but not the sort he had in mind. She often spent time with disgruntled exiles from court. They were always meeting at odd hours, most likely to avoid being noticed. A wise thing considering the kind of loose talk they engaged in. It was all play."

The actress sighed. "She always dressed as if she had been summoned to an audience with the emperor. Well, as near as she could given our circumstances. That's why she was accepted in those circles. She acted her part so well, you see."

John wondered whether that was the only service Agnes rendered. He kept the thought to himself. "When did Troilus leave?"

"He stayed for a long time, Lord Chamberlain. When you're young you can agonize over affairs of the heart for hours. Sometimes it's good to be able to discuss these matters with someone who is older and, sadly, wiser."

"I trust you are wise enough to be telling me the truth. If you are not, I will soon find out."

Chapter Twenty-Six

John paused outside Petronia's lodgings to decide in what direction the truth might be discovered.

From the street the sea was invisible, obscured by the structures rising all around. The low sun left the street in shadow except for a single, sharp lance of fire which found its way through some gap in the buildings.

If Petronia wasn't lying, which was far from certain, then Troilus could not have murdered Zoe. Whatever had been in the sack, Agnes had been seen alive hours after Helias had noted Troilus' late night labors.

In addition, Troilus had been baring his soul to Petronia when Agnes died, perhaps even as John was gazing down at her dyed and lifeless body in the cistern.

No matter the exact duration of his visit, Troilus could never have killed Agnes, attempted to obscure her identity with dye, and conveyed her body to the cistern unless he had in fact followed straight after her, which, according to Petronia, he had not.

No doubt Petronia had thought she was protecting Troilus by initially failing to reveal his argument with Agnes. He would have been one of the last to see the victim alive. An obvious suspect. As it turned out, Petronia had inadvertently concealed the innocence of the man of whom she was so obviously fond.

Her fondness for Troilus meant that Petronia could not be ruled out as an enemy of Agnes.

The lance of light crossing the thoroughfare faded as the sun sank lower.

John turned for home.

He walked up the short incline toward where the narrow street intersected a colonnaded thoroughfare.

It must have been the same direction Agnes would have gone on her way to meet him in the square. While John waited, she had been waylaid and killed.

By whom? And where?

If John were to attempt to retrace her route he might notice something useful. He would still be moving in the general direction of the palace. She would have kept to the main streets. There would have been no need to take shortcuts to a prearranged meeting, especially for a woman in predawn darkness.

Merchants were closing their shops. The torches they were setting into wall brackets would have rendered the colonnades relatively bright and safe even in the dead of night. Nevertheless, the shops were interrupted by gloomy alcoves, open doorways leading to apartments, archways opening into courtyards, and the black mouths of alleyways, all places where a murderer might lie in wait.

He spoke to a merchant, who jumped up, startled in the midst of locking the grating protecting his shop to the iron ring set in the pavement. No, there had not been any disturbances recently. He'd seen nothing out of the ordinary. He never arrived to open his establishment until dawn anyway.

Most shopkeepers would have been at home at the time Agnes passed by on her way to her appointment.

A familiar odor caught John's attention.

The smell of grilled fish, the sort sold on skewers by the docks. This street was a fair distance from the docks. He dismissed it as nothing more than hunger coupled with imagination.

The smell grew stronger.

Why would anyone be selling grilled fish in this part of the city at this time of the evening?

Then he saw the ragged creature huddled on the step of a doorway, surrounded by charred skewers from which hung mostly scraps of blackened meat, obviously unsold or ruined wares discarded by a vendor at the end of the day.

The beggar noticed John looking at him, grabbed an empty skewer, and waved it like a sword. "Get away, you bastard, or I'll have yer eyes out. It's all mine, this is. I didn't battle them mangy curs to stuff the chops of a worthless lout like you!" Bits of fish clung to the man's beard.

"I have a couple of coins for you, if you have certain information," John replied in an even tone.

The man squinted up at John suspiciously. One eye was blackened, the other watered profusely and he blinked it repeatedly. While considering the unexpected offer, he gulped down a bit of fish and nearly choked.

"My apologies, excellency," he gasped when he had stopped coughing. "I thought you was after my hard earned dinner."

"All I want is information." John angled his hand so the two copper nummi in his palm caught light from a nearby torch. "Have you noticed anything unusual around here lately?"

"No, excellency. This is a quiet street once the shops are closed for the night. There's no reason for anyone to be creepin' about up to no good and there's not enough taverns to attract them Blues and Greens."

"It's deserted here at night?"

"There's usually just carts, excellency, passing by on their way from the docks. In an hour or so no one will be around. Well, there might be something going on in the alleys, but it's the same all over, isn't it?" he leered.

The squeal and crash of another grate being lowered further up the street seemed to bear out the beggar's words.

The rags piled behind the beggar suggested the doorway was his residence. John asked whether he had been in the same spot a little more than a week earlier.

"Oh yes, excellency. I like this place. The last fool who tried to take it from me found out just how much I like it. Which is not to say I didn't do him a good turn because a one-eyed man gets more handouts and that's a fact." He gave a hoarse chuckle, his gaze fixed on the coins glinting in John's palm.

"You're observant. You must be to spot a bounty like that fish quickly enough to beat everyone else to it. Now, try to remember eight days ago, around dawn. Did you see anyone who might have seemed out of place at that time of the morning?"

"I'm not sure. Time does run together. I hardly know what day it is unless I'm due for an audience with the emperor." The fish eater emitted a coughing laugh. "What sort of person was you thinking about?"

"A young lady."

"Ah, yes. Now I remember. Yes, a young lady went by here just when you said." A greasy hand reached out.

John closed his fingers over the coins. "What did she look like?"

The beggar licked his lips. "Young she was, sir. A lady."

"As I've just said."

The beggar's good eye blinked rapidly. "No, excellency, I mean dressed like a lady, or rather dressed to look like one. A tart if you ask me. Some men like to pretend they're paying a lady for...well, that's surely worth them two coins in yer hand."

"What do you mean by saying she looked like a lady?"

"I mean she weren't a lady. But the first time I seen her, I thought, what's a high born woman doin' out here this time of the morning and with no attendants at that? Then, when she got closer, I seen her clothes was all bright colored like, but not much better than mine."

"You've seen her more than once?"

"Yes, excellency, every so often. She must live 'round here to be out on the streets on her own like that. Not respectable, is it?"

"The last time you saw this woman was about a week ago?"

The beggar nodded.

"Was anyone following her?"

"No, excellency. No." His voice trailed off. "Why do you want to know?"

John said nothing.

"Yer from the palace, aren't you?" The beggar shrank back into the doorway. "It's some trouble, isn't it? I din' have nothin' to do with it, excellency. Swear to our Lord."

"Nothing to do with what?" John demanded.

"With nothin', excellency, nothin' at all."

John bent, grabbed the front of the man's garment, and yanked him to his feet. "Nothing to do with what?" he repeated.

The rotten fabric tore and the beggar tumbled backward. John squatted down and addressed the blubbering figure, now groveling in the remains of his feast.

Tears streamed from the beggar's unclouded eye. "Mercy, excellency. Have mercy. I seen her. I don't know nothing more. I knew there must be trouble of some kind, what with one like you askin' about her. It were about a week ago. She came along here just before dawn. You can have me tortured, excellency, but I won't say different. Trust a tart to get a man minding his own business into trouble. If I see her again I'll—"

John stood. "Here." He added another coin to the two he still held and tossed them into the heaped rags behind the huddled, trembling man before him.

John strode away down the street.

The hollow feeling in his stomach had nothing to do with hunger.

He wished he could give up for the evening and return home to Cornelia.

He knew he had to keep following Agnes' footsteps.

Chapter Twenty-Seven

John continued through the alternating shadows and torch-light beneath the colonnade.

Only days earlier Agnes must have passed the same way. She might have been pondering whatever it was she intended to tell him. Did she realize she was in danger? Is that why she had arranged to meet in an obscure square while the city was still coming awake?

Here and there sculpture graced an alcove or a pedestal. Likenesses of long dead rulers and poets, the statues served as reminders of the empire's ancient heritage.

Where had Agnes' journey been interrupted? Had she gone past that marble Sophocles? Had she noticed him frowning at her? Was his bearded face the last thing she had seen before her attacker leapt from the black mouth of that nearby alleyway? Or had her assailant been hiding, masked behind the chiseled robes of the ancient playwright?

The red ruin of the woman's battered face floated to the surface of John's thoughts. He hoped it had been over too quickly for her to be aware of what was happening, that her killer had not dragged her away into darkness to complete his task in a leisurely fashion.

John brushed a spark from a sputtering torch off his shoulder.

There was no one to question. The only people on the street were of polished stone.

The thoroughfare crossed the street where Figulus kept his mosaic workshop and passed in front of the Church of the Mother of God, before running along the back wall of the law courts. To reach the square where John had been waiting for her, Agnes could have turned and gone past the courts or proceeded on for a short distance and gone up the street which went by the courtyard housing the make-shift theater, the dyer's emporium, and the entrances to the underground establishments of Helias and Troilus.

John guessed Agnes would have gone by the theater since it was most likely a route she took often to see her friends.

He continued toward the intersection, past Opilio's shop. A faint smell of spice drifted out through its lowered metal bars.

The giant, sausage-shaped sign looked even more obscene in the twilight.

The narrow way leading to the square, with its overhanging structures, was darker than the colonnade. The hot breath of forges and furnaces issued from archways.

In such an area why had the killer chosen to conceal his victim's identifying tattoo with dye? Perhaps he had not had access to a furnace. There was also the problem of the smell of burning flesh. Dye was easy to come by. Jabesh's establishment was not far from the alley leading to the cistern where John had found the body.

But then why not just carve the tattoo from the dead flesh?

Had Agnes come within shouting distance of the square? Surely whoever wanted to prevent the meeting would not have taken such a chance.

If, indeed, her ambush had been planned in advance.

Nothing moved in the square, aside from a dog which slunk away at John's approach. Scattered shop front torches hardly penetrated the gloom. The stylite's column rose from darkness into a gray rectangle of sky where a bright star winked between ragged clouds.

There was no light atop the column. No doubt the holy man would consider artificial illumination a luxury, a vanity of the world he had left behind. Would he, like Helias the sundial maker, be aware of the passage of time as the relentless sun drove his shadow around the top of the column or that of the column itself around the square?

John had completed the walk Agnes had failed to finish. He had learned little, observed nothing.

He looked up at the looming pillar. Might the stylite have seen something useful from his high perch?

From that height the holy man would be able to look down the street which John had just traversed, perhaps even into the courtyard where the theater was located.

A movement caught John's eye, and he whirled around. He expected to see the feral dog had returned. Instead a figure coalesced from the darkness.

It was the acolyte he had glimpsed in the square during previous visits or perhaps another like him.

"Do you seek Lazarus?" the man asked. The deep, raspy voice identified the figure as a man. His face was hidden in the shadow of a hood. "I have taken in the offering baskets, but I will gladly accept whatever you care to give to the glory of our Lord."

"I haven't come here for that purpose," John replied. "I do however wish to speak with this Lazarus."

"That will not be possible. Lazarus has dedicated his tongue to glorifying the Lord. He does not engage in worldly discussions and speaks not of earthly things. All of his words are of Heaven. Pilgrims from far and wide make their way to this city to hear Lazarus describe the beauty and joys to be found in the Kingdom of God."

"He will speak to me. I am a servant of Justinian, and the emperor is God's representative on earth, is he not?"

"The emperor is nothing to Lazarus, less than the scrawny mongrel that lifts its leg against the pillar. Lazarus is above them both," was the reply. "He prays to the Lord and the Lord protects him."

The acolyte made the sign of his religion before proceeding. "It may be that the emperor would threaten Lazarus with torture.

That is his way. Yet do you suppose there is any torment worse than those Lazarus imposes on himself? His own awareness of sin sears his soul more painfully than a thousand red hot pincers. If you return in the morning you may listen to his message, but Lazarus talks with no one except the Lord."

John craned his neck to observe the top of the pillar. The stylite would have retired to his tiny shelter by this hour. Every manner of religious zealot flocked to the Christian empire's capital. There was no reason to disbelieve the acolyte's description of the holy man's attitude to worldly authorities. John had encountered far more eccentric holy men.

He considered whether a coin or two might help his cause but decided it would not. In his experience the poorer the Christian the less susceptible to bribery—a trait a Mithran like John could respect.

He therefore asked the acolyte the same questions he had put to the beggar, and was not surprised to find that the former could shed no light on matters.

John had to admit to himself that he was tired. He could approach the stylite at some later time, if it still seemed worthwhile. He started back the way he had come. Night settled into the narrow passage between the buildings like a black fog. He lengthened his stride.

Soon he saw ahead the pallid light of the intersecting thoroughfare.

Again the image of the dead women returned. Agnes. An actress he had never known. A woman of poor repute. Or was she Zoe, the girl on his wall, his confidant and silent member of his household? He could not separate the two, but neither could he force them to merge and take on a single identity.

They were different shadows cast by the same person.

There was a scuffling sound behind him.

His heart jumped. He hardly had time to chastise himself for not being on guard against attack as he should have been when all thoughts ceased.

Chapter Twenty-Eight

John knew he was dreaming, even though he had never before dreamt of Zoe.

"That is because I was never dead before," she told him in an annoyed tone.

They were walking along a path in the grounds of Plato's Academy.

John had not returned to the Academy since his youthful studies there. It looked much as he remembered, except that now ancient stone grave markers jutted up between the olive trees shading their way.

"I have heard that the dead return in dreams," John replied, "but I never believed it."

Zoe wore the same solemn expression she exhibited in the wall mosaic. "Look," she pointed, "There is Justinian's tomb."

It struck John as remarkable the emperor would have chosen to be buried so far from the capital and on the grounds of the pagan school he had ordered closed. "Is that what you came back to tell me, Zoe?"

"Why would I want to grow up to be an actress?" she asked, ignoring his question. "I still live in our house, don't I? I should not want to be a woman like her."

"We cannot always choose who we grow up to be," John said. He found himself looking at the girl more closely. She smiled at him. "You are not Zoe!"

"Of course I am." As the girl spoke he saw that she was, indeed, composed of nothing but glass tesserae. "I will give you proof."

She lifted a hand to her face and plucked out a glossy eye.

"No!" John tried to cry out but an impossible weight bore down on his chest, preventing him from forcing out the slightest sound. He reached toward the delicate hand which held out the shining fragment.

He saw who she was now.

Cornelia.

"No!"

His voice was suddenly shockingly loud as if he had burst up from deep water into light and air.

He gripped a hand.

Cornelia's, holding a damp piece of cloth.

Sunlight forced him to briefly close his eyes. When he opened them again he saw he was in his bedroom, lying on the bed.

He remembered he had been sunk in thought while walking down a dark street.

Cornelia squeezed his hand. "Thanks to the Goddess," she said. There were dark circles around her eyes. "You've been unconscious since last night."

John realized his head throbbed with pain.

"Felix and several of his excubitors brought you home after dark, long after I expected you back. I feared the worst."

"Felix?"

"Didn't you hear me, John?" Relief sharpened Cornelia's voice. "When Felix arrived—"

"I'm sorry. I wanted to finish…what I was doing."

Cornelia wiped her eyes with the back of a hand. "Never mind. He said it was just a bump." She dabbed the damp cloth at a spot behind his ear, causing pain to lance through his head.

"What happened? Why did Felix bring me back? How did he know where I was?"

"Someone told him there was a dead courtier in the street. He wasn't very clear about it. I think he must have been rousted out of a tavern. He reeked of wine. He said when he got to you the City Prefect's men were already there."

"I wasn't far from the Prefect's offices in the law courts, the last I remember."

"As soon as he saw it was you, Felix took charge. He said you were fortunate some passerby spotted you or else you might have lain there all night."

Yet John had been assured that the area was not well traveled at night. He asked Cornelia who had made the report to the Prefect.

"No one seems to know and I didn't think to ask Felix under the circumstances. You'll have to ask him yourself."

John pushed himself into a sitting position. The movement made his head feel as if it would burst. His vision blurred.

"Did anyone see who attacked me?"

Cornelia shook her head. "Felix said it was a simple robbery. Your money was gone. But I think someone doesn't want you looking into that woman's death."

"Felix is right. It had to be robbery. If someone didn't want me investigating that murder they would have killed me."

"Perhaps it was meant as a warning. Isn't it just as I said? You can't go about unguarded—"

"There'd be no point in trying to frighten me, Cornelia. I could order others to investigate if I felt my life was in danger."

"Which is what you should have done, John. Why didn't you go to Felix about it? He would surely have set some of his excubitors to work for you."

"This is a private matter. I want to keep it private."

"Is it?" Cornelia snapped. "What is this actress to us?"

"I've known her for a long time, or so it seems. Don't worry, this had nothing to do with Agnes. It was a common street crime."

"Oh, very common, I am certain. It's common for high officials to stroll around the city in dark corners, all alone, just inviting someone to sneak up behind them and hit them over the head."

"Shopkeepers and laborers and clerks walk the streets by themselves," John pointed out, suppressing a smile at Cornelia's outburst, realizing her fiery outpouring masked concern for the man she loved. "Besides, I have the advantage of military training."

"Much good it did you!" Cornelia replied with a slight smile.

John put a hand to the tender spot on his skull. It was badly swollen. When he touched it pain brought tears to his eyes.

He noticed Peter standing in the doorway. There were two of him. Both frowned with disapproval. Both retreated into the hallway when John glared in their direction.

John squeezed his eyes open and shut several times, trying to clear his vision. "If people could creep up behind my back without my realizing it, I would've been dead long ago," he argued.

"You're not as young as you used to be, John." Cornelia leaned over and kissed his forehead. "We have spent most of our lives apart. I would quite like for you to stay with me for a while. And don't forget Europa. It's time we went to visit her. She's more important than a mosaic girl, or an actress, or whoever's death it is you want to avenge, because I can see clearly that's your intention."

"It is part of putting things in order, in the world, in my own mind. But I do think of our daughter."

"Not as much as you've lately been thinking about this Agnes."

John made no reply because she was right.

He saw that Peter had returned to the doorway, looking alarmed. "Master, I told him that you—"

A figure decked out in garish orange robes brushed past the servant.

It was Francio.

Before anyone would remonstrate, he yanked a cloth off the basket he carried, revealing a heap of coiled sausage links. "I heard about your accident, Lord Chamberlain. It's all over the palace. I immediately thought how disappointed you would be if you were unable to come to my banquet so I have brought the banquet to you. Or rather the sausages at any rate. Lucanian sausages, no less. You can't find them just anywhere. They'll have you up and about in no time."

Cornelia thanked him without mentioning the household had recently dined on the same hearty fare.

John threw off his cover and swung his legs over the edge of the bed. The room whirled around. "Lucanian sausages? Where were they purchased, Francio?"

"Where…?"

"Was it from a man called Opilio?"

Francio glanced around in confusion. "Opilio? It might have been. The name sounds familiar."

"Did he deliver them while Crinagoras was reciting his verse in your kitchen?"

"I'm not certain. It's possible. He made more than one visit to bring his wares. Now, John, make certain Peter cooks them well. Even eaten alone, they are perfection, and I am certain my guests—"

"Mithra!" John burst out. "That's where the sausage maker must have heard Zoe's name. Apparently Opilio still hasn't told me the whole story." He stood up and staggered.

"You're not fit to go out," Cornelia told him.

"Master," Peter cried, "let me fetch a physician."

"No need to consult a physician, John," Francio said. "Try these delightful morsels. They'll build up your strength in no time."

He thrust the basket toward Cornelia, who pushed it back sharply.

Francio lost his grip and the basket fell to the floor. He stood blinking, looking distressed, chains of sausage looped at his boots. "I was only trying to make you feel better," he said in a hurt tone.

But John was already out the door, closely followed by Cornelia and Peter.

Chapter Twenty-Nine

A crowd under the colonnade almost within sight of Opilio's shop brought John to a halt. He paused and waited for the pavement to stop tilting under his boots before attempting to plunge ahead through the closely packed bodies.

By the time his dizziness passed, Peter had managed to catch up again, not that the old servant would ever admit to finding it difficult to keep pace with John's loping stride. "Are you feeling unwell, master?" he panted.

John reassured him.

Cornelia had been furious when John insisted he interview Opilio immediately. He'd practically been killed and hardly had he opened his eyes when he was off to let the ruffians finish the job, she declared, although at great length and much more colorfully. She had been only slightly mollified by the prospect of Peter going along to keep an eye on things since if fisticuffs developed he would be there to summon help.

It was as well Peter had not heard her comment, as he would have been mortally offended.

"Master," Peter was saying, "it must be providence that brought us this way just now. Here is exactly what you need. One of Zachariah's melons."

John looked in the direction Peter indicated, toward the front of the crowd. He realized he had been so intent on simply forcing himself along that he had hardly taken note of his surroundings. That was dangerous in Constantinople, but how else could he have missed seeing the man who was lying on his back on the ground, juggling melons with his bare feet?

A young woman sold melons from a crate nearby. She caught sight of the Lord Chamberlain, whose height made him visible above most of the onlookers and whose expensive garments distinguished him from the others.

"Are you in need of a cure, excellency? Who among us does not have something that needs attention?" she asked. "And who is to say that these melons are not as miraculous as the ones which healed Zachariah?"

John glanced at the prone juggler, who was keeping three melons aloft. His legs worked frantically. The fist-sized melons barely touched the man's filthy soles before they were sent back into the air.

"The ones Zachariah juggles cost more," the woman remarked. "They are even more efficacious."

"I would like to buy you a melon, master," said Peter in an eager tone. "I've bought them before now, on my way to or from the market. They are always refreshing, and I hear their curative powers are undeniable."

"Certainly you've always had strength to return home from the market, however heavily laden," John replied. "I will buy one for each of us, but not the sort that has been juggled, if you don't mind. I shouldn't have made you rush out to accompany me."

John moved through the knot of spectators and completed the transaction with the melon seller.

"Look, all of you," she said loudly. "If our wares are good enough for this fine gentleman from the palace, why should you hesitate to buy them?"

The woman and the juggler looked well dressed for street per-formers. John imagined the juggler must be young also, though he had not managed a good look at his face, his muscular legs being more visibly presented.

John moved away.

"Do you want to wait for Zachariah's homily, master?" Peter asked.

"I think not. There is some urgency in talking to Opilio." John took his blade from his belt, cut a melon in half and handed it to Peter, then sliced his own. It was sweet. Whether it possessed miraculous powers was not immediately evident. "Why does anyone suppose these melons have special virtues?"

"Because they cured Zachariah," Peter replied. "Or at least ones like them did."

"From what affliction did he suffer?"

"He was born without the use of his legs. He grew up a helpless beggar, sitting in doorways. It's true, for I passed by him many times, before the miracle."

John inquired if the miracle had involved a melon.

Peter wiped his mouth with his sleeve. "It was a whole cart load of melons, master. It was early in the morning but Zachariah had already taken up a spot at the edge of the market where he had been eking out his living for some months. The place was filled with merchants and farmers. Many had come to know the poor crippled man who was not blessed as they were with the ability to labor long hours for his sustenance. A rickety old cart, too heavily laden no doubt, hit a rut as it passed where he lay against the wall. The axle snapped, the cart tipped, and an avalanche of melons came rushing directly at Zachariah."

John hefted the remains of the melon he had been eating. "I would hardly think even a cart load of these would pose much danger." He tossed the rind into the gutter.

Peter frowned. "But master, imagine the shock of seeing them all rolling at you if you were unable to escape. But that is when the miracle occurred. Without even thinking about it, Zachariah leapt up and raced to safety. He'd been healed. It's true! There were many in the market who witnessed his cure."

"I see." John recalled the story the mosaic maker Figulus had related concerning the spilled tesserae. "The streets of the city must be filled with miracles for those who can see them. I would never have thought produce a convenient means of divine intervention."

"The hand of the Lord is everywhere," Peter replied. "You have perhaps heard about the glass manna?"

John indicated he had not.

"An amazing tale, master!" Peter beamed. "A starving beggar, searching near the palace walls for scraps to eat, came upon baskets full of the finest banquet fare. There was fish and bread and fruits in endless variety, or so he thought. Ah, but on closer inspection he discovered this food was like none he had ever seen before. It was made entirely of glass. The man immediately fell to his knees and gave thanks."

It must have been the fruit Michri had mentioned, John thought. He didn't tell Peter it had been Theodora, and not the Lord, who was responsible for its appearance outside the palace. "And why did a starving man give thanks for baskets of glass food? Perhaps he was thankful he hadn't bitten into it before he noticed what it was?"

"But this food was beautifully made and highly unusual! He sold it off piece by piece to dealers in such things, and so the glass food filled his belly for far longer than the same amount of real food would have."

Peter might well have had many more miracles to relate, but they had arrived at Opilio's shop and John left the old servant to stand guard beneath the wooden sausage.

◇◇◇

Opilio was rearranging baskets of links that sat on the floor in front of the counter.

"You lied to me again." John said without preamble.

Opilio raised his balding head in alarm. "Lord Chamberlain! How good to see you once more!" His expression gave lie to the words.

"I seem to be meeting with you more often than with Justinian, Opilio. Unfortunately, it is because you persist in refusing to tell me the truth."

The stout sausage maker straightened up with a grunt. "I can't imagine what you mean, excellency."

"You said you hadn't seen Agnes for a long time after you banished her from your house. In fact, you saw your niece less than a month ago."

Opilio gaped at John. "But how...."

"Because less than a month ago you made a delivery to a courtier named Francio."

"Yes. I'm helping to provision a large banquet."

"While you were in his kitchen you overheard a piece of gossip. It concerned a certain chamberlain."

Opilio rubbed the bristles on his chin. "Something about a chamberlain...a Lord Chamberlain...." His face sagged into a look of horror. "Not about you, excellency? You aren't the Lord Chamberlain who....who....?"

"Who what, Opilio? Who talks to the wall? This is the third time I've spoken to you. Your refusal to be truthful suggests I'm now talking to the wall in this shop. I will have some answers now."

"Please, we should speak in private." Opilio gestured toward the archway behind the counter.

The room beyond smelled of herbs and spices, of savory, rue, and coriander. Bundled leaves and lengths of stalks hung from its ceiling and walls. It was a short time before John became aware of another underlying odor—a repulsive stench which came from stained and scarred wooden tables laid out with an array of sharp-edged devices such as might be seen in a surgery or a torturer's chamber, the skinned carcasses dangling from hooks, the iron pans brimming with offal. The work room opened on to a courtyard which contained fire pits and crude smoking sheds made of planks. A pair of plump pigs lay in a small pen.

The large gold painted cross nailed to the back wall of the courtyard struck John as incongruous. If sheep and goats and pigs envisioned an afterlife they must believe themselves destined for a heaven quite different from this sausage manufactory.

He wasn't surprised that Agnes, having grown up on the palace grounds in the house John now occupied, had not wanted to work in such a place.

A boy was sloshing lengths of entrails in a tub of water, cleaning out their contents, the very job Opilio had complained about his niece refusing. The sausage maker ordered the lad to mind the shop.

"You can see, Lord Chamberlain, that the birth of my delicious sausage is no more beautiful than any other birth." He waved flies away from his face. "As to that absurd and disrespectful verse. Such gossip does not bear repeating."

"You have repeated it, Opilio, and in front of Agnes. It is the only way she could have learned about the mosaic and whenever you saw her, it could not have been long ago."

Opilio paled. "She hasn't been spreading that tale around, has she?"

"Then you admit she got that verse from you?"

"I..er…well, I meant it as a lesson, excellency. An illustration of the depravity of the sort of people with whom she insists on associating. If our glorious emperor should discover such disrespect…." He clapped his hands together. When he opened them a enormous green fly dropped lifelessly to the floor. "That will be the end of you, just like that, I told her. But the foolish girl will never listen."

"I'm sure you've heard worse. How often do you see Agnes?"

Defeated, Opilio shrugged. "Not often. She comes and goes. When she has nowhere else to stay, she turns up here. She is my niece, after all, the daughter of Comita. If Agnes had been our daughter, rather than my brother's, she would have grown up differently."

John could understand why the sausage maker had not been able to disown his niece entirely.

"Opilio, I regret having to tell you. Agnes is dead."

Opilio looked at John mutely. The buzzing of flies sounded louder.

The sausage maker shook his head. He slumped down on the stool where the boy had been sitting to clean casings.

"She was found a little more than a week ago," John went on. "I have been looking into the matter."

"Looking into...but why...what happened? Was it an accident?"

"It appears she was murdered."

Opilio made the sign of the Christians. "I warned her many times, excellency. Thank the Lord her mother was spared hearing this. Perhaps they are reunited. Heaven is merciful, even to actresses. More merciful than I was." He wiped at his eyes with the back of his hand.

"You were correct to warn her against the life she took up and the associations she made."

"Was it to do with those foolish plots her friends were always chattering on about?" Opilio's tone was suddenly fierce. "If it was, I'll make sure—"

"Justice is for the emperor to dispense but you may be able to help its administration. You said you did not recall the names of any of Agnes' acquaintances, but then again you didn't remember talk of intrigues the first time we spoke. It may be that a name or two has come back to you. Troilus, perhaps? He was a close friend of your niece."

"Yes. Yes, I admit it. I saw that villain on occasion. He would come here looking for Agnes." Opilio's forehead wrinkled and he leapt off the stool. "Is he the one responsible?"

"There may be some connection between him and her murderer. Why do you call him a villain?"

"He was a malcontent, excellency. Every cloud that passed over the sun was directed by the hand of the emperor. Every cold wind that blew came from the direction of the palace. If his evening meal was not cooked enough...well...it would have been perfection if it weren't for the demon emperor."

Apparently Opilio's grief had unlocked his tongue and he was now talking without thought of the possible consequences.

"There was reason for his grievances?"

"Troilus was not a courtier. I know nothing of his family, but then why would I? Sedition's good business to him. Many of his customers are former courtiers so he adopts their viewpoint, or pretends to at least. People prefer to deal with one of their own, someone who thinks like them."

"People like Menander? Do you know him?"

"Yes, that's another name I had tried to put out of my mind, but I remember him now. Whenever Agnes would start chattering about whatever disreputable function she'd been so thrilled to attend, his name would come up. He's the worst of the lot. To him treasonous talk is entertainment. That and boys. Rather than cursing the emperor he should be thanking the Lord for his good fortune. I hear it was Menander who set Troilus up in business and even now he supplies half of his stock. No doubt he receives part of the sales price."

"You told me before you did not think any of these plots were likely to result in action."

"It's nothing but idle talk. That's why I dismissed it all from my memory. There's no harm in words which are only whispered to those who already share one's prejudices. Besides, even people who hate Justinian love sausage. And a healthy business enriches the coffers of the empire, does it not?"

"There aren't many men who would maintain such a strong allegiance to an emperor who had deprived their brother of his head."

"Perhaps Glykos deserved his fate."

A stray breeze carried a gust of fragrant smoke from the sheds in the courtyard into the workroom, rustling the bundles of dried herbs. John wondered if Justinian had taken the revenge on the sausage maker's brother that the Christian and patriotic Opilio had harbored in his own heart.

"When you told Agnes what you overheard in Francio's kitchen, was that the last time you saw her?"

"Yes, excellency. It was the very day I made the delivery. Otherwise, I would never have remembered even those few verses. I never could memorize my Homer, the seas like wine and such. Agnes talked about your house often. She thinks… thought…of it as home. I tried to give her and her mother a home, but my house is hardly comparable to a mansion on the palace grounds."

"It's understandable, Opilio. We all remember places where we were happy. What else did you talk about?"

The sausage maker sighed and blinked his suddenly brimming eyes. "Nothing of great importance. We argued and she left."

"Did she ever mention gossip about Theodora having a son? Troilus said it was the sort of thing that's bandied about."

"That's just the kind of scandal that fool Troilus would relish believing, Lord Chamberlain, and about as authentic as those curiosities he sells. Why don't you talk to Menander?"

Opilio's shoulders heaved as he suppressed a sob. "Please, excellency. I would like to close my shop now. I must arrange my niece's funeral. Where is she?"

"The funeral has already taken place, Opilio. I will tell you where she is buried so you can visit her grave."

◇◇◇

The boy barreled down the stairway leading up to the floor on which Menander lived.

John stepped aside to avoid a collision and grabbed a flapping sleeve, restraining the boy from crashing into Peter, laboring up behind.

"If you're here to see Menander, he's at home, but in no state for nothing," the boy blurted out.

"Explain," John demanded.

"He's drunk again. Took me ages to get him upstairs."

John released the boy who bounded away, almost knocking Peter down.

Menander's door was locked. John hammered on it until he heard shuffling on the other side.

"Who's that? Forgot something?" The words were slurred.
"Wait...."

The door came open to reveal white-haired Menander wob-
bling from foot to foot, gazing down toward where a boy's head
should have been. He jerked his gaze up, gave a startled gasp,
and staggered back.

His heel snagged on a rumpled garment and he toppled
over into the glittering wall of treasures that bisected the room,
dislodging a rectangular object.

Menander made a clumsy grab at it and missed. The artifact
hit a small table and vanished in a tinkling burst of color.

Menander stared down in horror at bits of glass littering the
embroidered wall hanging which served for a floor covering.

"There's a day! I have lost a day of my life," he wailed.

John realized the object had been the changeable mosaic
which had startled Crinagoras.

"Surely it wasn't that valuable?" John replied.

"You would be surprised, Lord Chamberlain. But then,
many people have no appreciation for them. Figulus takes full
advantage of those of us who retain our appreciation. They cost
a hefty sum, but he says he needs the money for a good cause."
Menander suddenly looked around in alarm, as if startled by
his own words. "What did I say? I am very tired, excellency. So
very tired. You must excuse me."

John gestured Peter to enter. The old servant glanced around
and immediately looked almost as horrified as Menander.

Menander gave a bitter laugh. "Another interview with the
Lord Chamberlain? Between you and Procopius I haven't been
so popular at the palace since the day I left."

Peter's expression changed to outrage at the manner in which
Menander spoke to John.

John ignored it. "Perhaps you have given a fuller account
of yourself to Procopius. Did you admit to him what you concealed from me? For example that you knew Glykos' daughter,
Agnes?"

"What? Agnes? I...I...."

"Is the wine clouding your thoughts, Menander? You moved in the same circles and did business with her friend Troilus."

"When did you ask me about Agnes and Troilus, Lord Chamberlain? Surely I must have mentioned them?"

"What I am interested in now, Menander, are these fanciful tales about Theodora's son."

"Procopius badgered me about that as well. It's an old story. He knew more about it than I do. That's what I said. I said you have just told me more than I know, Procopius, so go and ask yourself. My advice is to ask Procopius." Menander swayed.

John blinked. He did not feel too steady on his feet himself. His head began to pound again.

He realized Peter had taken hold of his arm.

"Master, forgive the familiarity but you do not look well. If I may say so, you won't get any sense out of that old wine-skin."

"What did you say?" Menander demanded. "Wine-skin? You called me an old wine-skin. Is that my fate? To be insulted by ancient menials?"

"My servant is right, Menander. I will return when you are capable of thinking clearly."

With the swift change of emotion of the intoxicated, Menander burst into tears. "Ah…my precious icon!" He crumpled to his knees. "A day of my life…gone…And how do I know it won't be the very day when the tyrant Justinian dies? A day I would have lived to see. Except for this…and now I have lost what would have been the happiest day of my life."

Chapter Thirty

Peter glanced into John's bedroom.

Through the crack left by the slightly open door he could see a form on the bed in the shadows.

John had remained in his room all day. It was deeply worrying.

Every time Peter checked, John had been asleep despite the noise caused by the workmen downstairs carting barrels and sacks of tesserae, plaster, and straw through the atrium.

It must have been the blow to the head.

The matter worried him. Long ago during his military days, a soldier Peter knew had been struck on the head by a Persian sword. It seemed the blow had left the man unharmed. For two days he showed his helmet around camp. The force of the blow had split it open.

It had been a miracle.

But on the morning of the third day, while the soldier filled his bowl with gruel and described yet again how he prayed each day to the military saints Sergius and Bacchus, he dropped dead.

This is how close to death we all are, Peter thought. We never can be certain we will finish our breakfast.

Death was close to old men such as himself. Some nights, alone in his room with the lamp extinguished and the only light that which came through his tiny window, the faint effulgence of the city, light from thousands of torches under colonnades and the glowing dome of the Great Church, Peter could sense the Angel of Death standing on the other side of his door. He would hold his breath, praying silently, waiting for the knock none could refuse to answer.

He heard nothing, could see nothing. Yet he could feel a presence. So far the angel had always chosen to go away.

Peter peeked around the edge of John's door, reassured when he saw John's chest rising and falling as he breathed.

He intended to prepare the sweetened cakes John liked but had found the jug of honey on the kitchen shelf was almost empty. Fortunately there was more in the storeroom at the back of the house.

Peter went downstairs. He wondered how the work was progressing. He'd be happy when he no longer had to repeatedly sweep away the straw and plaster dust the workmen dropped.

He sighed. Once again muddy footsteps pointed the way to the bath. Worse, the mud had been smeared all over the floor by whatever the inconsiderate fellow had dragged behind him.

Peter clucked in annoyance, then stopped himself. Cornelia might be in earshot.

Her residence in the house made him self conscious. He no longer felt free to sing his favorite hymns while he worked. The house had changed since she had arrived. He never knew when he was going to run into her rounding a corner or coming out a room. She was a kind woman, if ill tempered, he thought with a smile, and devoted to John.

For that latter he was grateful.

However, he knew both he and his master had become used to their solitude.

It was true that John had hired the Egyptian girl, Hypatia, who had once worked in the same household as Peter in the days when they were both slaves. But now she worked in the palace gardens.

He wondered if she might be persuaded to return.

Peter's trips in search of fresh produce took longer now. He had found a new market, farther away than the one he usually frequented, which, he had convinced himself, sold superior leeks. He also spent more time in the garden, trying without success to keep alive the herbs Hypatia had planted.

Perhaps John would ask her to return. Anyone who had lived in a house such as this would be dissatisfied with a cramped room elsewhere.

Perhaps....

The artisans were finished for the day, but had left tools and material littered along the hallway.

Good workmen would not be so careless with their tools, Peter thought as he picked his way between barrels.

Peter paused and glanced around.

Not that the mistress could have any objection to his checking to see how far the delicate task had progressed.

He opened the door and entered.

The activities portrayed in the mosaics, he noted, were shocking. Not anything a good Christian would take pleasure from. He hadn't seen their like outside a brothel.

His lips tightened as he suppressed a smile. The room always reminded him of an incident from his youth involving a pretty servant and his owner's bath. At the time he had cursed his stupidity for inviting punishment for the sake of a brief tryst with a girl he had never seen again.

Now, decades later, he could recall the young lady down to the smallest detail—and often did—while he could not even bring to mind the vaguest image of his owner's face.

The Lord would forgive him. After all, it was the Lord who chose to make young people the way He had.

Red light from the dying sun spilled down from the circular opening in the roof and caught the voluptuous torso of a marble Aphrodite, sparkled across a heedless couple depicted on the wall behind her, and limned the figure seated in the basin at her feet.

Peter stepped forward and took a closer look.

An old man sat at the bottom, a big fellow with a craggy face and bushy, white hair. A purplish bruise circled his neck.

His eyes were wide open but he was not looking at anything so earthly as the mosaics. He was clearly dead.

Chapter Thirty-One

The official sent by the Master of the Offices climbed out of the basin in John's private bath. "Menander, you say? I seem to recall the name."

The man's pinched features suggested he had suffered long employment by the prickly administrator. "A little too vocal about the emperor's revenue raising methods, wasn't he?" he added. "I suppose it's Menander who got the last laugh. He ended his days in the palace after all. I don't suspect you, Lord Chamberlain. I'm certain you have a servant who would do the job. Some sturdy, youthful fellow."

The official glanced at Peter who stood on the other side of the room, alongside Cornelia and Anatolius, both of whom had walked in on the unexpected drama. If there had ever been so many people in the tiny facility before it had been during the tax collector's ownership.

"I can assure you John didn't kill Menander," Cornelia flared. "Or for that matter order his death."

"Makes no difference to me," the official replied. "It would if it was Theodora lying there. A Lord Chamberlain's free to remove anyone who troubles him so long as the disappearance doesn't displease the emperor."

While his assistants wrapped the body in a length of canvas, the official studied the wall mosaics. His pained expression didn't change.

The body was pulled up out of the basin and strapped to a board. Before long Menander, the official, and his assistants vanished down the hallway, Peter leading them.

"It's not Peter's fault," Cornelia said. "He tried to keep an eye on the comings and goings today but there's only one of him. Not that I'd want an army of servants underfoot. It would make me nervous to have people waiting on me."

Anatolius laughed. "I've never seen such a household. You're both better suited to be hermits. A nice cave or a pillar might do."

"I wouldn't care to live on a pillar," John told him. "I like to walk while I think."

As they turned to leave, a glint from the bottom of the basin caught John's attention. He descended the steps and picked up the object. It must have fallen from Menander's garments.

A tiny glass portrait of an angel, similar to the icon in his room full of treasures.

"Menander has left a few of his hours behind," John observed. "He doesn't need them anymore. If you have a little time to spare, Anatolius, come up to my study."

Peter had not lit the lamp on John's desk so John did so. The bawdy gods on the wall mosaic took up where the ones in the bath mosaic had left off. As usual, as her maker had piously arranged, Zoe kept her dark eyes averted from the lewd activity around her, perpetually innocent.

"I visited to inquire about your health, John. Rumor has it you were almost killed."

"By tomorrow rumor will have me dead. I've got a bit of a headache," he replied.

"If you admit to so much as a headache, you're far from well."

"Please sit, Anatolius. You'll no doubt want to hear about my investigations."

John recounted his activities since they had last met at the seaside court where they had talked to Procopius. He spoke about his interviews with Troilus and the actress Petronia and how the latter had belatedly offered proof of Troilus' innocence. He described retracing the route he felt Agnes must have taken from Petronia's room to the square on the morning of her death, his visits with Opilio the sausage maker and the inebriated Menander. The attack on his person did not feature in his account.

It took a long time. Peter refilled the wine jug twice before John ordered him to bed.

"An untrustworthy bunch," Anatolius remarked. "I doubt you've got the full story out of them even now. This Troilus seems to be in the middle of it all. Everyone you've interviewed seems to know him one way or another. Although it appears he couldn't have committed the murder since I can't see how a sundial maker could mistake the time. Do you suppose Helias could have been lying about when he saw Troilus dragging that sack in?"

"Helias doesn't seem to be connected to this affair, except his shop is next to Troilus' establishment."

Anatolius grinned. "Well, he might have lied, given he's caused trouble for Troilus before. At least according to Troilus. And what about the sausage maker?"

"Opilio was trying to protect his niece," John pointed out.

"And Petronia was just trying to protect Troilus when she neglected to tell you he'd been to her room the morning Agnes was murdered."

John's lips tightened into a thin smile. "Unless they were both actually trying to protect themselves and still haven't given me the full story. Or even the truth."

"Rather like my clients. People invariably lie to their lawyers. Now there's no way of telling what, if anything, Menander was still lying about. This Troilus seems a suspicious sort to me, given he just walked into your house the other day. Plus he was doing business with Menander. Was there a quarrel over money from the sales of Menander's goods?"

"Perhaps."

"What about that rumor that keeps cropping up, John? The one about Theodora's alleged son?"

"I'm not sure what to make of that. Troilus was the first to bring it to my attention. I tried to question Menander about the story the last time I spoke to him but he wasn't as forthcoming as Troilus. Then again, he was very intoxicated. Menander might have been killed by someone who didn't want him speaking to me about this rumored son. On the other hand, he might have been killed before he could say anything about one of the other plots everyone talks about but nobody takes seriously."

"Or he might have known something about Agnes or Troilus and had to be silenced."

"That's true."

"But why go to the trouble to deposit Menander in your bath? Not to mention the danger of being discovered in the act."

"It's obvious, Anatolius. To link me to the plotters."

"You think so? If there really were an intrigue and you were involved you would hardly leave a treacherous co-conspirator lying dead around your house. The sea tells no tales for a start."

"It doesn't have to make sense as long as it starts people thinking, particularly when their thoughts turn to subjects like treason," John pointed out. "That's when reason leaves the room."

"By people you mean Justinian?"

John nodded. "More than one Lord Chamberlain has overreached himself. The higher the official the more plausible it is he may be working against the emperor. Don't worry, it would take more than one body in my bath to turn Justinian against me. But I may have to watch my step."

Anatolius frowned. "You think the murderer was warning you to give up your investigation? But what about the attack? What if that wasn't a robbery the other night? What if whoever knocked you over the head was interrupted before he could finish the job?"

"It's a possibility. My guess is that Menander and Agnes were both killed so they couldn't reveal to me whatever it is they knew. In which case Petronia and Troilus, and Opilio for that matter, might also be in danger. Perhaps that is was why they all tried to avoid telling me anything useful. Perhaps they feared for their lives. You should warn Crinagoras to be careful. He visited Menander's room with me. And you might be in danger yourself, Anatolius."

"And don't forget Cornelia and Peter."

"I haven't. I am beginning to feel as if I am carrying the plague."

Anatolius took a sip of wine. "Do you think there's something in this business about the empress having an illegitimate son?"

"Judging from how little people have to say about it and how emphatic they are that it means nothing when they are forced to confront the rumor, I would not be surprised."

"I've always considered it as nothing more than a palace legend. The story's been around forever. I would have thought if there was any substance to it, we would have known the truth of the matter long ago."

"People don't usually go searching for the truth about legends. I intend to look into it."

"You can't question Menander further."

"No. But he advised me to ask Procopius, which is what I intend to do."

John picked up Menander's angel icon from his desk and turned the tiny artifact around in his hand. "Menander hoarded his time, but he should have been more concerned with his safety. Strange that he should end up in my house, surrounded by Figulus' mosaics. The last time I saw him he broke one of those changeable mosaics and was lamenting how much time it had cost him. I wonder if he sensed how little he had left?"

"Menander owned a mosaic by Figulus?"

"Yes, about the size of a codex. It turned from a simple cross into something quite obscene, to judge from Crinagoras' reaction."

Anatolius looked thoughtful. Then a faint smile quirked his lips. "Now I understand the icon at Isis' place!"

"Isis has an icon?"

"Indeed she has. It must have been one of Figulus' works. Mithra only knows what that stern old mosaic holy man got up to in the evenings when the light shifted, particularly since Isis mentioned it probably wasn't displayed in the best light."

"Figulus apparently does a brisk trade in those mosaics. When I visited his workshop to see him it was clear from his wife's reaction that she thought I was looking for one, and that such customers were not at all uncommon."

"It must be a lucrative business. Isis said hers cost a fortune, and you know she's not averse to spending lavishly on her decor. But didn't you tell me Figulus is a pious man?"

"Cornelia says he has tried more than once to persuade her to allow him to fix the bath properly, as he put it, or in other words make the mosaic more proper."

"Isis said he needed the money for a worthy project," Anatolius mused. "I wonder what it was?"

"Menander told me the same thing. I wouldn't have thought Figulus was in financial straits, busy as he seems to be."

"People will accommodate Lord Chamberlains," Anatolius pointed out. "But it does seem peculiar. Was it really a coincidence Menander owned one of those mosaics, and ended up murdered and left in your bath? Or that this whole affair is linked to the mosaic on the wall behind you? Could it be that Figulus isn't raising money for himself?"

John nodded. "I had thought of the possibility. Could he be aiding the conspirators? Helping finance their plans?"

"Those who have lost their position at court tend to be short of money, given everything they used to own is usually in Justinian's treasury."

"On the other hand, they may have required another service from Figulus when they realized he had access to my house. Do you suppose it is too late an hour to speak to the mosaic maker again?"

Chapter Thirty-Two

John and Anatolius waited in Figulus' workshop for a long time before the mosaic maker appeared. Light glittered off tesserae in the barrels against the wall, and struck sparks here and there on the dark floor where stray bits of glass had fallen.

"Lord Chamberlain! Is there anything wrong? Have my workmen caused some damage?"

The mosaic maker ran a hand over his eyes. Had he been asleep? He wore only a thin, unbelted tunic. The servant who had stayed with the unexpected callers stepped away into the shadows but did not leave.

John peered around. From the little he could make out, nothing looked different from his previous visit. He hadn't expected to barge in on a band of conspirators. He would not have been shocked, however, to have found the mosaic maker dead.

"I was able to clean a considerable portion of the mosaic today, excellency. In particular I brought out some of the details in the depiction of the Olympian palace of Zeus. If that it is not to your taste—"

"How well do you know Menander?" John cut in.

"Menander? I can't—"

"Don't lie, Figulus. It is not advisable. You sold him one of your special pieces."

"Special pieces?"

"Whatever it is you call those particularly lewd mosaics. I'm aware of that part of your business. My colleague tells me you sold one to Madam Isis." John nodded toward Anatolius. "I wouldn't have expected a religious man and a good family man to be dealing in such wares, and certainly not selling them to brothels."

Figulus glanced around. "Please, excellency. If you could not speak so loudly. My boys...."

"What can you tell me about Menander?"

"He's a customer. A big, white-haired fellow, isn't he?"

"He used to hold a position at the palace."

"Yes, I suppose so. There are a lot of people like that living in the area."

"Do you do business with such people on a regular basis?"

"Lord Chamberlain, I cannot answer since I don't question my customers about their background. I suppose some may have been at the palace at one time. Many still are."

"Including one of your customers who was found dead in my bath after you and your workmen left today. Menander."

Figulus blinked in bewilderment. The hand holding the lamp shook, and the flame guttered and hissed as oil splashed on it. "Dead?"

"Indeed. I believe the body was taken into my house concealed in one of the sacks or barrels in which you move your plaster and tesserae."

Figulus protested, asking surely the Lord Chamberlain did not think him guilty of murder.

"I wouldn't have imagined you were a purveyor of lewd pictures."

"You don't understand...I only sell them because...well...."

"To finance a worthy undertaking."

"Yes...but how did you know?"

"You are in the habit of making apologies for yourself, Figulus. But what exactly is this worthy undertaking? Something a disenfranchised official, like Menander, might approve? An attack on the emperor, for instance?"

A look of terror crossed the mosaic maker's face. "Nothing like that, Lord Chamberlain."

"What then?"

"I'll show you." Figulus walked hurriedly to the barrels of tesserae against the wall. Setting his lamp down on one, he pushed two others aside without any sign of exertion. They must have been empty, the pieces of cut glass piled on a false top to give the impression they were full.

The action revealed an opening half the height of a man in the wall.

"Please, excellency, follow me." Figulus ducked through the aperture.

"Be careful, John," whispered Anatolius.

But the Lord Chamberlain was already following the mosaic maker.

He found himself in a cramped vault sided with crumbling concrete. Underfoot were broken bricks of the sort used to fill up the interiors of walls.

A ladder extended from an uneven hole in one corner. Figulus scrambled on to the ladder and vanished downward, obviously used to the procedure. John followed, cautiously, and Anatolius came after him.

Below, a gloomy chamber led to another, similarly bare.

Then they emerged at their destination.

John was not certain of the original use of the space, which was too narrow for a cistern or warehouse but too wide to be a corridor, with a curved roof perhaps three times a man's height. It bore a resemblance to the huge corridors leading down into the storage areas beneath the Hippodrome. The far end of the place was lost in darkness.

Here and there scaffolds hid the walls. Nearby, where there was no scaffolding, John could see mosaics.

Even in the poor light of Figulus' lamp, it was obvious that they were as finely wrought as those in the Great Church, and they would not have been out of place there. So far as he could tell they depicted scenes from the Christian's holy book.

A garden which looked remarkably like parts of the grounds of the Great Palace, but even lusher—the foliage so thick as to practically conceal the two figures entirely, let alone expose any of their nudity—represented the paradise from which mankind had been expelled. There was a ship, not unlike the merchant vessels to be seen in city harbors any day, but far larger, to judge from the tiny size of the animals shown on board. A weird tower, reaching up into cut glass clouds, might have been the lighthouse visible from one window in John's house, but as seen in a nightmare. The stars scattered across the curved vault overhead would have made it resemble the ceiling of a mithraeum, except for the hovering angels.

"You see, excellency," explained Figulus, "tesserae are expensive. I could not afford this except for those evil pictures. It is a torment to me to make them. But I am not responsible for the lusts and sinfulness of other men and here their vices are transmuted into a tribute to God's glory."

"This is magnificent," exclaimed Anatolius. "But no one can see it down here."

"The Lord sees it," Figulus replied. "That is enough, isn't it?"

"You should be working in one of Justinian's new churches or at the palace," Anatolius told him.

"Alas, I do not have the proper connections to obtain imperial contracts even though many from the palace are well satisfied with the lesser projects I have undertaken for them personally."

"Do you know the original purpose of this room?" John asked.

Figulus shook his head. "I discovered it shortly after I bought the workshop, which was badly in need of repairs. I explored the area carefully. This room appears to be completely sealed off on its own. I took it to be a gift from the Lord. It extends for a long distance. Before I leave this world I hope to have shown the whole of the events related in our sacred writings."

It occurred to John that given the scope of his ambition, Figulus must be hoping for a very long life indeed.

Anatolius meantime had walked up and down, inspecting the walls. He paused for a time in front of a large space where there seemed to be nothing on the wall but shadows.

Figulus bought his lamp to where Anatolius was standing. "I see you are admiring my best work, sir. This was the most difficult scene yet. I labored over it for years longer than the Lord labored over the real thing."

"But there's nothing here," Anatolius replied.

John, moving closer, saw that the apparently blank wall was in fact covered with tesserae, but they appeared uniformly black.

"This is the beginning," Figulus explained. "The darkness out of which was formed light and the world." He began to move the lamp. As the light shifted the wall became alive.

It seemed to John that black shapes coalesced and evaporated. Vague, shadowy possibilities of men and animals and vegetation swirled and flowed across the glass. Dark smoke in a starless night.

Or perhaps it was nothing but shadows and John's imagination.

"Mithra!" The admiring oath escaped before he realized it. He looked away from the wall, toward Figulus. If the mosaic maker had heard, he gave no indication.

Chapter Thirty-Three

When John returned home he could not sleep. Every time he began to nod off he dreamed about the strange, living darkness in Figulus' wall and came fully awake with his heart pounding.

Words came back to him that he had heard once, during an official ceremony he could not recall, in a church he could not immediately place. Something moving upon the face of the deep. What did that mean? Had it been Figulus' intent to capture that?

The face of the deep.

The very phrase made him shudder.

He needed to walk, to think.

He left the house without waking either Cornelia or Peter. He had learned to move in quiet fashion as a mercenary patrolling the empire's border and had maintained the skill. He was naturally quiet in his movements. He startled people without meaning to do so by appearing at their elbow as if springing up from the underworld. However, he reminded himself, if palace residents feared the Lord Chamberlain might be with them before they knew it, that was to his advantage.

It was earlier than the time he usually took long morning walks. He followed his accustomed route and had almost reached the square where he had met Agnes before the roofs of the city began to emerge from the night, a mountain range of massive blocks and escarpments, surmounted by countless crosses.

He heard a scuffle, and turning quickly, caught a glimpse of movement. He had the impression something had vanished into a doorway on the opposite side of the street. A feral dog or a cat?

Then it occurred to John that he was near the spot where he had been attacked.

He stepped back against the wall of a closed shop. His side of the street was still sunk in impenetrable shadow.

He waited.

A figure burst out from the doorway and raced across the street at an angle, this time disappearing under an archway. The echoing footsteps seemed to linger in the narrow space between the buildings.

John's hand went to his blade. Had he been followed? Was the figure he had glimpsed attempting, not very artfully, to outflank and then creep up on him?

He moved toward the archway.

The figure rushed out.

John raised his blade and stepped into the man's path.

The other came to a sudden halt.

It was the maker of sundials.

"Helias!"

"Lord Chamberlain." The voice had the same pitch as the squeak of a terrified rat.

"Have you been following me?" John demanded.

Helias threw panicked glances this way and that. "No! I'm just on my way home."

"You have a stranger manner of it."

The diminutive sundial maker shifted from foot to foot. "Please, do you mind if we continue while we talk?" Without waiting for a reply, he headed off a trot.

John caught up easily with his long stride. "Why were you darting back and forth like that? Were you trying to elude someone?"

"No, excellency. It's because of the shadows. Can't you see them? They'll trip you up. Nasty things, they are. They move fast."

To John the street appeared uniformly dark, aside from the deeper shadow along the side they were walking on. He said as much.

"But you don't work with shadows every day as I do, Lord Chamberlain. My sundials are specially made to display them. You might call my creations shadow traps. Or perhaps time traps. It's the same thing, you see. It's all to do with the sun crossing the sky, pulling shadows along with it. It's enough to make you giddy if you can't help noticing, as I do."

During their first meeting Helias had confessed he didn't like being out in the sun because he couldn't help calculating the time from the shadows, but it struck John now there was something more to the matter than that.

Or else Helias was lying.

Helias turned and went through the archway leading to the courtyard and his subterranean shop. He stopped abruptly at the edge of the open space and jerked his head around, averting his gaze. "I'm too late!" His squeaky voice rose to an even higher pitch. "I had business to attend to and I lost track of the time."

The irony of the statement was not lost on John. However, he contented himself with questioning Helias why he conducted business in the middle of the night.

"My clients value my services. They are willing to make arrangements to suit my needs." Helias replied. "Time is important. They depend on me to supply them with time of the best quality." The sundial maker kept his gaze pointed toward John's feet, or perhaps at some indeterminate point on the pavement behind John because the Lord Chamberlain would certainly cast a shadow.

"Time is the same for all of us," John observed.

"I fear it is not so, Lord Chamberlain. For example, consider the senator who decided to install an antique sundial in his garden. Suddenly he was missing important meetings. The sundial was set for hours in Rome. It wouldn't work in Constantinople…I don't know how I'll get to my emporium now. The courtyard is swarming with shadows. They're creeping everywhere."

In fact, John could make out poorly defined shadows, including that of the exedra used by the troupe. "Helias, do you claim you can see these shadows moving?"

"But I can! I can't help it! Anyone'd see how they move too if they spent all day incising the lines of the hours, each perfectly in their place so shadow fingers would cross them exactly when they should."

John remained unconvinced on the matter of whether or not Helias had been following him and advised him in a curt voice to admit it if it had been so.

"No, Lord Chamberlain, it is just as I say. And now, I must…try….If I fall, would you pick me up?"

It was evident the little man's fear had made him forget he was talking to one of the most powerful officials at court.

The sundial maker backed hesitantly into the courtyard. John watched in amazement as Helias crept backward, eyes squeezed shut. He began to veer off course.

"Move the other way," John instructed.

Helias finally blundered into the wall some distance from the doorway leading to the underground shops. He scuttled crab-like along the wall with his shoulder blades pressed firmly to it, managed to open the door without turning, fell backward into the dark maw revealed, and was gone.

John pondered the strange events. This was the second extremely odd explanation he had encountered for someone's suspicious actions. Figulus, at least, had obviously been working on his enormous mosaic for years, but Helias might have manufactured his excuse on the spot. Still, John felt Helias was telling him the truth.

Who would make up such a ridiculous ruse to disguise his actions?

Chapter Thirty-Four

The rasp of a bolt being drawn back and the creak of the front door opening carried up the stairs and into the kitchen where John and Cornelia had just sat down to a breakfast of bread, cheese, and hard boiled eggs.

"It must be Anatolius. I wasn't expecting him this early, not after we were out so late last night. I kept dreaming about that black glass wall." John took another bite of bread and stood up.

"Don't think I didn't notice you going out for a walk," Cornelia remarked, getting to her feet. Her eyebrows knitted in concern. "I hope it's not about that girl."

"Agnes wanted to talk to me, Cornelia, and now she's dead. Probably because of what she wanted to tell me."

Cornelia sighed. "Be careful. The Goddess has watched over you so far but…."

"We're going to speak with Procopius. Nothing dangerous about that. We won't be leaving the palace grounds."

"They can be dangerous too."

"So I've been told." John picked up a sliver of cheese and chewed it as he went downstairs to the atrium.

Peter had closed the door.

He was alone.

"Who was that, Peter?"

"I can't say, master. It took me a little while to get here and when I looked out there was no one there. Only this." He held out a rolled bit of papyrus no longer than John's finger.

"You didn't see anyone in the square? No one near the excubitor barracks?"

"No, master."

Whoever had left the papyrus must have raced away to vanish before Peter got to the door. On the other hand, Peter was slowing down.

John took the papyrus and unrolled it.

The message had been penned in Latin:

> *"At the second hour, two conspirators will meet beside the Milion."*

The Milion sat at the edge of the Augustaion. From the Mese, John could see the four pillars, connected by arches and surmounted by a pyramidical roof. Pedestrians hurried past on their way to the Great Church, Samsun's Hospice, the law courts, the Baths of Zeuxippos, and the palace.

No one lingered near the Milion.

John walked slowly to the monument. There was no one inside either.

The morning light, slanting in through the archways, illuminated inscriptions on the pillars stating the distances from the capital to the important cities of the empire.

John pretended to study them.

When he first lived in Constantinople as a slave he had searched for places he had lived—Athens, where he briefly attended Plato's Academy, Bretania, one of the places he had served as a mercenary, Alexandria in which he met Cornelia. There had been no city in the border region where the Persians had captured and emasculated him before selling him into slavery.

The distances, vast as they were, did not begin to describe the gulf which lay between John and those places. No journey, however long, could return him to the man he had been.

He waited. No one stopped near the monument. He was certain the second hour had passed. Perhaps he had arrived too late.

The light dimmed as a figure stepped through an archway. A burly man with a bushy beard and familiar face.

"John!" said Felix. "What are you doing here?"

"I might ask the same of you."

The excubitor captain tugged his beard and glanced around. "I...um...."

John produced the bit of rolled papyrus. "This was left at my door a short while ago. It said two conspirators would be meeting at the Milion."

"I received a similar note," Felix admitted.

He compared his papyrus to John's. The wording was the same and the handwriting appeared to be identical.

"For all we know our informer may have alerted half the palace," John said. "The emperor himself is liable to come strolling along within the hour."

"There doesn't seem to be anyone here but us, John. The villains might have been frightened off. Maybe we should wait over the way and see if anyone appears."

John followed Felix to the other side of the Augustaion. They climbed the tier of steps surrounding the base of the towering column there.

Sunlight glanced blindingly off the column's copper sheathing. There was no stylite atop the pillar but rather an equestrian statue of Justinian.

The emperor's bronze steed had one foot raised, as if about to gallop off toward the east. A few people sat on the steps, as if upon theater seats, to gaze down on the drama of the city.

From where John and Felix stood, the Milion and all approaches to it were clearly visible.

"I'm surprised you didn't bring armed excubitors with you, Felix," John observed.

His companion grunted with disgust. "I thought it was a jest by someone who has an odd sense of humor."

John raised his gaze to the mounted Justinian. "If a couple of conspirators wanted to meet, they might find it amusing to do so right under the gaze of the emperor himself."

"They'd be perfectly safe with the emperor staring off into the east," Felix replied. "It strikes me he'd best stop keeping an eye on the Persians when the real dangers to his rule are right here in the city."

Crowds surged back and forth through the open space before them. No one paused at the Milion. City dwellers took the monumental milestone for granted. They knew they lived at the center of the civilized world. The distances to its other parts were irrelevant.

After a while, the pair decided to leave.

Felix suggested visiting a tavern close by and they repaired to it, taking their seats at a table in the back part of the room. From there they could see into the street.

The tavern was plain, most of its patrons dressed in a manner showing them to be workmen. Its plaster walls were black with smoke stains and its wine cups not of the cleanest.

Perhaps the proprietor felt no need to make an effort to entice patrons, being located so close to the busy Augustaion.

"Do you think there's someone laughing at our folly right now, Felix?"

The excubitor scowled over the chipped rim of his cup. "No doubt about it, John. If you really wanted two villains caught would you send the Lord Chamberlain and the Captain of the Excubitors? No, you'd alert the city authorities."

John took a sip of wine to which far too much water had been added. "Yet we both came to the Milion, didn't we? A little more than a week ago I was approached by a woman in a square in the Copper Market. She wanted to meet me the next morning. It was suggested to me that the arrangement was a jest by some fool at court. The next time I saw her she was dead. Murdered."

"It's the woman who called herself Zoe you're talking about?"

John looked away from the door. "Yes. Her real name was Agnes. How did you know?"

"Anatolius mentioned it to me, although he didn't go into details."

"I'm glad to hear he has gained some discretion, although not nearly enough."

"You say she's been murdered?"

"Yes. Furthermore, I've come to believe that the woman had something to tell me, something someone else didn't want me to know."

"Why didn't she tell you right away instead of making an appointment?"

"Perhaps she feared she was being watched."

"Why didn't you come to me? I'd have assigned a few of my excubitors to help. That is if I could find any to spare. The emperor has my excubitors serving as personal bodyguards for every minor dignitary that shows up in he capital. They're nothing more than ornaments. Still, I would have found someone to assist you."

"I thought it was a private matter and should remain so. I had the impression there was some connection to me personally."

"Because she knew the name you gave the mosaic girl? I'd have thought you would have confided in me after I'd rescued you from the street. The attacker must have intended to kill you. Was there any connection to Menander?"

"News travels fast," John remarked.

Felix ran a big hand through his beard and laughed. "When a corpse is found in the Lord Chamberlain's residence the whole palace is agog over the sensation within the hour."

John nodded and resumed his observation of the tavern door.

The tavern itself had almost emptied while they sat there. A man with a basket full of vegetables came in and gulped down a cup of wine while standing at the counter. A servant taking time to have a drink on the way back from market, John thought.

"I tried to question Menander shortly before he was killed," John went on. "It's no wonder we received anonymous notes. Our informant—if he was genuine—must value his life. As I said, I had thought this matter was a private affair, to do with me personally. I am beginning to suspect there's a lot more going on."

"You might deign to allow me to be of assistance then?"

"I can certainly use it, Felix."

John recounted events since his meeting with Agnes and the results of his inquiries. He spoke in low tones and kept a watch on the street.

Felix nodded and scowled and emptied his cup twice. Finally he growled, "This rumor about Theodora's lost son replacing Justinian is absurd. Granted, she hasn't managed to give Justinian an heir, but that doesn't mean anyone would accept the claim of one of her blood rather than the emperor's. For every man who hates Justinian there are ten more who hate Theodora. Admittedly the populace would be glad to be rid of the imperial couple, but I don't think they'd want to replace them with her evil spawn."

"You're thinking of the tales about the empress enjoying congress with demons?"

"Who can say what she was up to in Egypt, when she wasn't sharing the stage with hungry geese?" Felix grinned. "Besides, what claim to the throne could an illegitimate son of the empress possess?"

"Power proves its own legitimacy. Theodora is powerful. More than a few consider her to be a true co-ruler. Were Justinian to be removed Theodora would doubtless claim to be his appointed successor, and not without justification. To placate her enemies, she could offer to stand aside in favor of her son, and thereafter rule through him."

"That sounds far fetched," Felix observed.

"It would sound convincing if backed up by enough swords and there were enough weak-willed men who would wish to remain in favor with Theodora."

Two middle-aged men entered the tavern. They surveyed its cramped space and selected the table furthest from where John and Felix were sitting.

After they were served they leaned toward each other to talk. Both wore fine garments and unhappy expressions.

"I'll have our jug refilled," John told Felix. He moved quickly and quietly. He had passed the table where the two sat almost before they noticed.

John returned with the wine. "I have just learned Senator Corvinus will soon be involved in an exceptionally unpleasant divorce."

Felix smiled. "From the law courts, are they? Lawyers often look as guilty as criminals. You should put that nonsense about Theodora's son out of your mind."

"Admittedly, it would take a lot of swords to make an argument in such a son's favor. But what if the son himself believes he is destined to rule? Whereas the truth of the matter is more likely that certain parties only want to prove his existence in order to rid themselves of the imperial couple, and after that, well...."

Felix asked him what he meant.

"You recall the general opposition to Justinian marrying an actress? His uncle Justin, even though he ruled at the time, wouldn't pass the law that allowed it until his empress died."

"Eudoxia did hate Theodora, it was common knowledge, but I'm certain if Justin had thought it best for the empire he would have passed the law sooner."

"That may be," John said, aware of his friend's admiration for the emperor who had risen from the same position Felix now held. "But what if her enemies had proved she was mother to an illegitimate child? Would the church have accepted the marriage? Could Justinian have ruled and commanded the loyalty of the army and aristocracy, while in a marriage to a former actress, condemned by the Patriarch?"

"It might have been difficult." Felix stared into his cup.

"The city is overflowing with people who have grievances against the imperial couple. Luckily for the emperor they all have different grievances. Should they agree to come together over a shared outrage and rise up together...well...consider the sort of trivial events that spark riots."

Felix set his cup down on the table so hard the lawyers looked up. "We could come up with a hundred possibilities, John, and every one as likely or unlikely as the next."

"There is no way to predict exactly what might happen, but if an illegitimate son of Theodora's does exist, he poses a danger to the emperor. Besides, if I find him, I may also discover who killed Agnes and Menander."

Chapter Thirty-Five

John and Anatolius intercepted Procopius halfway across the nave of the Great Church.

"I see my friend's informant was right," John said. "He indicated we could find you here."

Anatolius had been waiting for John when he returned home following his discussion with Felix. He had inquired at the palace as to where Procopius might be found.

"I just finished speaking to a deacon," Procopius replied. "I was interested in hearing his comments about the effect this wonderful structure has on worshippers. How else to describe the Great Church except by its effect?"

He waved the wax tablet he carried at their surroundings. His garments were as pristine as when John and Anatolius had recently seen him, and his hair as neatly arranged. John imagined that no matter where he came upon the man nor what time of day, Procopius would be just as perfectly garbed and coiffured.

"You're researching for that work about Justinian's buildings?" Anatolius asked.

"Yes, but I intend to finish my history of the wars first. Relating historical events is an easy task compared to describing such magnificence."

"It would take a poet," John agreed. "A skilled poet."

Although John had attended innumerable ceremonial functions there in his capacity as Lord Chamberlain, the church never failed to surprise him whenever he visited. Its complexity was such that it could not be fully absorbed, let alone recalled in every detail. To enter the soaring space for the fiftieth time was to enter for the first.

Columned aisles and galleries rose up into a bewildering assortment of intersections, in the center of which the impossibly huge central dome floated like a golden sky. Light flooded in through countless windows, reflecting at every conceivable angle from gilt and marble, precious metals and glass, until the air shimmered with a glow which seemed to emanate from the walls themselves.

"I am only a thin-voiced scribbler," Procopius said. "My desire is to describe what the emperor has wrought as simply as possible. The weight of the slightest verbal encrustation would bring my whole structure tumbling down."

"And what did the deacon have to tell you?" asked Anatolius.

"Why, that we can easily imagine the Lord in this place, can we not? There are those who say we are no more than fleeting ideas in His eternal mind, and here, in the golden light from which every shadow has been banished, we might be at the very center of that mind. Do you know, it is said there are pagans who choose to worship in places made to resemble caves? I speak of Mithrans, who worship a sun god in such sad subterranean environs. What sort of man would worship in a cave who could commune with God here instead?"

Anatolius sneezed. The sound echoed around the vast space. "My apologies. It's the effect of the incense."

Procopius scratched a note on his wax tablet.

"I have been told you are a repository of rumors, despite spending most of your time off on campaigns with Belisarius," John said.

"When I am in the city I make it my business to learn as much as I can. I have many works yet to be written. Who can say what may turn out to be useful? Did you know the wife of

Senator Maximus is having an illicit affair with a minor func-
tionary from the tax assessor's office? The Senator came upon
the two in his own residence, if you will believe it."

"I have no trouble believing it. That's the second such infidel-
ity I've heard about today," John said.

Anatolius looked thoughtful. "Perhaps I should abandon
untangling matters relating to estates and concentrate on domestic
disputes."

"It depends on whose side you prefer to take," Procopius said.
"These days faithless women run straight to the empress and cry
they've been slandered. They start countersuits. The husbands
don't even get a trial. It's well known the empress sees to that. The
unfortunate men are fined, whipped, and sent to prison. When
they are allowed to finally trudge home their wives are often found
entertaining lovers in the garden or the marital bed."

He paused and smiled. "Or so it is claimed. All preposter-
ous. These statements are merely the vicious lies of malcontents
jealous of Theodora's goodness and beauty. I studied at the law
school in Berytus, you know. I am glad I do not pursue the profession any longer. I find writing to be more rewarding by far."
He regarded Anatolius. "Perhaps you should consider writing
rather than law, young man."

"You appear to spend a lot of time talking with malcontents,"
John put in. "I hear you recently interviewed Menander again."

"Poor Menander. Very sad news. I'm sure he still had many
interesting stories. There was one he began to tell me, about a
garden in the palace quarters occupied by the empress. A concealed garden, no windows overlooking it."

Procopius licked his lips and pitched his voice lower. "This
garden contained a number of large carved stone phalli, and
Theodora was in the habit of taking moonlight strolls in it. But
was Menander your house guest, Lord Chamberlain? What was
he doing in your bath?"

"Don't you know, Procopius? You seem well informed on
most matters."

"I only know the tales Menander related, which naturally never involved him personally. He was a careful man. He stored up anecdotes as well as treasures. He enjoyed showing them off in the same fashion. A prelate's nasty predilections here. A pious lady's dark little secret there."

"And perhaps an illegitimate son of the empress?"

Procopius' broad forehead furrowed. His gaze met John's. His eyes were dark. They did not seem to catch the surrounding effulgence. "That? A cheap bauble, not worth bothering about."

"Did Menander repeat the tale to you?"

"I have heard about this alleged son but you will appreciate I cannot divulge my source. If someone were to take this libelous information seriously the fact that someone possessed it might be, shall we say, misinterpreted."

John thought a man might find he could divulge his sources quite easily when questioned in the emperor's dungeons. It was, however, a reasonable excuse for concealing information.

"I am being honest with you when I say I know little about Menander," Procopius continued. "He was an excellent source of gossip. He spent years living in the Copper Market among others who had once enjoyed the comforts of the court. Every sordid tale they are afraid to whisper while at the palace they are happy to bellow forth once they have been disgraced. They thereby prove they were indeed unworthy of our esteemed ruler's loyalty. By their own vile tongues they demonstrate the emperor is not a petty and vindictive tyrant, casting them out on the flimsiest of pretexts. He is merely prescient. They are fortunate to be still alive."

"Would you say any of them might be inclined to do more than just talk?" John asked.

"As I have already indicated, it was nothing but talk. There is no doubt that Justinian has set too many enemies loose. He forgives his opponents too readily, as everyone knows. An admirable trait for a Christian, but one that's dangerous for an emperor. Yet the scoundrels have so far not risen against him. Thanks, perhaps, to the protective hand of God."

Anatolius sniffed. Faint vapors snaked through the glowing air, eddies in a haze of incense and lamp smoke. John felt his eyes beginning to burn.

Procopius went on. "I form no opinion on matters for which I have no evidence, such as what we are discussing. Your legal friend will agree with me that is the best policy, Lord Chamberlain."

"Indeed. Now, tell me about a matter for which you have no evidence. The matter of Theodora's illegitimate son."

"If you insist, I will tell you the story although it pains me to repeat such slanderous tales about our dear empress." The sparkle in Procopius' eyes gave the lie to his pious words. "While Theodora still lived in Egypt and performed on the stage, she accidentally became pregnant by one of the many men with whom she is said to have dallied. She realized her misfortune too late on this occasion and her efforts to abort the child failed."

He leered at John. "I find it incredible that a woman of such reputation should either have failed to notice her condition, or that she did not possess the artifice to rid herself of what must have been a frequent inconvenience. Yet that is what some evil persons would have us believe about our devout empress."

"I do understand that you do not approve of this story, Procopius, or believe in its veracity. Continue."

"Thank you, Lord Chamberlain. I would not want to be thought disloyal. It transpired she was forced to bear the child. She was beside herself with rage and exasperation. How could she care for an infant and maintain her accustomed activities? Wantonness and lust left no room in her for motherly love. Even common whores, I am told, shed tears over their abortions and plead that the children they do bear not be sold as slaves. The father suspected, no doubt rightly, she would do away with his son before too long. So he took the baby and sailed to a far-off land. John was the name he gave to the boy."

"The commonest of names," John observed. "Is anything known of the father of this mythical child?"

"Nothing, except that the boy was supposedly told about his mother when the father was on his death bed. The boy was around fourteen by then. Theodora, as we all know, had repented her sinful life and made her way from the brothels and stages of Alexandria to the bed of the emperor in Constantinople as his devout and charitable wife and benefactor of the city."

Procopius sighed. "It's said the boy set sail for Constantinople as soon as he'd buried his father. Wouldn't you, if you suddenly discovered you were the son of the empress?"

"Not knowing Theodora as I do," John stated.

"Surely you do not give any credence to those who would have us believe she is now less than a Christian paragon, Lord Chamberlain?"

"No more than you do."

Procopius may have smiled. It was hard to tell. "To finish the story," he continued, "the young John presented himself to the empress's chamberlain. When informed of the child's presence, Theodora was stricken by fear. What if Justinian found out about the lad? Many had opposed his marriage to a former actress in the first place, and an illegitimate son would be fresh proof of her immorality. Gossip is one thing and easily ignored, but a young man in the flesh is another matter entirely. He'd also present a political liability, and then there'd be Justinian's reaction when he discovered what had been concealed from him."

"If he did not already know," John replied. "The same sort of problems would arise if he were to reappear today."

"Indeed. However, despite the rumors there is no chance of that happening. Theodora summoned this John to an audience. If the poor child expected some show of motherly affection he was sadly disappointed. The empress put him in the charge of a servant, a fellow employed for his loyalty, discretion, and brutality. The boy was never seen again. No one knows by what means he was removed from this world. No decent person would want to know."

John's lips tightened. "You are wrong, Procopius. I want to know. I am beginning to believe this tale is partly true, that Theodora's son was removed from the palace, but not from the world."

Chapter Thirty-Six

There were within the empire many former actresses who had planted Christian crosses upon their doors. Most such doors were modest affairs of unfinished wooden planks, opening onto the stark cenobitic cells into which many of these fallen women had retreated in search of salvation.

The cross-emblazoned doors to Theodora's quarters in the Great Palace were altogether different. Massive, elaborately worked bronze portals—beyond them lay a glittering maze of corridors, reception halls, and sumptuous private rooms, some unglimpsed even by the emperor. They might have been the doors to a splendid church or the servants' entrance to heaven.

The Lord Chamberlain was known to everyone at the palace and passed into the outer realms of Theodora's environs without challenge.

He had sent Anatolius back to the courts. He wanted to conduct the interview he sought on his own, for he knew he would be uneasy and he did not want to display it to a friend.

Brilliantly robed attendants with smooth faces swarmed in the hallways like flights of angels.

They were eunuchs.

One, chattering away carelessly to a companion, brushed against him.

John stepped away and gave the creature a black glare that sent it scurrying off like a frightened girl.

John realized his fists were clenched. He tried to force himself to relax.

He did not like eunuchs. As a former military man who had been grievously wounded, he hated any comparison between himself and those pitiful beings who had never attained manhood. He was only too aware how many of the men with whom he dealt believed because his condition was the same that he shared the eunuchs' propensities for dissembling and treachery, although they would never dare say it to the Lord Chamberlain's face.

After traversing the halls for a short time he found an armed guard beside a doorway leading toward the inner sanctum, a soldier rather than a eunuch. He gave John directions to the office of Theodora's head chamberlain.

Kyrillos rose languidly from a padded chair in front of an ivory inlaid desk, as if weighed down by his garments, heavily embroidered as they were with a confusion of bright, geometric patterns overlaid with golden crosses. Like many of his kind, he was unnaturally tall but hollow chested with the puffy, characterless face of an overgrown child and the pallid skin and soft hands of a woman.

"Lord Chamberlain, do you wish an audience with the empress? It can be arranged, provided she does not have a prior appointment."

"I am not seeking an audience. I am here to speak with you."

John's eyes watered, so thick was the air with perfumes. The exotic, masking scents spoke of one who lacked the discipline required to control the functions of a mutilated body.

"I am profoundly honored," said Kyrillos. "What is it you wish to talk to me about?" His voice was thin and sexless.

"I require information concerning an incident which occurred some ten years ago."

"A long time ago. I may not remember."

"You will remember, I am certain, especially since the emperor's life may depend on your recollection. Not to mention your own life."

Kyrillos waved his hand in a dismissive gesture. "Everything is life and death in my position, Lord Chamberlain. You can be assured if eggs are boiled too hard I will be stoned to death with them, and I will doubtless be slowly strangled in any silken attire in which our dear empress discerns a wrinkle. But that is as it should be, for perfection cannot but demand perfection."

As he spoke, the eunuch did not meet John's gaze but stared over his shoulder across the spacious but cluttered room. A variety of chairs, sofas, and tables made it appear more like a private dwelling than an imperial office. A small fountain, its waters strewn with rose petals, gurgled between the windows of one wall.

What surprised John, however, were the statues, large and small, occupying tables and wall niches and the floor space between the furniture. He picked up a bronze statuette. The figure, half covered by animal skins, reclined beside a tree stump. "You are interested in satyrs?"

"As you see." Kyrillos' gesture took in his small army of goat men.

A porphyry satyr played a flute while another carved from ivory danced nearby. A large torso, the remains of a life-sized sculpture, sat in a corner, while a pedestal supported the head of a youthful satyr whose forehead displayed nubs rather than horns.

"It amuses me to contemplate the poor monsters, driven by their appetites, like men," Kyrillos went on.

"It must have cost a great deal to accumulate such a collection. Many of these works look ancient."

Kryillos shrugged. "Most of them were gifts. From high officials. The very sort of men who will sacrifice their heads to satisfy their loins. We are fortunate not to suffer from such a repulsive and dangerous weakness, are we not, Lord Chamberlain? We did not attain our positions by rutting like common beasts."

"I did not bring you a satyr, Kyrillos, but I expect you to answer my questions regardless."

"I never take bribes. Can I help it if men think I do? You must know what the common people think about us eunuchs. What information do you require?"

John felt heat rising in his cheeks. He hoped he was not visibly reddening. "Around a decade ago a boy arrived here," he said, struggling to keep the anger out of his voice. "He claimed to be the son of Theodora. He subsequently vanished."

Kyrillos' eyes widened. His gaze darted about without settling on John. "How many children of Theodora have I heard about over the years?" he asked in a plaintive whine. "You'd think she was a hare before she married Justinian. I've never taken them seriously, and as far as remembering any particular—"

"Every beggar in the streets seems to know about this boy."

"I can't recall the last time I ventured outside the palace. I rarely visit the gardens, let alone the streets. Besides, I never talk to beggars. They're always so filthy and smell in the most dreadful way."

"This was a boy named John, aged about fourteen. He arrived following the death of his father. The man had known Theodora when she lived in Egypt."

Kyrillos was silent. There was no sound but the splashing water in the fountain. "Why is it men suppose that the conjoining of loins imparts entitlement to the issue?" he finally said, his voice even thinner than before. "How absurd to imagine an untutored, rustic child might expect a place at the court simply because of the coupling from which it resulted. Why, by my training and experience, I am more a son of Theodora than any such bastard could be."

"You do remember such a boy?"

"I would have to ask the empress if I do," Kyrillos smirked.

John offered a grim smile. "I understand you are in a difficult situation. I appreciate that you are loyal to the empress, but as I have explained, the safety of the emperor is involved. Would you choose to betray him?"

Kyrillos pursed his lips. "Lord Chamberlain, I believe we both know while the emperor may forgive those with whom he becomes angry, once we attract the enmity of Theodora, she will pursue us straight through the gates of heaven, and indeed often arrange for them to be opened for us."

"Would the empress fault you for helping to preserve the throne?"

"I have only your word that the throne is at stake. If it is not, I could be—"

"I could order you executed myself," John cut in. "I am the emperor's Lord Chamberlain, whereas you are merely chamberlain to the empress."

It seemed to John that Kyrillos trembled. "I will give my life for the empress if necessary," said the eunuch all but inaudibly. "But where is your sealed order written in purple ink? If Justinian had sent you, you would be able to show me such a document."

John's heart had begun to pound. "And what if your fine mistress had sent me, to see whether you would put the emperor to death by your own treacherous folly and insubordination?"

"If you have approached me in the emperor's name without his knowledge, both he and the empress shall know of it." Kyrillos' faint voice quavered. "But if I do you a service by saying nothing of this visit, there will be a reward, will there not?"

So even abject terror could not allay such a creature's greed.

John felt his muscles tense. He was aware of the weight of the bronze statuette he still held. He restrained himself from lashing out in a fury, striking the repulsive eunuch with the satyr, knocking him backward into the fountain, watching the puffy face gaze up from beneath scattered rose petals on the surface of the water. The thought reminded him of his discovery of Agnes.

The image brought him to his senses. He set the satyr down. "I will see you have a reward."

Kyrillos slumped down into the chair in front of his desk. He looked exhausted. "Thank you, Lord Chamberlain. Now that I think about it, I believe I may indeed recall the boy you mentioned. He was brought into my office by one of my slaves. The child had been wandering around the palace asking after his mother, if you can imagine that. He was questioning a servant when my slave overheard him. How he slipped into the palace I don't know. A large number of guards were executed afterward for dereliction of duty."

John asked for a description of the boy.

"He was a child and children all look the same. I don't pay much attention to them. They aren't important at court. Strange that he said his name was John." A sly smile flickered over his face. "There was nothing to his claim, but he had been searching from one end of the palace grounds to the other. The empress would doubtless hear about it so I wished to tell her first. To my surprise, she ordered me to send him to her at once."

"That must have suggested to you that his story was genuine?"

"Not necessarily, given Theodora's strange humors. I thought it was possible she was bored and looking for amusement. Afterward I knew the boy was not her son."

John asked how Kyrillos could be certain.

"Because...." Kyrillos paused and dabbed his suddenly bright eyes, unable to control his emotions like all of his kind. "Because no mother would slaughter her own child, Lord Chamberlain."

"Theodora killed the boy?"

"Not with her own hands. But...I heard about it later, you understand...I was not present. My slave escorted the boy off to a private audience with Theodora and that was the last I saw of him. No one knows what passed between empress and child. After a short time, she summoned a favorite of hers, a rough, illiterate brute. No better than a beast, but as loyal as a cur. She placed the child in this monster's hands. John has never been seen again."

"And you believe Theodora ordered the boy killed?"

"What other conclusion can one draw? The brute, Theodoulos, could be trusted to carry out the task. It is well known he had done so on other occasions."

John suppressed an oath. "And Theodoulos?"

Kyrillos shook his head and stared at the floor. "You doubtless expect him to have been executed? But no, there was no reason to do so. He would no more betray the empress than a dog betray his master. And, as I told you, he was her favorite, a pet, like that bear she used to keep caged....

"Theodoulos is a dwarf and you know how she dotes on them. Why would she destroy a plaything like that? No, she merely had his tongue cut out. I doubt a beast like him even misses it."

And yet the grim story had traveled on other tongues from the palace grounds into the city, thought John.

Chapter Thirty-Seven

As he strode through the narrow white-washed hallways of the servants' lodgings, John's head throbbed with pain, more, he suspected the result of his infuriating confrontation with Kyrillos than any lingering effect of the street ambush.

No splendid tapestries, mosaics, or frescoes decorated this dimly lit palace warren, only crosses provided by a benevolent empress as a reminder of the greater riches waiting in another world.

There were as many eunuchs here as in Theodora's own quarters. They made way nervously for the tall man with a military bearing and a dark look in his eyes.

"Where can I find Theodoulos?" John demanded of one servant after another.

He was directed this way and that and eventually upon turning a corner nearly tripped over a bow-legged, barrel chested little man with massive arms.

The dwarf's coarse features contorted when he saw John. Theodoulos must have been warned by someone who had made a swifter way through the maze of corridors ahead of John.

Theodoulos put his shoulder down and plowed it into John's stomach, then barged past and raced down the corridor, scattering eunuchs as he went.

"Stop him!" John ordered. The eunuchs, useless creatures, merely gaped and cried out.

Cursing, John set off in pursuit.

The clamor brought more servants into the hallway. Theodoulos dodged and ducked between them. John shoved bodies aside and increased speed.

He closed ground, flung a hand out, and almost grasped the back of his prey's tunic.

Theodoulos veered through a doorway.

John followed and burst into a kitchen.

Theodoulos scrambled onto a table and kicked a covered wicker basket toward the long brazier. The lid flew off as the basket and the chickens it contained tumbled onto the hot coals.

There was an explosion of feathers and flaming fowls, accompanied by a cacophony of screams from the cooks and the outraged cackling of prematurely roasting chickens. John knocked one of the burning chickens out of the air. Another flapped against his legs and scrabbled at his robes, shedding sparks.

John loped across the long room but it was too late.

Theodoulos had already exited via a door leading into the kitchen gardens.

John raced across herb beds to a covered walkway and down to its end.

Theodoulos was nowhere in sight.

No doubt he was familiar with every part of the grounds of the Great Palace, a vast, bewildering confusion made up of paths, plantings, buildings, courtyards, pavilions, colonnades, pools, and fountains laid out on terraces descending to the sea. A beggar had once got into the grounds and managed to elude guards for two months while living off scraps of food and an occasional loaf stolen from an unattended kitchen.

If John did not locate Theodoulos immediately he would never find him.

Glancing around, John saw an opening in a high wall of bushes. It was the way Theodoulos must have taken.

The gap led to a sculpture garden, a frozen crowd of deities, in which stood every god and goddess imagined by the classical mind.

There was no time to catalog the collection.

Movement drew his gaze to the back of the garden.

Theodoulos was creeping away between Mercury and Jupiter.

John went after him, narrowing the distance between them as the two emerged from the garden and began pounding along a wide mosaic walkway depicting mythical wildlife.

Theodoulos suddenly left the path and plunged into a stand of thickly interlaced bushes pruned into domes.

John lunged after him but whatever opening beneath the bushes Theodoulos had found was too small to accommodate John. Branches ripped at his face as fought his way forward.

His foot came down on air.

John grabbed at the surrounding branches as he started to slide over the edge of the parapet. He felt his hands sliding down, ripping off twigs and skinning his flesh.

His forward motion stopped and he pulled himself back from the edge.

Some distance below leaves fluttered toward the flag stoned courtyard on the next terrace.

Theodoulos scrambled along the low parapet over which John had almost fallen and leapt onto the steep stairway at its end.

Cursing, John followed.

His prey had increased the distance between them.

The pain in his head had become almost unbearable. Every footfall as he ran down the stairs communicated itself directly to his skull.

By the time he reached the lowest of the terraces Theodoulos had already crossed most of the equestrian field laid out there and had almost reached a line of yews through which the sea glittered.

He intended to throw himself into the sea.

The realization hit John with a sickening, hopeless certainty.

He tried to call out, to promise protection.

As if anyone could be protected against the wrath of Theodora.

The dwarf vanished between the trees.

Blackness flickered at the edge of John's vision by the time he had followed Theodoulos to the path between the yews and the parapet wall.

He stopped.

Impossibly, Theodoulos stood in front of him. His coarse features, wide lips, and squashed nose were scarlet with rage as he strained futilely to escape from the grasp of the two excubitors who held him.

Felix put a hand like a bear's paw on John's shoulder. "Are you all right, my friend? It's fortunate I happened to be passing by just now."

Chapter Thirty-Eight

The single, narrow window in Felix's office offered a view of a courtyard with a fountain which had been dry for years.

John, Felix, and Theodoulos sat at the table which served as a desk. The plaster walls were bare except for a silver cross, the required decoration of every administrative office.

John reflected that no doubt some prosperous metal worker in the Copper Market was even then hammering out another crateful of pious artifacts.

A visitor might wonder why the religious symbol in the excubitor captain's office had been allowed to tarnish, but such a person would not know that, like John and Anatolius, Felix was a secret follower of Mithra.

Felix had stationed two guards outside his office door. Theodoulos appeared resigned to his fate. He perched silently on his stool, giving his captors angry looks.

"So our mistress has removed your tongue," Felix said. "I hope she was kind enough to have it cut off rather than ripped out."

John thought he looked more nervous than Theodoulos.

"You can answer my questions by nodding yes or else shaking your head no," John said.

The dwarf made a guttural, growling noise.

Felix frowned. "You have no choice but to cooperate with us. I can use the same torturers as the empress. You are already missing your tongue, but they are talented men and can find plenty of other body parts to remove."

Theodoulos' hands unclenched. He opened his left hand, turned it palm upward, extended the stubby forefinger of his right hand, and began running it across the palm. Then he growled again.

"He wants a kalamos." John said.

Felix grunted. "Likely to stab you with. I thought he was supposed to be an illiterate brute?"

Theodoulos shook his head.

"Well, there's two of us and only half of him." Felix got out of his chair, opened a chest beside the table, rummaged through its contents, and pulled out a roll of parchment. He glanced at the writing covering one side and slapped it down on the table. "Request for extra supplies from six years ago. The other side's blank."

He brought an ink pot and a kalamos from a shelf, hesitated, and then handed the sharpened reed to Theodoulos.

The dwarf dipped it into the ink, carefully marked the parchment, and turned it around so John could see what he'd written.

"'Thank you, excellencies,'" John read out. "I notice you write in Latin."

The kalamos scratched across the parchment again. 'I was taught by a bishop. A friend of the empress.'

"One of those monophysites she's got lodged in the Hormisdas, I'll wager," Felix grumbled. "You learned to read and write after your tongue was removed?"

Theodoulos nodded.

"Does the empress know about this unexpected talent?"

A shake of the head indicated she did not. He wrote again. 'Every man needs to be able to tell his story if necessary.'

Felix grinned. "You're right there. So you're not the beast you've been made out to be."

Theodoulos' thick lips curved into a broad, grotesque smile as he scratched out his reply. 'I would gladly kill you both were I able. I am a literate beast but a beast nonetheless.'

John handed the parchment back. "And an honest beast, I see. How was it you came into Theodora's employment?"

It took the dwarf some time to frame his answer. 'My father was a baker,' he wrote, 'and a good Christian. When I was born he thanked the Lord for blessing him with a son. When I did not grow like other children he prayed to the Lord to make me whole. When his prayers were not answered he cursed me as the spawn of demons and sought to cast me into the street. But I was stronger than him, and that is how I came to the attention of the empress. She can always find a use for a boy who strangled his own father and hung him from his own bakery sign. The fact that I was a monster amused her.'

"You have killed for Theodora?" John asked.

'More times than I can recall.'

"He enjoys it." Felix's voice was thick with disgust. "Soldiers kill but few enjoy it."

The pen moved furiously, leaving blots of ink. 'Do you know what it is like to be mocked as an abomination, to be loathed by your own father? The bishop taught me that mankind was evil. And so it is. I am happy to punish mankind for its sins.'

"Indeed," Felix observed. "And you are punishing mankind one victim at a time."

"Why did you flee when you discovered I wanted to speak to you?" John asked.

'I guessed what you wanted to know,' Theodoulos wrote. 'Too many people have been asking questions about the same matter.'

"What people?"

'Ask the excubitor captain.'

Felix glared at their captive. "I made inquiries after you mentioned a certain matter to me, John. I instructed my men to be discreet. It would appear they were not."

"And you really intended to throw yourself into the sea, Theodoulos?" John asked.

'Rocks and waves are kinder than the torturer. I am already a dead man. If I can, I intend to dispatch that eunuch chamberlain before I go into the next world.'

"A journey you will not be taking any time soon unless Theodora realizes you can tell your story. What is your story? You must remember the empress' son?" John said.

Theodoulos dipped the reed in the ink pot and stared down at the parchment for some time before he began to write again, slowly and pausing now and then to think. When he was finished he pushed what he had written across the table to his interrogators.

'I recall the boy named John only because I did not kill him. He was alone with the empress when I was summoned to the most private of her reception rooms, a room hung with heavy tapestries which allow no sound to escape. The tapestries depict scenes from the Bible and these are often among the last things visitors to that secret chamber will ever see....

'On this occasion the empress did not seek entertainment. She instructed me to take the child away and show him the usual courtesies. By this she meant I was not to inflict more pain than was necessary. He looked at me most haughtily, and then asked the empress if a mother could not spare her son a more presentable servant?...

'I was not surprised by his words. I could tell you where to find the bones of others who thought to present themselves as heirs to the throne. I was, however, offended by the insult and resolved to show the boy less courtesy than he could have otherwise expected....

'I took him by the arm and led him out of the palace through a corridor known to few. We emerged in the gardens. There is a secluded spot near the sea, surrounded by wind bent olive trees. It has served my purposes well....

'Darkness had fallen. I took the path that runs behind the banquet hall, along the parapet, because it is little used....

'I was thinking how best to accomplish my task, whether to break his neck or smother him. Or perhaps a little blade work beforehand would be an enjoyable interval. The boy chattered on like a mindless bird or a prelate. He gave the impression that he thought I was taking him to be measured for an imperial crown. He was shrewder than I realized.

'Suddenly he twisted out of my grasp and flung himself over the parapet. I heard his scream as he fell.

'I cursed myself for inattention. I rarely get the chance to dispose of children. I hurried to the nearest stairway. There was no question of anyone surviving a fall to the next terrace but I feared someone might come upon the body.

'There is little light in that part of the gardens but my eyes had grown accustomed to the dark. I made my way along the bottom of the wall. There was no body to be seen.

'I became aware of someone looking at me. I peered through the darkness, and saw a pair of horns and a bestial face. For a heartbeat I thought Satan himself had arrived, no doubt to visit Theodora. Then I saw it was a statue of Pan, presiding over an ornamental pool.

'Or perhaps it was Satan in the guise of the pagan god for this pool was newly built and its deep water had saved the boy who claimed to be Theodora's son.

'As you can imagine I began to scour the surrounding gardens. I was not unknown at the palace, even then, and so was able to enlist the aid of several of the night guards.

'It was nearly dawn when we spotted him. He had managed to find his way to the Chalke and was about to escape into the city. One of the fools assisting me raised the alarm. The soldiers who stand watch at the great gate are on the alert for miscreants seeking access to the palace grounds. The boy was past them before they knew what was happening.

'I sent the guards after the boy and was told later they pursued him into the Copper Market where he vanished into thin air. They swore to me that he was running ahead of them and then suddenly he was gone. He was a demon, they said, as if that excused their failure.

'I returned to the empress and reported that the boy had escaped. I was relieved when she had my tongue removed. I had expected to be killed, but I am valuable to her.'

John finished reading. "If you thought you would be killed why did you report to Theodora at all?"

'Where does a person like me hide from the empress?' Theodoulos wrote. 'Besides, as I described the circumstances, the fault lay mostly with the guards. Naturally they were all executed. I particularly enjoyed that little task.'

John studied the face across the table from him. It displayed no remorse or any other emotion. How long must it have taken him to learn to write? And for what purpose? To tell the story he had just told? "Are you certain you did not loosen your grip on the boy's arm on purpose, Theodoulos? Did you intend to show the boy some pity?"

Theodoulos did not nod, neither did he shake his head in the negative.

John turned to Felix. "I'm surprised you don't remember guards being executed by order of the empress."

Felix grunted. "If they'd been my excubitors, I would remember. The Master of the Offices is in charge of guarding the gardens. A fine job he does of it too!"

John nodded. "Now, Theodoulos, has Theodora ever mentioned this boy since then? Has she had him searched for over the years?"

Theodoulus shook his head to indicate she had not.

"What makes you think that?"

The kalamos moved again. 'If the empress had searched she would have found him and if she had found him she would have ordered me to finish my work.'

"I don't imagine she expected him to show his face again, considering what he knew would be in store for him," Felix said. "And conducting a serious inquiry would only have lent credance to his dubious claim."

John addressed Theodoulos again. "Do you know anything about a woman murdered and left in a cistern a little more than a week ago?"

"Or a former silentiary named Menander?" Felix added.

Theodoulos raised the reed pen, snapped it in half, and dropped the pieces onto the table.

Felix leapt to his feet. "I can order done what Theodora didn't unless you tell us all you know!"

"I don't think he knows anything else," John said. "Let him go. He won't mention this interview to Theodora. To do so he would have to reveal he can still communicate her secrets."

◇◇◇

When Theodoulos had been escorted out Felix paced over to the window and stared out. His expression was as bleak as the wind-swept courtyard outside. "He could've choked the life out of the girl and Menander easily, John. Did you see the size of his arms? It's not just that his job is killing people for Theodora. He's safe so long as she protects him, and he's made it plain he enjoys the filthy work. We should let the torturers persuade him to tell us more."

"We know what's most important already. Theodora's son—if he is her son—is almost certainly still alive."

"From what you told me, you went all over the Copper Market searching for information about the dead girl. Now you propose to go back and search for the boy?"

"It would seem the logical course. There are more disgraced courtiers there than anywhere else in the city except the cemeteries. They are the only ones who might know more."

"Might be harboring him, you mean? I can assign some of my excubitors to scour the area."

"Have you been following me, Felix?"

The excubitor captain stared at John in amazement. "Following you? Why would you think that?"

"Was it merely a coincidence you happened to run into Theodoulos as he was about to jump into the sea?"

Felix growled unintelligibly and pulled at his beard. "You did ask me to help you investigate this matter of the missing son."

"And you thought to do so by having me followed? Or were you interested in what I might be looking into? Or perhaps for other reasons?"

"Mithra! How can you say that, John? I knew you when I was just a pup in the excubitors and you were—"

"A slave. I am no longer a slave, and you are no longer a young excubitor, Felix. I know how much you admired Justinian's uncle Justin. After all Justin was captain of the excubitors before he was emperor."

"It's not an uncommon path to power. Everyone knows that. Everyone also knows that I am loyal to Justinian. As you are."

"Yes, it's a most uncommon occurrence, for an emperor to boast both an excubitor captain and a Lord Chamberlain, neither of whom are seeking to put a blade into his back. Or haven't been until now. Are you sure you haven't become bored, Felix? As a military man you can't be satisfied with guarding doors and making out requests for supplies." John tapped the parchment on the table in front of him.

"You talk to me as if I'm a stranger." Felix regarded John with an expression of puzzlement.

John leaned back in his seat. "Friends can become strangers. You brought me home after I was attacked in the street. That's what you told Cornelia. I don't remember what happened."

Felix flushed with rage. "You think I had something to do with that attack? The blow on your head's affected your reasoning powers, my friend."

"I merely wondered if you had been following me at that time also. Should I now suspect you of having a hand in the attack as well?"

Felix started to speak, stopped, and remained silent for a while. It took a visible effort. "You need to go home and get some rest," he finally said. "Your humors are upset. You are making up tales even the cleverest spinners of words would envy."

"Consider the situation, Felix! We have the illegitimate son of an empress—a former actress—who should never have been permitted to marry Justinian in the first place. The city harbors a virtual army of malcontents—former high officials and courtiers who have lost their positions, senators who have had their lands confiscated. In many cases those who fell into disfavor were executed but the emperor is not in the habit of executing entire families. Those who remain behind, condemned to scratch out a living on the streets, are naturally bitter. It's a golden opportunity for an ambitious man."

"Then you'd better explain it to me."

John was aware of an increase in the throbbing in his head. A wave of dizziness hit him. Two Felixes were standing by the window, tugging at a pair of beards.

John squeezed his eyes shut and when he opened them again only one Felix remained. "Rumors have killed more than one innocent man, as we both know. I am telling you to be extremely careful in what you say in public or indeed private," he said. "I would not care to see a close friend condemned to death."

Chapter Thirty-Nine

"**D**o you know how many girls are in my charge?" said the abbess. "And considering their earlier lives, how many do you suppose might have a tattoo of one sort or another?"

Anatolius had taken a boat across the Marmara only to run aground on the rock of the abbess.

The head of Theodora's convent for reformed prostitutes rose ponderously from the cushioned chair behind her desk. She was dressed in shapeless black robes. The veil covering her head fastened beneath her chin, and revealed a weathered granite face.

"Now, sir, I have duties awaiting me," she went on. "I serve one far more exalted than yourself, whatever your position at the palace."

Although John had discovered the identity of the dead woman and was now directing his investigations toward the whereabouts of Theodora's supposed son, Anatolius could not let go of the idea that the tattoo was somehow important. Agnes' history was, after all, mostly gaps. It was entirely possible that a clue to her murder might be found in her past.

It seemed to Anatolius that he had visited every brothel in the vicinity of the Copper Market. He knew, however, that some had been shut down by Theodora, their residents sent to the convent.

What if the tattoo had not been a scarab overlain by an ankh? What if Agnes had reformed and sought to renounce her past by having a cross drawn over the pagan symbol? She might very well have spent time in Theodora's convent. Someone there might know her.

It was worth the short journey to investigate. Or so he had thought until he came up against the abbess.

"This is a matter of considerable importance," Anatolius persisted.

"What goes on in the sinful world outside is of no consequence inside these walls. It is my job to ensure that my girls do not concern themselves with such things. I cannot have them reminded of their former ways."

Rising from cliffs overlooking the water, the convent had the appearance of a fortress protecting those within from all invaders, particularly those of the male gender who were not permitted to venture far into the building. Anatolius had penetrated no further than the administrative office, escorted there by an elderly gatekeeper.

He wondered about the abbess' own background. Had she been in charge of a brothel or plied her trade in the alleys of the city? "Do you by any chance know Madam Isis," he asked. "Or rather did you know her?"

"You're referring to a brothel keeper?"

"Well, she's well known in the city and I thought perhaps...."

The nostrils in the stony face flared. "You are acquainted with her, it would seem. I suggest you avail yourself of our visitors' chapel on your way out, sir."

The abbess summoned the gatekeeper and instructed him to show Anatolius to the chapel for a cleansing prayer and then escort him from the building.

Anatolius went out into the hall, feeling sheepish. He could hardly wrestle the abbess to the floor and make a run for the living quarters.

The gatekeeper could not provide any information either—or would not—as he led Anatolius down a side corridor and indicated the chapel door.

"I'll wait for you here," he wheezed, sitting on a bench under a window opposite the door.

Anatolius hesitated. Perhaps if he spent a little time in the chapel the abbess would be more inclined to cooperate with further inquiries?

It seemed unlikely, but it was worth consideration. Perhaps the elderly gatekeeper would go to sleep—or expire—allowing him to reenter the premises.

He entered a small domed room with a raised platform at one end. A cool sea breeze carried the cries of gulls through slitted windows. Looking up he saw that the dome was adorned by frescoes of two haloed women who might have been twins.

"Theodora's the one with the chalice. Mary's got the baby, see?" The speaker rose from scrubbing the flagstones. She was dressed in black clothing like the abbess but the pale oval face was decades younger.

"I thought none of you were allowed to talk to men?" Anatolius whispered, conscious of the gatekeeper sitting outside.

The penitent smiled. "Don't worry about Simon, he's half deaf. You're from the palace, aren't you?"

Anatolius admitted it was so.

"I knew it! I learned to tell what part of society men came from in my former employment!"

"According to the abbess, you should've forgotten all that," Anatolius replied.

"I wish I could. I wish I'd never been hauled away from the city. If they aren't preaching at us, they're making us pray. I pray they'll release me, but you might as well talk to the wall." She went over to one of the narrow windows. "Some girls have thrown themselves into the sea from sheer boredom. The authorities keep that from public knowledge."

"You're not considering killing yourself?"

"No, not usually, but when I see one such as you, it reminds me of the real world. They named this place Repentance. What I repent is having to live here." She leaned forward and light reflected off the waves below flickered across her face.

Anatolius tried to imagine the youthful features highlighted by cosmetics. Isis would doubtless consider her an ornament. "Don't be foolish," he said. "One day perhaps you will return to the world."

The girl stepped back. "But when my broken body is embraced by rocks and waves, my immortal soul will soar up to heaven, or so I'm told. My name's Agnella, by the way."

"And mine's Anatolius. Why such gloomy thoughts, Agnella? Didn't you come here of your own accord? To be…um… reformed. It must be less of a hard life than working, better than a hand to mouth existence?"

"I'd rather live hand to mouth in the city, sir, sinful as that might sound. What is the point of locking yourself up? As long as you're in your flesh you're in the real world, no matter how many locked doors surround you."

The girl gave a harsh laugh. "But how could I refuse Theodora's imperial invitation to live here?" she went on. "One backed up by a company of excubitors, who pulled me right out of the arms of a rustic boy on his first visit to the capital. I hadn't even showed him the glories of Constantinople. The empress sent enough armed men to put down a riot. When we all realized what was going to happen to us, they did have to put down a riot. The abbess had arranged for them to swoop down on us while we were, well, distracted, see? At her age she was ready to wear black. Miserable old crow. At least she got to enjoy her life."

Anatolius asked how long Agnella had been pursuing her profession.

"Nearly three whole weeks, sir," she replied.

"A few months longer and you might have been happier to retire here."

Agnella pursed her unpainted but full lips into a pout. "I'm so bored I can't bear it. Now if you're bored too, sir, there's a room where we store buckets and such. Perfectly private. The abbess would as soon pick up a snake as scrub a floor."

"I must decline, Agnella," Anatolius replied, not certain if she was jesting or not.

"But, sir, if we got caught, they'd throw me out of this wretched place."

"And if we weren't?"

"If I was to, er, well, be discovered as being with child, they'd banish me just the same."

"No, I…I really can't, Agnella…."

"You can't?"

Anatolius shook his head. "No."

"You don't mean you're one of them—"

"Yes. I'm a eunuch."

He wasn't sure why the excuse had suddenly popped into his head and he immediately regretted his words. They had the intended effect though. Perhaps even too strong an effect. He saw her jaw clench and her eyes narrow. He could almost sense her shrink away from him. Nothing pained him more than the disapproval of a pretty woman. He realized he didn't much like being a eunuch.

"I didn't mean to offend you, sir." Agnella's voice shook.

"Don't worry, I won't report you to the abbess, if that's what you're afraid of. We're not all treacherous and deceitful beings, you know."

"I was so hoping…."

"Never mind, doubtless another man will arrive to carry you off in good time."

"Yes, a man to take me away from here, that's what I'm praying for."

Anatolius had a sudden thought. "Doesn't anyone ever leave this place except in disgrace or out a window? I've been told about a woman who arrived here of her own accord and renounced her profession, but then left. Agnes was her name."

"It's not one I've heard," the girl replied. "If she was here, she managed to get away. Who was she?"

"She was the daughter of a tax collector. Her father ran afoul of the emperor. He lost his head and the family was thrown into the street, which was where Agnes found work. She had herself tattooed with a pagan symbol. When she decided to change her ways she declared her intent by having a cross overlaid upon it. She must have been bored here also, to wish to leave such sanctuary." This history was mostly conjecture and invention, but Anatolius did not reveal that.

Agnella knelt down again and made a few desultory swipes at the stones, as if deciding to resume her cleaning. "I've never heard tell of a woman like that. It must be even harder to come here once you've lived at the palace. There was a girl who arrived a while ago fleeing someone from the palace. Imagine that! I don't know what her name was. I heard about it, never talked to her myself."

"What was said about this woman?"

"The story I heard was while she was working, a regular customer of hers—a high official—took more than the usual sort of liking to her. He insisted he wanted to marry her. Some day, not right away, and yet talk that any girl would hope to hear, I should think."

"High officials are not usually free to marry prostitutes, whatever they might say."

Agnella's expression was one of disapproval. "That's what she thought. I say you take your chance. What better opportunity are the likes of us going to get? But she fled here, hoping to be forgotten. She didn't like it any better than I do. Finally she left."

"She was allowed to leave?"

"Only because this official wouldn't let her alone. He kept appearing here and pressing the abbess to release her. I suppose the abbess was tired of being annoyed."

"Or she feared the palace might get involved. "

"The abbess isn't likely to give any of us girls any reasons. All I know is she let her leave."

"When was this?"

"Oh. I have no idea. It was just a rumor. Recently, I believe."

"I don't suppose you have any inkling of where she intended to go?"

"Why yes, sir, I do. It caused much tongue wagging. She knew an actress in the city and was going to stay with her. And the abbess let her go, despite all the talk about our souls."

Agnella directed a mournful stare at Anatolius. "Such a pity when I am so terribly bored and you have such a nice face. But then, I suppose, in your condition, you are never bored in that way."

Chapter Forty

The boy had fled into the Copper Market and vanished into thin air.

It was as if he was a demon, according to the guards who had pursued him. Or so said Theodoulos, who had not himself witnessed the pursuit or disappearance.

John had not been able to locate and question the guards concerned. Perhaps they had been executed, just as the dwarf had said. John did not trust Theodoulos.

The Copper Market was not an enormous quarter, but its streets and alleyways seemed without end. John had lost track of how many thoroughfares he had hiked up and down, wide streets and narrow, straight and twisted, a few boasting colonnades, most without.

He had spoken to shopkeepers, servants on their way to market, beggars, laborers going to and from their jobs, and prostitutes, not to mention several members of the Blue faction swaggering around in search of a reason to start a fight.

No one recalled seeing a boy pursued through the streets by guards from the palace. Was it surprising? It had been at least ten years ago. In that time riots, fires, and the recent plague would have buried such a trivial incident deep beneath more dramatic and horrific memories.

Still, it was not every day a boy vanished into thin air.

"What did you say? Palace guards?" The wizened man in the candle shop turned his head toward John, as if straining to hear the question. "Yes, I remember that, sir. I looked out and saw soldiers. There was a big man with a beard. Someone was lying in the street. Couldn't make him out too well. He wore dark robes. He was probably some dandy from the court who came looking for trouble and got more than he bargained for."

John thanked the shopkeeper and returned to the street. What the man had recalled was the aftermath of the attack on John.

Somewhere in the labyrinth of shops, tenements, and foundries there was someone who would have reason to recall a minor event from years ago. Perhaps the boy had knocked over a servant on his way home from the market and scattered a perfectly good basketful of vegetables onto the street and the guards chasing the lad had trampled most of them before he could retrieve them from the cobbles.

Unless the servant could somehow replace the goods, he would remember such an incident.

Especially if he was employed at the palace, where discipline could be harsh.

That was grasping at phantoms, John realized. The chances of him finding such a witness were almost non existent.

He had come to the entrance to the courtyard where the theatrical troupe was located. He had already passed the spot once. Troilus was too young to have maintained his establishment at the time of the chase. What was now used as a theater would have been a brothel. Should he interview the dye maker Jabesh? Perhaps not. Those John was seeking in the crowded, cramped city—plotters against the emperor and Agnes' murderer, or murderers, one and the same or not—could not be far away.

Unless they had fled Constantinople.

Word might have already reached them, since he had spent all morning and half the afternoon trudging around the area repeating the same questions. By tomorrow morning rumors would begin to spread and people would be convinced a boy had been seen fleeing soldiers from the palace. So and so had heard it from a most reliable source.

The tale of the fleeing boy might well replace the inevitable gossip about a tall stranger who had been seen again and again in the Copper Market.

John walked on until he found himself at the square where he had met Agnes, the center of the entire affair.

Rising up over the rooftops at one end of the square was the granite column of the stylite.

Who had lived up there for how long? The stylite would have been able to see not only the square, but the surrounding streets and alleys as well.

He had this same thought days ago. Then he had wanted to question the holy man—Lazarus, his acolyte had called him—to establish whether he had noticed anything on the morning Agnes had been killed.

The acolyte had said Lazarus would not speak of worldly things and at the time John had not considered it worthwhile to press the matter.

Now he would not be deterred.

Let Lazarus speak for himself—or not.

John craned his neck to look upward.

He could make out the stylite's motionless, bowed head through the window of his ramshackle shelter. How did he pass the time? Did he meditate on the evils of the world? Pray silently?

A life so constrained, such rigid self control, was not unknown. John had seen a stylite glistening in the morning sun on a bitter day, the man's emaciated body covered with a sheen of ice from the driving rain of the previous night.

A lifetime of bodily suffering was a transitory inconvenience compared to the eternal glory such men anticipated.

The door in the back of the column swung open when John pushed. Lazarus and his acolyte put more faith in their god than in locks. He ducked under the low lintel and started up a stairway resembling a stone ladder. Light filtered in from above. There were two landings, both almost blocked by wicker baskets. John did not pause to examine their contents. When he reached the second landing he could see the open trapdoor leading out to the platform atop the column.

Cautiously, he poked his head into the open air and looked around.

There was something wrong.

What?

John sniffed.

That was it.

There was no smell.

He had been on top of the stylite column more than once in the past. He knew that to glorify their god such solitaries dwelt for years amidst the decaying refuse from their scant meals, dead vermin, and their own filth. When the breezes were in a particular direction, standing downwind from such a pillar was enough to take away the appetite.

Yet here there was no odor at all. The air smelled fresher than it did in the square below.

John pulled himself up onto the platform. It was wider than most. There was room for a man to lie down, but not much more.

Constantinople stretched out around him. He could see the dome of the Great Church, the Hippodrome, and the palace grounds. Sunlight struck sparks off the water on three sides.

A man perched up here would have been able to see a great deal.

On the other hand, the acolyte had insisted Lazarus would never talk about what went on below him.

John turned carefully to face the shelter. It was hardly more than a few weathered planks. The door which made up the front was shut.

"Lazarus," John called out. "I am sorry to intrude on you. The matter is urgent."

He was not surprised that there was no reply.

"I am seeking to bring a murderer to justice," John went on. "I am hoping you will be able to help me."

John grasped the edge of the ill-fitting door and gave it a tug.

It opened a crack and he peered into the enclosed space.

Lazarus lay rigidly, at an awkward angle, head against the back wall and feet against the door.

John opened the door wider.

The holy man slid out onto the platform feet first.

His head hit the platform with a clank and came off.

His arms remained bent at the elbows, fingertips pressed together just under his chin in an attitude of prayer. His face, sitting beside his shoulder, appeared frozen in an expression of eternal beatitude.

Sunlight glinted off the smooth, bronze features.

Lazarus the stylite was an automaton.

Chapter Forty-One

A sound caused John to look up from the automaton lying at his feet.

He was not alone atop the stylite column.

A man emerged from the trapdoor leading to the stairs.

John recognized the acolyte who had advised him that Lazarus would not speak of anything but heaven.

"You are the man who claimed to be from the emperor," the acolyte said in the same raspy tone John recalled from their brief conversation in the square.

"You deceived me," John stated, indicating the metal figure. "Explain."

"I told you Lazarus would tell you nothing. That was the truth. Yet you still sought to violate a holy man's solitude."

"You indicated Lazarus was not concerned with what the emperor might order done to him," John replied. "I can see you were perfectly truthful about that as well. But can you say the same of yourself?"

The acolyte blanched. "I am not Lazarus. Flesh is weak."

John glanced down at the metal figure. The joints which would enable arms, legs, and mouth to move were cunningly wrought.

He had recently seen a similar mechanism among Troilus' antiquities and curiosities.

Like Troilus' automaton, this one wore armor. It was odd attire for a holy man, but it would not be noticeable from the square.

"Lazarus here was not one given to human weaknesses," John remarked. "What is your name?"

"I gave up my name when I came to serve Lazarus."

The garment the acolyte wore was too large for him. The skin of his hands appeared weathered when they emerged from his overly long sleeves.

"Your name?" John ordered.

"In my former life it was Stephen," the other admitted.

A swirling breeze carried the smell of fresh bread from a bakery hidden in the welter of buildings laid out below them. The shadow of the column sliced across the square. John could see the tops of pedestrians' heads as they hurried by without looking up.

Few paid attention to stylites apart from their followers and the occasional pilgrim. Those men perched atop pillars were always there, part of the city landscape, like the statuary lining the streets.

John half expected the other to rush at him suddenly. There was little space between them on the small platform. The iron railing was low and insecure and the ground was a long way down.

It would be an easy matter to arrange an accident.

"Where was this automaton obtained?" John asked.

"I can't say," came the reply. "I found it up here."

John gave him a stony stare.

"No, it's the truth," the acolyte protested. "It's been many years since then. I'm not sure how many. My days are all the same. One morning when I came up here, Lazarus was gone. This metal creature had taken his place. Perhaps it was a miracle?"

"You don't really think so." It was not a question.

Stephen bent his head. "No."

"Now explain to me how you came to be spending your time shifting an automaton around on top of a pillar. I observed

Lazarus outside his shelter, or so I thought. I assume that was your intent?"

"Yes. I moved him in and out of the shelter and stood him in different places. People don't look very hard at stylites."

"But someone might eventually notice if the pillar remained unoccupied?"

"Yes," the other acknowledged. "And also the pilgrims would have been disappointed."

"Not to mention you would have been without employment," John pointed out.

"I can't deny it. Yet it seemed to me the Lord must have left the automaton here for a reason. In that way, it was a miracle. If God had simply wanted to call Lazarus to his reward, I would have found the top of the column empty. As his acolyte I felt it was my duty to continue his good works."

The fact that a holy man might appear to remain motionless for much of the day would not be at all unusual, John realized. The mortification of the body that many of them practiced included standing in one position for hours. He suspected they endured their harsh existence by remaining in a self-induced stupor much of the time. "How did you come to hold your position, Stephen?"

"Through the grace of God. When I was a boy I found myself living in the streets. I don't know why. I don't even remember my parents. One day I stole a leg of lamb. As I raced off, delighted by my cleverness, a huge black dog came loping after me."

The acolyte looked down into the square. "It was Satan in the shape of a dog. I should have given the beast what it wanted, but the lamb tempted me. I was hungry, I'd been eating what I could find in the gutters, dead fish that had washed ashore, that sort of thing. So I ran, foolish child that I was. You can't run from Satan. That monstrous dog savaged me. I should have died, but that was not the Lord's plan. The man who served Lazarus at the time found me bleeding in an alley. He'd grown feeble with age and needed a helper. After I healed I assisted him."

"And you eventually took his place?"

Stephen nodded. "He died a year or so after he rescued me. I had learned my duties by then. They're simple enough. I arrange the offering baskets in front of the column in the morning and keep beggars away from them. Lazarus shared edibles with me and I bought more with the coins left by pious pilgrims."

"And now you do not need to share the offerings," John observed.

"There are far fewer than there used to be. Scarcely enough for me to keep body and soul together. Fewer pilgrims visit these days and they are usually older. Whatever fame Lazarus had in his native land, a fame which at one time drew people to this city, has faded away. Those who witnessed his works and were inspired by his teachings, before he journeyed here and mounted this column so as to give his earthly husk over to God, are gone. Even their children are gray and bent, as are most of those who heard him preach from where we stand."

John suggested that Lazarus had simply decided to leave.

"No," said the acolyte. "His legs were all but paralyzed from living in such a confined space, and besides, they were so deformed from disease and hardship he would have had to be carried down the stairs. He couldn't have walked away unaided."

John looked down once more at the soldier with the gleaming metal face, hands frozen in eternal prayer.

Stephen stepped over to the railing, put a hand on it, and gazed out across the city. "Lazarus was not like other men. Perhaps…." His voice was unsteady. It had been a shock discovering John up here, finding his secret had been uncovered after so many years. What would he do now if John chose to make his deception known?

John had climbed to the top of column in search of a missing boy and learned instead of a stylite who had vanished just as mysteriously. "How long ago did Lazarus disappear?"

"As I said, all my days are the same. The seasons blend into one another. It might have been ten years ago."

"Did you have any forewarning? Did anything unusual happen before the automaton appeared up here?"

"Only that Lazarus stayed in his shelter for a long time. That's why I finally decided to investigate. I thought he might be dying. Or dead."

"You didn't communicate with him regularly?"

The other shook his head. "Lazarus said little. The man I replaced described the sermons Lazarus had once given. He knew them word for word, hearing them every day. He could recite them like a pagan can recite Homer. Lazarus painted the most glorious vision of heaven, but as the years went by he fell silent. Sometimes he talked to the Lord, but his words made no sense to me."

John thought anyone's humors would become unbalanced after perching atop a column for years. He could understand why the acolyte had not wanted to simply take the holy man's place. "How long did he remain in this shelter before you decided to investigate?"

"A week or two. Lazarus sometimes retreated into his shelter to meditate for long periods. In the evenings, as usual, I sent baskets of food up by means of the rope and pulley you see attached to the railing and in the mornings the baskets were returned empty. So far as I knew he was avoiding the sun while he pondered. They say there are those who worship the sun rather than the Lord. He used to denounce them most vehemently. But then several days passed and the basket I had sent up remained up here, untouched."

The sun whose worship the stylite had abhorred, and John had embraced, had begun its daily descent. Two moving shadows—low flying gulls—swept across the platform.

"And what did you do when you found the automaton in your master's place?"

"I thought it must be a miracle. Yet the world seemed the same. The city still stretched around me. I could hear gratings being pulled up in front of shops, dogs barking, see the ships on the water moving, just as always. If I had witnessed a miracle wouldn't the world feel different?"

The acolyte sighed before going on. "Then I feared some villains had abducted Lazarus. For all I knew they might have been trying to extort money from the Patriarch or even the emperor."

John thought that if that was the case they would have soon and in a very painful manner learnt their error. He said he would have been surprised to learn that this had been the case.

"But he was a holy man and the Patriarch and Justinian would be concerned about his welfare," Stephen said. "The kidnappers would have left the automaton there so as not to draw attention to the fact that Lazarus was missing, and yet, if they sought to benefit from his kidnapping, they had to announce he was gone. I soon realized such actions were contradictory and dismissed the notion. Then it occurred to me he might simply have been murdered. The Blues and Greens are often involved in mayhem. One of them might have killed Lazarus for the sheer enjoyment of it. Or perhaps they were blasphemers who wished to see if he would return to life as did his namesake."

His own words seemed to upset the acolyte. His rasping voice quavered. "Or it may be a thief suspected Lazarus had been offered valuables which could be stored up here. Whoever killed him left the automaton so that no one would notice for a time."

John nodded. "The longer the time that passed, the smaller likelihood of the culprit being caught."

"That was my thought. Then when some weeks had gone by and nothing happened I decided to continue Lazarus' ministry. There's nothing more I can tell you."

John looked down at the automaton again. It resembled the one he had seen in Troilus' shop. On the other hand, he had purchased much of his stock from Menander. Might both have been in Menander's collection about the time the boy purporting to be Theodora's son had escaped?

If only everyone kept as precise a track of time as Helias the sundial maker.

John moved toward the trapdoor. "If it is necessary for me to question you again, where can I find you?"

"Here at this column. I have no home. I usually sleep in a doorway." The acolyte clasped his hands together in distress. "What is to become of me? What will you do?"

"You have no need to fear, Stephen. There are no laws against moving automatons around," John replied as he swung himself down through the trapdoor.

Chapter Forty-Two

Had the automaton on the pillar come from Menander's collection?

Menander could no longer answer the question.

However, Alba, the pious woman John had interviewed at the hospice, had mentioned she'd first known Menander when they were both newly exiled from the palace.

The flooded alley leading to the wooden tenement behind the Church of the Mother of God had dried out. Tracks of foraging dogs and feral cats criss-crossed the hardened mud. The rent collector sat in the same place at the bottom of the rickety stairs. After John spoke to her and went up she made the usual charcoal mark on the wall.

This afternoon Alba was not at the hospice. She met John at the door of her cell-like room on the top floor of the tenement.

"You tell me Menander's room has been emptied of his possessions, Lord Chamberlain?"

"Whoever was responsible left the door open. They didn't leave behind so much as a cobweb. You didn't notice anything?"

"No. It would have been better for Menander if he had put aside his earthly goods long ago. Now I fear the weight of them has dragged his eternal soul down into the fires of hell. Let us pray that the Lord will show him mercy."

Alba wore the same black attire as at the hospice, the veil fastened under her chin so that only her bone white face showed. She let John into the room and sat on the edge of a low cot. "Please make yourself comfortable, Lord Chamberlain. I can offer you nothing better than a stool. I do not entertain visitors." She spoke with the well bred tones of a woman raised at court. It was the sort of voice that usually invited one into lavish reception halls or beautiful private apartments.

John sat down near the brazier. His knees almost touched the cot. Through the room's single window he could see the brick wall of the church, an arm's breadth away. A window there gave a glimpse of a wall where vestments hung from pegs.

"Alba, you told me that you tried to persuade Menander of the error of his ways. Did you ever see his collection?"

"Only once. He insisted. I have no interest in such vanities but I did not want to be impolite."

"Do you recall any automatons? Men made of metal?"

"Indeed I did. How could I forget such monstrous works of blasphemy? An artist may depict a man in stone or bronze or bits of colored glass. Such things are clearly meant to be nothing more than representations. To seek to mimic the living flesh with metal that moves…that is to pretend to a creation that is God's alone." Her tone remained even but her pale, unlined face tightened as she spoke.

John asked her how many automatons she had seen.

"Two, Lord Chamberlain. They were a pair. They represented the martyred saints Sergius and Bacchus. Whatever beast created such a mockery of those devout soldiers will burn beside Menander."

Then the automaton on the pillar had almost certainly come from Menander's collection by way of Troilus' shop.

John's gaze went to Alba's window and to the diamond paned window of the church beyond. A ray of light falling through the narrow gap between church and tenement gleamed on the silver embroidery on the vestments hanging there.

"I understand you have devoted yourself to religious works, Alba. I have seen you laboring at the hospice. There is a stylite in a square not far from here. His name is Lazarus. Do you know anything about that holy man?"

John saw Alba's sharp intake of breath. "How remarkable that you should ask! But then we are often guided by an invisible hand. It was what I saw in that very square that saved me. I had hoped it might save Menander as well, but it did not, for my words fell on stony ground."

She sighed. "Lord Chamberlain, I sense you do not worship the one true God, or perhaps you simply do not call Him by His rightful name. Yet you are a spiritual man. You will appreciate that wisdom can come to us in dreams and visions such as I have had. Things that seem unreal to those who are not spiritual by nature, who are bound to the earth, have their own reality to we who are willing to acknowledge and commune with them."

John recalled her earlier mention of visions and asked her to explain her comments.

"It was a miracle. A message from God. They are not uncommon, you know, but we usually do not recognize them for what they are. That was true of what I witnessed that morning. Only afterward did I understand."

"When did this event take place?"

"It must have been ten years ago. I regret to say I had not yet reconciled myself to my new life. I still lamented my fallen state, not realizing what a blessing it was. I was on my way to market. The sun had risen and was bathing God's great works in glorious light, yet all I could see was the dining room I'd left behind, the silver plates, the painted vineyards on its walls. All I could think of was how I had been transformed into one of my own servants, treading the morning streets with a basket."

She sighed. "But I felt worse off than my servants. I had sent them out in search of the finest ducks and freshest greens, newly caught fish, the best fruits, fresh baked bread. But I would be fortunate to be able to purchase a hard bit of cheese or a dried out parsnip or two to choke down in the solitude of this poor room."

Alba smiled and shook her head. "How foolish I was then, Lord Chamberlain. How many there are in this city who would thank the Lord to have such a fine room as this and coins enough for both parsnips and cheese."

"That is true enough," John agreed. "What was this miracle that opened your eyes?"

"I saw a boy drawn straight up to heaven."

"From the square where Lazarus lives?"

Alba nodded. "I had just entered it when I heard a commotion. Shouts, the sound of running footsteps. I drew back against the closed grating of a shop that had yet to open. I was trembling in terror for I was not inured to the sudden storms that sweep the streets outside the palace walls."

"Into the square raced a boy. He staggered as if exhausted. He reached the column upon which Lazarus stands and collapsed. I didn't know what to do. He might have been a criminal or an innocent pursued by ruffians. He looked back the way he'd come. The shouts from that direction grew louder. Then he vanished behind the column."

"There is a door in its base," John said.

"Yes. I saw that, later. But just then a number of palace guards burst into the square, swords drawn. Understand, Lord Chamberlain, that what I have described took no more than an instant. They raced across the square and disappeared from view. I remained where I was, afraid to move. Fearful that they'd spot me and think I could tell them about the boy. After a short time some of the guards reappeared and went off down other streets that ran into the square. A little later, when everything was quiet, I continued on my way. I noticed that there were still guards prowling about and one was posted in the square when I returned from market with my cheese. There hadn't been a bunch of parsnips I could afford."

John shifted uncomfortably on the low stool. His long legs had begun to cramp. "Surely that wasn't a miracle, Alba? The boy obviously hid himself inside the pillar. I admit it may have been a miracle the guards didn't think to investigate that possibility."

"The Lord clouded their eyes and their thoughts," Alba replied.

"On the other hand," John replied, "the guards might have believed the boy had outdistanced them. A stylite's pillar is not something one thinks of as affording shelter. Holy men occupy them and they aren't of any use to anyone else. We tend not to notice things that are of no use to us. But why did you consider the foiling of the boy's pursuit a miracle?"

"Because he vanished, Lord Chamberlain. He was drawn up to heaven, as I said. The next day, Lazarus sat in his shelter as usual, and ever since Lazarus has emerged from time to time just as he always did. But the boy has never been seen again."

"The boy merely waited for the guards to leave, then emerged. There are numerous places to hide in the city, after all."

Alba shook her head. "That would not have been possible. There were guards posted in the square for several days. And after they had gone, others returned more than once to ask questions. I made inquiries of the shopkeepers all around. No one had glimpsed this boy except me, nor did anyone ever see him again."

"You were interested enough to inquire?"

"Because I sensed that what I had seen held a message for me, Lord Chamberlain. Miracles are happening all the time, but only those to whom they are addressed notice them."

The ray of light which had illuminated the vestments visible in the church had shifted so that it slanted in through the narrow window of Alba's room. It cut across the end of the cot on which she sat and over the brazier before tracing a line of orange fire up the wall where there hung a elaborate, jeweled cross fit for a palace.

"Isn't the message clear? A boy is pursued by guards from the palace. He ascends a pillar and afterward there is no boy there but only the holy stylite. Does it not demonstrate how those pursued by wealth and power may yet escape if they forsake the earth and choose instead to rise up to heaven? It was a sign telling me I had not been condemned to a hard life outside the palace walls, but rather had been granted freedom from the wealth and privilege which bars our entry to the Kingdom of Heaven. My soul had escaped. I tried to explain this to Menander. He laughed and said he would have had to see it with his own eyes. Sadly, I do not think his eyes would have been capable of seeing."

John rose stiffly from his stool. "Do you have any idea who this boy was?"

Alba shook her head. "No. I was afraid to inquire too closely of friends from the palace after what had happened to my father."

John did not ask what that had been, or who her father had been or what office he had held. He offered her a few coins for her information. She refused, until he persuaded her that charitable works could be accomplished and accepted them with a blessing on him.

The shaft of light which had illuminated the room began to fade. John could not help asking a final question. He indicated the jeweled cross. "That is the sort of artifact that would have been in Menander's collection. Did he give it to you perhaps?"

"No, Lord Chamberlain," came the reply with a smile. "It has been in my room for as long as I can remember, since when I was a little girl. I cannot bear to part with it."

Chapter Forty-Three

The establishment belonging to Madam Isis, with its lavish wall hangings, bright frescoes, and lewd statuary, might have occupied a different world than Alba's austere quarters. Yet, after Anatolius' servant delivered the message, it took John no longer to walk from his house to Isis' than it would have taken him to walk to Alba's room.

Anatolius greeted him at the door of a room strewn with cushions and dominated by a large figure of Bacchus. "John, I'm sorry to ask you to meet me here, but I returned home very late last night. I wanted to ask Isis some questions without delay. Besides which, I didn't think a written communication was wise, although I'm afraid I've learnt little."

John wondered too if his friend didn't care to face Cornelia's wrath if she found him at the door, apparently intent on dragging John out on more investigations.

They crossed the room to talk to Isis, who was watching the diminutive self-styled magician, Dedi. The rosy-cheeked, plump madam, dressed in multi-hued silks, hardly seemed the same sort of creature as the pale, black-garbed, pious woman John had spoken to the day before.

But even among birds there were crows and there were peacocks, John reminded himself.

Isis clasped her pudgy, beringed fingers over John's hand. "I was beginning to think I'd never see you again, John. I was afraid you'd joined our friend Captain Felix in spurning my house."

"I suspect Felix has been as busy as I have of late, Isis. I'll visit so we can talk when I've straightened out…the situation."

Isis waved her hand and laughed. "Oh, Anatolius has told me all about it. You don't have to worry, you know nothing that goes on in my house is spoken of outside it. If it did, I'd soon be out of business."

She gave Dedi a pointed look. He was setting the contents of a leather bag out on a table. He grinned, exposing wildly crooked teeth. "You may rely on my discretion, Lord Chamberlain. Demons could not pry anything from my lips."

"I wish I could be of more help," Isis continued. "Alas, no one I know claims knowledge of a prostitute with a tattoo such as described. But then I don't reveal much about my girls to my competitors, so I can't expect them to tell me about theirs, can I? However, I'm not surprised it was an Egyptian design. Tattoos are more popular with the girls there. Didn't you find it to be so when you lived in Alexandria?"

"I was a young man then," John replied. "I hardly remember what it was like being myself, let alone what tattoos the girls wore."

Isis clucked her disapproval. "If they had been my employees, you would remember them! But I was young then too, and just a working girl myself. I'm just as happy we didn't meet in the course of business. If we had, our reminiscences would be far different."

"Indeed." John did not add that he had no memory of them meeting in Alexandria, as Isis always maintained they had, her accounts embroidered with colorful details. It was said that the past became clearer when one grew old. Perhaps someday he would remember and realize she had been right all along.

"Won't you stay for Dedi's next performance?"

John expressed his regret he could not do so.

"That's a pity, John," Anatolius said. "I know you've seen his work before, but he has unveiled some new magick. What I witnessed was quite remarkable. There's an urn which supplies either wine or water or a mixture of both, not to mention a talking skull that vanishes! Tricks, of course, but how they're done eludes me."

Dedi removed a skull from his leather bag. "I do not mind revealing a few of my secrets, sirs. In fact, it is prudent to do so in case someone seeks to persecute me as a demon, which has occurred on more than one occasion. The urn, for example, employs a cunning arrangement of tubes and vents, based upon writings by Hero, another Alexandrian. Apparently that city was and remains a popular place to live! As for the skull, it can be made to vanish only because it isn't a skull."

The magician handed the object to John. It might have been made out of parchment, it was so light.

"Be careful," Dedi told him. "It's nothing more than the molded caul of an ox, wax, and gum, all of which burn much more readily than bone. The better to vanish when surrounded by coals and enveloped in thick incense smoke!"

"But how do you make the thing talk?" Anatolius asked.

Dedi looked serious. "Ah, I admit I have tricks. I did not say I have no knowledge beyond mere trickery. How the skull speaks must remain a mystery."

"Nonsense," put in Isis. "It is a question of speaking without moving the lips! But of course that information will never leave this house!"

Dedi moved his lips into a grotesque pout of displeasure.

"But there is some information which must leave this house," Anatolius said. "And I need to convey it to John rather hastily."

John followed Anatolius out into the hallway. Anatolius repeated he had not established any facts, but went on to explain what he had learnt during his visit to the Repentance convent. "I tried to speak to the abbess again, but she refused to see me. No doubt you could have convinced her."

"I've never tried to question an abbess." John recalled his glimpse of the tattoo. Agnes had reached up to push her veil aside, bringing her momentarily bared wrist in front of his face. When she had voiced the name "Zoe" and offered confirmation by revealing the strangely familiar features, other thoughts had been driven from his mind.

It was true John had examined the tattoo more closely after finding the body in the cistern. By then it had been largely obscured with red dye although not completely obliterated as the murderer must have hoped.

"Yes," John continued, agreeing with Anatolius' conjecture, "that might have well been a cross drawn over the scarab. And if this woman you speak of intended to seek shelter with an actress she knew, the circumstances would fit Agnes' life, with what we know of it. Petronia told me Agnes lived with her. She said nothing about Agnes having fled Theodora's convent. I shall talk to Petronia again."

Chapter Forty-Four

"Agnes was never in a convent, Lord Chamberlain! She did not flee to my apartment from such a place! Nor was she a prostitute." Petronia stood, arms folded, in front of the painted Greek temples on the curtain which divided her room.

She was dressed in a gaudy tunic and a mantle glittering with glass beads which would pass for precious gems when viewed by an audience. Her patrician features were hardened into a look of imperial scorn natural to whatever personage she was about to play.

John couldn't help wondering whether it was more convenient for her to get into costume at home or whether she enjoyed the stares she must attract walking the streets in such forged finery.

"You lied to me to protect Troilus," John said. "Are you now trying to protect Agnes?"

Petronia laughed, a little too dramatically. "Agnes is beyond protection now. I am very late for my performance. I really cannot linger."

Anatolius sat in the chair resembling a throne and observed the actress with obvious admiration. "I hope you'll have as large an audience as that holy melon juggler who's performing practically at the door of this building," he offered. "I wouldn't have supposed this part of the city would be quite so...well...theatrical...."

Petronia's eyes narrowed. "You mean Zachariah? He's back here again?"

"That's the man. John was telling me he passed him nearer to the palace not many days since. What was it Peter said, John? Something about the miracle of the melons?"

"There's really no time to discuss street performers," John replied.

"That's what Zachariah is," Petronia snapped, "a performer. He used to juggle with the troupe, when he wasn't drunk. He much preferred drinking to working."

"But the Lord Chamberlain's servant insisted Zachariah had been born crippled," Anatolius said.

Petronia laughed. "One morning Zachariah woke up on the street, too inebriated to move and babbling incoherently. Some passing pilgrims, likely newly arrived from a dusty little rural village, thought he was afflicted and tossed him several coins. Gold, mind you. They were probably inebriated as well. So Zachariah decided it was easier and more profitable to just sit and beg for coins rather than work."

Anatolius smiled. "Until the accident with the melons caused him to forget his supposed paralysis in front of too many people who knew about his affliction?"

"That's right. I understand he's doing even better now, selling magickal melons that supposedly cure the sick." She moved toward the door, but John stopped her.

"I thank you for clearing up the mystery of Zachariah but I am more interested in Agnes," he declared. "You will be permitted to leave when you have answered certain questions. What do you know about the tattoo on Agnes' wrist?"

"Agnes did not have one," Petronia declared.

"You are lying. It is not advisable."

"Why would I lie about anything so trivial?"

It was a good question, John thought. But was she so skilled an actress she could lie in such a convincing fashion that most would accept the lie as truth? "What of her history?"

"So far as I am aware she came here more or less directly after being thrown out by that bastard of a sausage maker. She continued to go back from time to time. Who knows why. She was never away long enough to work as a prostitute, be removed to Theodora's little sanctuary, and then change her mind and leave. It's ridiculous. Now, please, may I go?" She picked up a brightly painted diadem from a table littered with statuettes of deities.

John was reminded of the clutter in Menander's room and Troilus' shop. Had the statuettes come from one of them? It was hard to believe that Petronia knew as little about Menander as she had insisted previously. He was a patron of the theater after all, and actresses were notoriously friendly with such men. Also she knew Troilus well enough that he had spent hours pouring out his woes to her while Agnes was being murdered.

"Petronia, you told me that you only knew Menander by reputation, as a benefactor of the theater. This being so, you will not know that he was murdered recently."

The actress stared at John. Her pale features remained calm but her grip tightened on the diadem. "Murdered?"

"Strangled, as was Agnes."

"But for what reason?" Petronia asked in a faint voice.

"It is not known, but they were both well acquainted with Troilus, a name which I have heard often during my investigations."

"I haven't seen Troilus for days, not since he and Agnes argued here."

"Tell me what you know about Menander," John ordered. "It may help Troilus."

"Yes. He might be in danger." Petronia shook her head. Her laugh was tinged with bitterness. "I expect you think I've been protecting Troilus because of some fondness I feel toward him." She glanced around as if to be certain that Anatolius was listening as well.

"How could you think that, gentlemen? It isn't what you imagine." She turned the diadem over and over in her hands. "What I feel for the young man is a motherly affection. Nothing more, or should I say nothing less? I looked after him, you see, for several years. Menander asked me to. He found me this fine place and decorated it lavishly, as you observe."

"You were Menander's mistress? Are you claiming Troilus is your son?" John asked.

"Certainly not! Neither! It's true I am old enough to be Troilus' mother, but no, I am not his mother. I've always thought Menander was Troilus' father. He treated him like a son, but he told me never to reveal that there was any connection between himself and Troilus, aside from what everyone could see, which is to say their business dealings."

She paused and frowned. "Many thought Menander was taking advantage of an inexperienced young man, selling him items from his collection for a better price than a shrewder merchant would've given. Some even supposed Troilus was one of Menander's boys."

She gave a sad smile. "I could tell that was not the case. Oh, I often wanted to explain. Because it not only made Menander look grasping but also made Troilus appear to be a fool."

"You say you were not Menander's mistress. Why did he entrust the boy to you?"

"Perhaps he considered me more responsible than most. He could see that I avoided troublemakers."

"He could see, because they were the people with whom Menander chose to associate."

Petronia's wan smile indicated her agreement. "That, and the fact that I am from the palace myself. Do not question me further on the matter. I refuse to discuss it."

John felt he should have guessed her background from her manner of speaking and the way she carried herself. He had put it down to artfulness.

"When did Menander bring Troilus to you?" he asked.

"It would have been around ten years ago. Troilus was about fourteen then. I don't know where he lives now. He doesn't come to see me very often. In fact, the morning Agnes was murdered was the longest time I've spoken to him in years."

"Are you certain he remained here for hours?"

Petronia confirmed it was the case. "He and Agnes were inseparable. They met while he was still living with me. She was living with the sausage maker."

"You told me Agnes spent time with those who once lived at the palace. She enjoyed play acting, pretending she was still part of the imperial court."

"A young woman's fancy. They all enjoyed play acting, imagining they were still respected members of the court. Poor Agnes was only a child when her father was executed. She was never to live the life of a fine lady, even for a little while."

Petronia looked down at the diadem she held. It must have reminded her that she was dressed like an empress herself. "We help them relive what their lives were once like," she continued. "That's why they love the theater."

"What do you know about Troilus' background?"

"Nothing at all. He could have been a fish seller's son for all I know. He had to pretend to be well born for business reasons. People who have been at court are more comfortable dealing with those who share their attitudes."

"Did those attitudes include a dislike for the emperor?"

"I would prefer not to say anything about that. You are, after all, Justinian's servant."

"I am well aware Justinian is not universally loved. I have also been given to understand that the various alleged plots hatched in the Copper Market amount to little more than scurrilous mimes."

"Then you know all there is to know about Troilus' attitudes," Petronia replied.

Chapter Forty-Five

John and Anatolius left Petronia and turned their steps to the thoroughfare that led toward the Augustaion and the Great Palace. John walked a few paces ahead. He was turning matters over and the harder he thought, the faster he walked.

"Troilus is Theodora's son," John muttered.

Anatolius managed to catch up to John. "What did you say? Troilus is Theodora's son?"

"Yes. Or at least he holds himself out as her son, when it suits him. I've finally managed to piece most of the mosaic together. I've been listening to people for days. Their stories are all interesting enough by themselves. Like the tesserae I saw in Michri's shop. Colorful in isolation, but the picture they form when assembled correctly is much more fascinating. Listen to my argument and see if you can rebut it. It will be good legal practice."

"I will if I can keep up with your stride," Anatolius complained.

John did not diminish his pace. "I've recounted all the facts to you more than once, my friend. Now, consider that according to the empress' servant Theodoulos, the soldiers who pursued the boy reported he vanished as if into thin air in the Copper Market. Alba told me she'd watched a boy chased by men in military garb hide inside Lazarus' pillar. Afterward she considered what she saw to be a miracle because the boy was never seen or heard of again. In fact, she told Menander about it while trying to convince him to change his ways."

"That might have piqued Menander's curiosity about the pillar."

"I believe it did. About the same time the stylite's acolyte discovered Lazarus had disappeared from the top of his column and been replaced by an automaton. Menander had at least two automatons, Alba told me. One she remembered must have been the Sergius I saw in Troilus' shop. The automaton on the pillar was also a soldier, the other half of the pair of military saints. Everyone knew Menander had sold much of his collection to Troilus over the years, but it appears their connection was closer than that."

Anatolius agreed it was likely, given the information just provided by Petronia.

"I am taking a leap into darkness," John admitted, "but I believe Menander was intrigued by Alba's story. Alba said there were guards posted in the square for several days, but Troilus was up on the pillar with the body of Lazarus for longer than that. After the guards had gone, Menander must have climbed up into the column during the night, if only to be in a position to contradict Alba the next time she mentioned it to him. He must have been surprised to find Troilus. He sent the boy to live with Petronia, as she just told us. He wouldn't have wanted him staying in the same building as Alba because she might have recognized him."

Anatolius grinned. "I have it! Just as the acolyte guessed, someone left an automaton behind so no one would notice the stylite's absence for some time! And who do we know who had not one but two of those useful artifacts?"

"Indeed. Menander didn't want attention drawn to the pillar, in case anyone from the palace was still looking for the boy."

Anatolius frowned and asked John about the whereabouts of the missing stylite.

"That's part of the mosaic I haven't yet filled in," John admitted. "The square isn't much traveled at night, particularly after the shops are closed, not to mention the local populace can't be relied on to be forthcoming when questioned, as we've discovered ourselves. It wouldn't have been difficult to take an automaton to the column or to smuggle a boy or a body away after the guards were no longer stationed in the square. In the meantime the boy could have eaten the stylite's food."

"But what could Menander want with this boy?"

"Menander had grievances against the imperial couple. No doubt he thought that a son of Theodora—even if one only purported to be such—would be useful to him one day."

Anatolius stepped around a dog eating offal. "And Agnes involved herself with actors and disgruntled former courtiers and officials and the like, the same circles in which Menander and Troilus moved. But what conclusions do you draw from this? Is a plot really being fomented or is it just more play acting?"

John and Anatolius passed basket-laden shoppers, begrimed laborers carrying the tools of their trade, and twittering clerks. If any of them heard Anatolius utter the word "plot" they pretended to be deaf. It was not the sort of information you admitted to knowing if you valued your life.

"If Troilus is Theodora's supposed son then he must be one of the plotters, since they cannot proceed without him," John replied.

"He doesn't appear to be the one who murdered Agnes, since she was alive when the sundial maker Helias spied Troilus dragging a sack about in the middle of the night, given she was arguing with Troilus in Petronia's room the next morning," Anatolius said. "And indeed why would Troilus murder Agnes? Petronia said they were inseparable."

"Think of Dedi's vanishing skull act, Anatolius. It appears to be magick only because a skull would not burn the way it does. Once you realize that what you thought was a skull isn't one, but rather a thin, flammable counterfeit, then it does not appear so remarkable. Fostering a false assumption or two and some skilled misdirection can make perfectly unremarkable events appear quite sinister. Or, for that matter, make sinister events appear unremarkable."

"What do you mean, John? What misdirection? And where are we going in such a hurry?"

They had crossed the Augustaion, and were walking toward the Chalke. Gulls flapped out of their way, protesting as they were forced to abandon the city's discarded debris on which they'd been dining.

John glanced at his companion. "Do you remember you mentioned you saw Felix entering a tavern not far from the cistern where I found the girl's body and on the very same morning? A coincidence, it would seem. But how was it he happened to be on hand to rescue me when I was attacked in the street, not to mention being at the right place at the right time to prevent Theodoulos from throwing himself into the sea?"

"But surely...I can't believe Felix...."

"People often see what they wish to see, not what is actually there."

"But if Felix is involved," Anatolius protested, "who sent that message about two conspirators meeting at the Milion...well, if you are right you did meet a conspirator there...but you aren't a conspirator!"

"No. And I know I'm not, and so do you. But consider again Dedi's act."

They passed through the magnificent Chalke gate, entered the palace grounds, and made their way to its far less imposing maze of administrative buildings.

Felix was not present in his office, although a mismatched assortment of rugged excubitors and callow clerks milled in the antechamber.

John stopped a thin man who visibly trembled at the touch of the Lord Chamberlain's glare. "Where is the captain?"

"I...I...don't know....uh....excellency. He's gone off with a contingent of excubitors. Trouble of some sort...a riot...."

"Mithra! It's started! I have to warn Cornelia!"

Chapter Forty-Six

"The Lord Chamberlain is not available," Cornelia told the stranger at the door.

"We know that. I've come here to speak to you."

The caller was a man of average appearance, aside from his immaculate dress and perfectly trimmed hair and his exceedingly dark and chilling eyes.

"He refused to give his name, mistress," said Peter, who had answered the insistent knock.

"I hope you are not offended," the stranger said to Cornelia. "It is not possible for me to give you my name. It would not be safe for either of us."

"Give your blade to Peter, and come into the office," Cornelia replied.

The room beyond the foot of the stairs, furnished with cushioned chairs and a desk of inlaid wood, opened on to the garden. John rarely used it. He preferred to meet visitors in his stark upstairs study.

Cornelia posted Peter beside the door. The visitor refused the proffered seat so she remained standing.

"What did you mean when you said that you knew the Lord Chamberlain is not here?"

"Only that we have been watching him."

Cornelia forced herself to breath slowly. She could not stop her heart racing. John was in grave danger. She was certain of it. The mild-voiced stranger chilled her in a way that finding Menander's body in the bath had not. The dead man's identity had been known. Whatever peril his death represented to the household could therefore ultimately be traced.

Confronted with this unknown caller she could not tell from which direction danger might come.

"Who has been watching?"

The stranger offered a faint smile. At least Cornelia interpreted the expression as a smile. "My apologies, but I simply cannot say."

Where was John now? He had been gone all day again. Was he safe? Was he…? She pushed the thought away.

"Say whatever it is you've come to say." Somehow she kept her voice steady.

"Please believe me, we have your best interests at heart. The Lord Chamberlain—your husband—has spent a great deal of time lately in the company of people with whom he would not seem to have any legitimate business."

Cornelia did not correct his misapprehension that she and John were married. If, indeed, he really believed it. "As Justinian's representative he might have legitimate business with anyone in this city or indeed the empire," she pointed out.

"That may well be, but these people I mention are like pieces of colored glass—innocent enough singly but when arranged together they form a picture. In this case, a most sinister picture."

"What people are these?"

"Why, Felix for one, the excubitor captain who controls a contingent of armed men within the walls of the palace itself. Did you know that General Belisarius is also in the city? Justinian relieved him of his command, so he has a grievance against the emperor, and the loyalty of a great many soldiers. I have it on impeccable authority that your husband has consulted an associate of the general."

Cornelia noticed a look of outrage appeared on Peter's face. Evidently he too had grasped the implication contained in the smooth words. She glared at the visitor who continued unperturbed.

"The Lord Chamberlain and the excubitor captain have been friendly for years and would hardly be expected to oppose one another if they became, shall we say, ambitious. And then there are all these persons your husband has been meeting in the Copper Market. A seditious rabble, to be sure. He has been present at clandestine meetings, or meetings those attending foolishly imagined were clandestine. You surely realize all this."

"Are you implying the Lord Chamberlain is involved in some intrigue against the emperor?"

The visitor sighed and made a vague gesture with his hands, the fingers of which were perfectly manicured. "If you step back a pace or two, you will have to admit the picture formed by all these circumstances is very suspicious, particularly since one of the scoundrels known to be involved was found dead in your bath."

"You insult the Lord Chamberlain's loyalty by even suggesting he would be part of such a conspiracy!"

"Perhaps he wants us to think he could not be involved because if he were he would not be so stupid as to call attention to himself by leaving the corpse of one of his co-conspirators in his own bath? That by doing so we would overlook the remarkable amount of time he has spent in the Copper Market recently?"

"Investigating the death of a young woman. I am certain I'm not telling you anything you don't know, whoever you are."

The stranger smiled again. Or was it a sneer? "Investigating a murder makes for a fine pretext for being in places palace officials would best avoid. And if the victim who supplies the pretext is a person who needed to be put out of the way...."

Cornelia felt her face flush with fury. "You dare to say John murdered her to give himself a pretext to visit with a band of plotters?"

"If your husband was really investigating such a death, why did he not inform the emperor?"

"He considered it a private matter!" Cornelia regretted her hasty words as soon as she had spoken.

The man gave a contemptuous smile but remained silent.

"Why are you telling me?" she demanded. "Confront the Lord Chamberlain with this outrageous nonsense, if you dare."

"I suspect you may be more amenable to reason, Cornelia. You have a daughter, don't you? Yes, she is quite fond of Zeno's horses. She was out riding yesterday."

Cornelia stifled the cry that formed in her throat. Out of the corner of her eye she saw Peter move. She motioned him to remain where he was. "If you will not reveal who you're working for—"

The stranger's voice remained quiet. "At the moment, I am working for you. For you and your husband and your family. A family which may be in danger. I am only trying to help."

He paused and stared thoughtfully out into the garden. "I had hoped we might talk in your husband's study. I would be curious to see that mosaic girl I've heard about. I understand when Justinian executed the former owner of this house he spared Glykos' family. I have it on good authority that he is not likely to be so forbearing this time."

"I fail to see how your threats and insinuations are of any help to anyone in this house. Watching John, trying to manufacture a case against him out of nothing...."

"Ah, but you assume we are the only ones watching, the only ones who have observed your husband's actions these past days. Not so. Perhaps the emperor's ire cannot be avoided. So long as the emperor is Justinian. The Lord Chamberlain is a man of principle. A man who would surely put principle above all else, perhaps even his family. This is why I wished to speak to you, Cornelia. I must leave now. Your husband will be back soon and you will want to discuss these matters with him."

Chapter Forty-Seven

John found Cornelia sitting in his study, staring at the wall mosaic.

The lowering sun spilled red light across the glass country scene, a place upon which the sun set, but never rose. Zoe stared out, silent as ever, while Cornelia told John about her visitor. He had a suspicion who it might have been, but he said nothing. It might only alarm her more.

"Could you be implicated, John? Would Justinian believe you are involved in plot against him?"

"It's impossible to say what Justinian might believe. It can change from hour to hour. He believes whatever he wishes and what the emperor believes might as well be true so far as the rest of us are concerned."

"You must continue to do whatever is proper," Cornelia said.

John put his hand on her arm. "Even if I didn't worry about you, there is still our daughter. Felix has already set off with a contingent of excubitors. The city is liable to be in flames before the sun comes up tomorrow. I want you and Peter to leave while you can. Go straight to Zeno's estate and join Thomas and Europa. It will be safer for you all."

"You'll come with us?"

"No. Justinian would conclude, or be persuaded, I had fled because of guilt, in which case there'd be nowhere in the empire we'd be safe. I have given Peter his instructions. You need to hurry now."

He started to take his hand from her arm but she grasped it. There was more anger in her eyes than fear.

"It's all because of that girl—that woman! You've told her things you'd tell no one else!"

"Because she is no one, Cornelia, merely pieces of glass. Do you really think I talk to her? I am only talking to myself."

Cornelia squeezed his hand and let it go. "She's destroyed everything, John. You would never have gotten involved in any of this, except for her."

"A woman died because she wanted to speak to me. A real woman, not a mosaic figure. Justice must be served."

John realized he was gazing at Zoe. He went to the window and looked out. Would he have paid the slightest attention to the prostitute in the square had she not identified herself as the model for Zoe? Was there any possibility he would have agreed to meet her the next day? Couldn't the Prefect have investigated her death? Cornelia was right. It was only because of Zoe that he had become involved. Or was it entangled?

"Did you know there's someone watching the house?" he asked.

Cornelia came to his side.

"Look," he told her "Just past the corner of barracks. In the shadows." He turned abruptly. "I have to go. There are things I need to do. Don't worry about me, but call Peter and leave as soon as you can. It is still possible now, but it won't be for much longer."

He strode out without looking back and Cornelia did not go after him.

As he left the house, he laid his hand on the blade in his belt. He could see that the shadowy figure remained beside the barracks. He walked directly toward it.

Rather than fleeing the figure stepped forward.

She stepped forward.

A shade.

Agnes.

Zoe.

The fading red light robbed the face of detail so that it resembled the mosaic even more closely than it had the first time John glimpsed it.

Had the little girl, Zoe, known what was about to happen, that she was to be deprived of her father, she and her mother thrown onto the street? Was that why she had appeared so sad? Or had Figulus, the mosaic maker, known what was in the store for the innocent child and depicted her in mourning for her future?

A torch on the barracks wall threw her shadow across the square and part way up the side of John's house.

John glanced back and saw Cornelia—only a shadow herself now—beyond the ruby tinted window panes. The brick front of the house was the color of blood.

Or red dye.

He looked back toward Agnes.

She stood still for a heartbeat, then fled.

John went after her.

She cut down a paved path that led off into the imperial gardens. She wasn't moving fast, but each time John accelerated to catch her, she responded by running faster herself.

She veered off into a gap in a line of towering shrubs making a solid black wall in the twilight. She might have evaded him, but when he emerged from the shrubbery he saw her dark figure making its way across a glimmering flag stoned court, angling in the direction the palace gates.

John's boots clattered across the stone. Black and white tiles formed an enormous sundial in the center of the open space, but at this hour the gnomon was nearly lost in darkness.

Then they were in the vast hall leading to the Chalke. The sound of the crowd of workers leaving the palace grounds for the night or returning from the city echoed up into its lofty vaults.

Agnes had slowed almost to a walk, dodging in and out through the clerks and laborers and servants spilling toward the gates. She kept looking back over her shoulder. John moved straight ahead, cutting through the crowd.

No one dared to block his path.

Should he alert the guards?

If they went into action there would be chaos. She would likely escape in the confusion.

Besides, the longer he watched her, the more glimpses he had of her face, looking back at him, the more convinced he was that the woman was indeed the same who had accosted him in the square.

The body in the cistern therefore had not been Agnes.

Who then?

It must have been the prostitute Anatolius had learned about, the young woman who had fled the convent.

Which meant that the corpse had been dyed to make it appear that the person responsible was trying to hide the tattoo that would identify her. So that John would overlook the fact that the battered face could have belonged to anyone.

Was that possible? A tattoo could be painted on a living wrist, especially if it needed only to be seen for an instant.

Agnes was outside the palace now, moving down the Mese, not quite at a run. A shadow flickering in and out of the pools of light cast by shop torches under the colonnades.

John followed, keeping her in sight.

He became aware of a sound that was not the usual clamor of hurrying crowds anxious to be home. A sound as of wind sighing around columns and statuary in enclosed squares.

A formless sound, more rhythmic than wind gusts, akin to waves washing against the sea walls.

Had the rioting begun?

Agnes turned off onto a narrow street, turned again.

John followed her through an archway connecting one street to another and plunged into a surging mass of humanity.

He reached for his blade, then realized he had not stumbled into a melee. The chanting mob was marching along in an orderly fashion.

It was a procession, a common enough occurrence. This one was obviously on its way to a church, for here and there he saw men in ecclesiastical garments. Most of the crowd wore the rough clothing of the poor or of pilgrims who have traveled far. Some carried torches. Gilded icons ascended toward the heavens on poles. Stern bearded figures stared into the night, images of the Christian god. Torchlight struck liquid fire off the golden figures.

The monotonous chanting washed over John, filled his head, as if he had fallen into deep water. Was he still feeling the effect of the attack he'd suffered?

He couldn't see Agnes.

Had he lost her again?

A shouted curse caused him to whirl around. A gem-studded silver angel tilted precariously on a platform borne along by several husky acolytes, who were now trying to maintain their grip while at the same time keeping the angel from falling. No doubt the angel was a reliquary, holding the bones of a holy man.

Over one glittering wing John spotted Agnes, staring back at him from the far side of the procession.

He forced his way through the crowd, but when he reached the opposite side Agnes was gone. Just behind where she had stood was a dark, irregular opening in the wall of a derelict shop.

John squeezed through into darkness. Faint light from the street illuminated a steep slope of debris, the remains of collapsed floors. He picked his way down through splintered shelves and broken pottery.

When his eyes had accustomed themselves to the dimness he was aware of a faint, undulating radiance. Light reflected off water.

He had entered a building built over a cistern, perhaps the upper part of the very cistern where he had found the body. He could still hear muffled chanting from the world above.

Then he heard her voice, resonating amid the rows of pillars against which water lapped.

"Lord Chamberlain! At last we can talk."

"What do you want to tell me, Agnes?"

"Not here. We can't talk here."

Where was she?

Her voice seemed to come from no particular direction. Distorted by the echoing space, it sounded hardly human.

He peered into the dimness. Reflected light wavered and pulsed over the columns and walls of the cistern.

There she was, at the far end of the concrete walk which ran down the center of the cistern.

As quickly as he dared, he loped along the narrow path, all too aware of the water waiting for him.

At the other side of the cistern a brick archway opened into a cavernous room echoing with Agnes' receding footsteps.

He followed her through a series of basements and sub-basements. In places stinking swamps of stagnant water soaked his boots, while other areas were dust dry. He could hear rats skittering in darkness relieved by scattered shafts of light.

Agnes remained in sight. John realized that if he caught her, he would not discover where she was leading him.

However, he could now guess their destination.

They passed corridors which slanted upward and skirted piles of rubble. One, a huge mound of shattered tiles had obviously been part of an elaborate floor. Pieces of couches stuck out from the mass, wooden arms broken, cushions gutted by rats. A fountain basin filled with rust-colored water sat amidst fragments of monumental statues. A pale, naked Aphrodite stood in a niche, pristine, as if whatever calamity had befallen this place had feared to touch her.

This must be what remained of the palace of Lausos.

Then abruptly they had passed through one last doorway and John saw they had arrived at the destination he had expected.

They were behind Troilus' subterranean establishment.

Armed excubitors milled around the dry cistern.

A hand clamped down on John's shoulder. He turned to face the man whose familiar voice spoke his name.

It was Felix.

Chapter Forty-Eight

Felix escorted John to Troilus' emporium. The excubitor said nothing and looked straight ahead, avoiding John's gaze.

The abandoned cistern at whose center the ramshackle structure sat had taken on an aspect different from that presented during John's previous visit.

Then it had been a dim, empty cavern. Now a crowd of shadows moved between its rows of pillars glimpsed through a shifting fog of smoke. Torches shone like hazy suns or threw out shafts of light as the miasma eddied to and fro.

Even in that uncertain illumination John could see many of the figures were armed.

Not all of them were excubitors.

John recognized several faces. Men he had seen from a distance, meeting with Menander at the court near the sea, an actor from Petronia's troupe, and, sitting on a fallen column, staring insolently in his direction, the boy who had led him from the stylite's square to the cistern where the dead woman lay face down in the water.

The corpse that had not been Agnes.

Agnes stood beside Troilus in front of his shop, her face flushed from exhilaration or perhaps the physical exertion of leading John here.

They had been leading him from the very beginning but he should have realized it sooner than he had, John thought. Would have realized it, had he not been so eager to track down Agnes' murderer and learn something about the model for the girl who had served as his confidante for so long.

There was nothing of Zoe left about Agnes now, except for the haunted eyes.

Troilus stepped forward. The torchlight accentuated the lines in his face and silvered the gray hair. Despite his youth he looked old and careworn.

"Lord Chamberlain! I see you are still in the habit of carrying out pursuits in person. Most high officials would summon servants for that sort of exertion. Nevertheless, I am pleased you have chosen to join us."

"Us? Who do you mean, Troilus?" John replied.

"Why, those who have rebelled against Justinian's vicious rule! Men and women of courage who have met with each other in secret until now! Men like yourself!"

John glanced at the purple trim on the garments worn by both Troilus and Agnes. The structure they stood before had gained the appearance of a military command post. Guards were stationed at its door and two artifacts from the shop stood ceremoniously outside.

The Sergius automaton and a life-sized satyr.

"As you well know, Lord Chamberlain, appearances count for everything," Troilus went on. "What Justinian believes is more important than the actual situation."

Felix had moved back a few paces. John could feel his silent, watchful presence.

Agnes stared at John with Zoe's eyes.

Her gaze was full of hatred.

Had John always misinterpreted the mosaic girl's dark-eyed countenance? He had supposed it evidenced a knowledge of the world beyond her years. Was it merely her loathing for the man who sat at his desk and contemplated her? The man who lived in the house where her family should have lived?

"If you abandon whatever foolish plan you've concocted, Troilus, it may be possible to convince Justinian that this has been nothing more than play-acting. Foolish, certainly, but not treason." John looked around at Felix. "Isn't that so, captain?"

Felix made no reply.

"It would not even be necessary for you to arrest these prank-sters, my friend," John persisted. "Return to the palace with me and we can laugh about it over a jug of wine."

Felix's gaze remained obstinately fixed on some distant hori-zon.

Troilus laughed. "Don't imagine that either General Felix or I am so faint of heart as to abandon what we have set out to accomplish, Lord Chamberlain. Do you suppose these armed men are my only accomplices? Fate is on my side also, or perhaps you would say Fortuna? Not to mention gods much older and more powerful than the stripling godlet on which Justinian depends."

"Indeed? And what causes you believe it to be so?" John replied in a tone indicating he doubted every word Troilus had spoken.

"Why, everything that has transpired in my life! What dreams I had after my father revealed my lineage! I remember when the ship bearing me came within sight of Constantinople. It was near sunset. The lights of the city were beyond counting. It seemed to me that I stood outside the sphere of the heavens and saw the stars blazing on the inside with the brilliant dome of the Great Church glowing sun-like at the center. This was to be my world, by right of birth, as the son of an empress!"

"Poetic words, but proof of your lineage," John demanded, "where is that?"

Troilus' eyes narrowed. "Do not interrupt me, Lord Chamberlain. You are accustomed to listening to your emperor, are you not? You will speak when I give you permission to do so."

"But I am most interested in your tale!"

Troilus smiled coldly. "As well you should be! First, you must understand the effect of my only meeting with my mother. Can anyone conceive what it did on the innocence of a child to be greeted, not by motherly love, but by demonic hatred? I came as a babe to the breast, only to be cast into the grip of a murderous monster."

John shrugged. "You did not know Theodora's reputation?"

"Silence!" Troilus shouted. "You are speaking of my mother!" He paused and gathered his thoughts before taking up his story. "And yet that was only the beginning of the horror. I ran away. I was pursued through a nightmare of dark and unfamiliar streets, every one of which could lead only to my death."

John pointed out that his present course was leading him to that dark destination.

Agnes stepped forward. "Troilus, I advise you to have the Lord Chamberlain's tongue removed."

"Afterward, perhaps, when we have extracted all the information he can provide," Troilus replied. "If he chooses not to cooperate with us, that is. But first let me finish revealing my history to the fool. It will be spoken of for decades, celebrated in song, and if he refuses to join us, he should not go to his death without hearing it."

Turning toward John, he continued. "And then when in my flight I sought refuge on a stylite's column, as I reached the top, there descended upon me a demon. A foul, black bird. Flapping and screeching and scratching at my eyes with its filthy talons. Its stench was like the pits of hell. I fought, though I was nearly senseless with terror. The demon died and in doing so took the form of an old man."

John remained silent. The remaining mosaic pieces were rapidly joining together.

"I was afraid I would be seen," Troilus continued in a quieter voice, as if talking to himself. "I hid the body in the shelter atop the column and huddled beside it. Dawn came. How would I know when my pursuers had ceased to search for me? I had nowhere to go. If I were discovered I would die. Besides, all my senses left me. For a while I did not know where I was. Perhaps I actually was dead and in hell."

"You have not seen Justinian's dungeons yet," John offered, calculating how near he would have to get to be able to leap on Troilus and disarm him.

Troilus paid no attention. "There was no room to move. I was thrust against my dead companion. His glazed eyes stared at me. He wheezed, as if some foul thing were trying to speak with his corpse mouth. And more than once I saw his expression change, but now I realize it was only the mass of flies crawling across his sunken face."

Agnes began to interrupt, but Troilus waved his hand and she fell silent.

"Yes, Lord Chamberlain, my shelter was alive with flies. Their buzzing filled my thoughts and the formless drone became the tormented cries of dead souls, too loud and horrifying to be grasped by a mortal man. So overwhelming that it made me unable to think. And then there was the smell of death. I gagged ceaselessly. When I tried to breath through my mouth to avoid the stench, I inhaled flies."

Felix stirred restlessly. Knowing his friend as he did, John realized he was tired of listening to Troilus and wished to move into action.

Troilus, however, was determined John would hear his story. "It was during that endless damnation that details of my flight came back to me as a dream I had forgotten. In the palace garden I broke away from the monster into whose hands my mother had delivered me and threw myself into an abyss. I had no thought but to end my life in my own way before death was inflicted on me in some manner too dreadful to contemplate."

"It would have been an honorable death," John said quietly.

"Ah, but my destiny was shown to be greater than that! For I was saved by falling into an ornamental pool. I stood in the water, hardly believing I was alive, wondering if I were really still falling and the world would wink out in an instant to end my hopeful dream. I felt a gaze on my back. Turning, I saw a figure glimmering in the darkness."

Troilus paused, took a few steps to the statue of the satyr, and patted the chiseled fur on its marble flank. "It was the god Pan, Lord Chamberlain. He had spared my life by arranging for me to fall into a pool guarded by his image. Clearly I had been chosen to overthrow the foul representatives of the new religion, whose mothers throw their babes into the arms of demons. That is also why I ascended toward heaven and replaced the so-called holy man on the pillar. These were miracles, you see. Miracles arranged for me."

John thought of Alba, who had also thought the boy's ascent a miracle, although interpreting its message in a different fashion. He made no comment.

Troilus moved to Agnes and grasped her hand. The girl continued to stare darkly at John.

"The miracles did not end with my being transported to safety atop the pillar," Troilus went on. "Before too many days had passed, the gods sent to serve me a man who had also been cruelly banished from court and now as you see...."

He fell silent.

"John!" The rumbling voice belonged to Felix. "The emperor has surely convinced himself you have turned against him."

"I cannot imagine that," John replied.

"It's true. I'm certain of it. You must protect yourself by joining us."

"What if I refuse, my friend?"

"Don't think to test me, John. I can do nothing for you except to see...to make sure...you don't suffer....You were warned, why didn't you take notice?"

"You mean Cornelia was threatened. It was Procopius who visited her, wasn't it? Did you send him, Felix? You could hardly warn me yourself."

It was Troilus who replied. "We were and are concerned about the welfare of you and your family."

"Felix must have told you I was loyal to Justinian," John said. "And I remain so."

Troilus smiled. "Then there is no reason for me not to have you killed, Lord Chamberlain. In fact, now you've seen what is about to happen and can betray those involved, there is every reason to order your execution. You will become half a centaur skeleton, like the stylite who once lived atop a pillar but now passes his days underground!"

"Soldiers die if it is necessary," John replied.

"You might choose to die, but is your family as loyal to Justinian as you are? Even if our plans fail—which they cannot, for it is the will of the gods that they succeed—you have been implicated so far as Justinian is concerned, just as we planned by the method Procopius revealed to your wife. In the past the emperor has not treated kindly the families of those who displeased him. As for myself, a good ruler is merciful, but a ruler must sometimes give orders he might find distasteful for the preservation of the empire."

"Such as murdering the man who rescued you from the pillar and treated you like a son?" John snapped.

Troilus' jaw clenched.

It was Agnes who spoke. "Menander was untrustworthy. He talks too much when intoxicated. He had to be silenced. Besides, being like a father to Troilus was just good business on Menander's part, wasn't it?"

Here her voice was not distorted by echoes as it had been in the water-filled cistern. It sounded not unearthly but merely strident, not at all like the voice with which John was familiar.

Zoe's voice, which had only been the sound of his own thoughts.

"But as to you, Lord Chamberlain," Troilus was saying. "I offer you one more chance of life. If you are willing to aid me in—"

"The answer is no, Troilus," John interrupted. "And as for Menander, however he died, your hand was in it."

"I don't dispute it, Lord Chamberlain."

"And what about that young prostitute whose body you dragged into your shop and took from there to the cistern where I was led to discover her? You used the underground route I have just followed. Did you meet her when she came to the theater looking for her actress friend? How did you lure her to her death?"

"Mithra!" Felix drew his sword even as he uttered the oath. He took a step toward Troilus. "You said you'd paid a madam for a body. You never said you'd murdered an innocent woman."

Troilus raised his hand in what he must have supposed was an imperious gesture but resembled, rather, an actor aping a ruler. "These are matters of no concern to us now that the time has come," he said.

"What was her name? Was it Vigilia?" Felix demanded. "It was Vigilia, wasn't it? You said you hadn't seen her since the day she'd arrived at the theater."

"We can discuss this matter later, General Felix," Troilus replied, "when the imperial couple has been deposed. Now, order your men—"

"The last time I went to visit her at Theodora's convent, I was told she'd fled and where she'd gone," Felix persisted. "When I came looking for her, you told me she'd been to the theater but had left and that you would ask after her whereabouts. You'd help me search. Then you introduced me to Menander and his ambitious friends. And all the time...."

Felix's voice cracked. His gaze was suddenly as wild as his brimming eyes, reflecting the torchlight.

John had understood the situation correctly. Vigilia had been the prostitute who had come to Anatolius' attention. It wasn't surprising Felix was the man from the palace who had pursued her. It wasn't the first time he had been smitten with a young prostitute.

How cleverly after Vigilia had visited the makeshift theater in the Copper Market the plotters had grasped their opportunity to further their plans.

"It was a stroke of good fortune for you," Troilus told Felix. "And for me also. You saw your chance for glory and joined us. When all this is over, we will find your—"

Felix's knuckles whitened as he gripped his weapon tighter. "You're a liar, Troilus, as well as a murderer," he said in a cold, flat voice. "She's dead. Vigilia's dead, and you killed her."

"That's true, Felix," John said. "And then Troilus left her in the cistern, in order to draw me into a situation which could be presented as a plot to overthrow the emperor, doubtless expecting me to join it to protect myself and my family."

Felix glanced from Troilus to John and back to Troilus. "Do you deny killing her?" Felix took another step toward Troilus, lifting his sword slightly.

John moved between the two men and addressed Felix. "Now we have heard these confessions, the time has come to reveal a certain secret to Troilus and his misguided followers. You are here not to assist these miscreants, but rather to arrest them all, are you not?"

The look of bewilderment that flickered across Felix's broad, bearded face was replaced almost instantly by a ferocious scowl.

"Indeed! That has always been my plan, Lord Chamberlain. I was simply allowing these two to condemn themselves by their own words as well as gathering up their followers in one swoop."

"And just as well," John told him. "When I guessed what was happening, before I returned to warn Cornelia I sent Anatolius to Justinian with an urgent message. Soldiers from the palace are already on their way."

He paused. "You would have had to dispatch me on the spot if you were really involved in this matter, Felix."

Before Felix could give orders to his men, a murmur filled the cistern and smoke coiled and swirled like fog in a sudden stiff breeze.

The emperor's men had arrived. Dark figures poured through the door leading from the corridor.

Agnes grabbed Troilus' arm and looked at him in alarm.

He remained expressionless, as motionless as the sculpted satyr behind him, staring fixedly at the world he had built in his imagination.

"This cannot be," he said. "The will of the gods shall be done. These men have come to join us! General Felix, kill the Lord Chamberlain immediately!"

Agnes glanced rapidly around. She tugged at Troilus' arm. "Hurry!"

John expected her to bolt back into the labyrinth through which he had followed her. It would not be difficult to escape in the maze beneath the city.

But Troilus refused to move, even as Felix strode forward to grasp him.

Now he was as good as in the hands of Justinian's torturers.

Agnes looked around again.

John saw her tense.

Flee, Zoe!

Where had the unworthy thought come from?

Had John spoken it aloud?

No. Or if he had, the girl had not heard.

Agnes did not move. She squared her shoulders. She had chosen to stay with Troilus.

John moved to her side. "Agnes, if—"

Her hand shot out and her fingernails raked down John's face.

"Filthy eunuch bastard!" she screamed and spat at him.

As the first of the emperor's men reached the group and formally placed the treasonous pair under arrest, John felt blood welling up and running down his cheek.

Agnes' eyes remained dark and cold as she was escorted away with Troilus.

Epilogue

"There are some points on which I am not clear," Anatolius said, taking another honey cake as gusts of wind rattled the dark panes of the window in John's study.

John poured more wine. He noticed Anatolius kept his eyes averted from the wall mosaic as he munched on the cake, dropping crumbs on his lap. Was he trying to avoid looking at the lewd deities revealed by the flickering lamplight or at the mosaic girl, the innocent cause of so much trouble?

"What is it that puzzles you?"

"For a start, your foolhardy behavior in following that girl back into an underground maze. Suppose Justinian had refused the request I took to him, to send a contingent of armed men, or they had taken too long to arrive? I would've put your apparent stupidity down to that knock on the head except, and as an old friend I say this without rancor, you were behaving as if you had been knocked over the head even before you were actually attacked."

"From time to time it occurred to me it was possible I was being deliberately herded in certain directions," John replied. "I had obviously been led, in the first place, to the body that was supposed to be Agnes. Had it been meant as a warning to me? Yet the tattoo could have so easily been removed with a sharp knife. Why dye the corpse in an attempt to hide it? It seemed an overly dramatic touch. Then again, there is no guarantee criminals will necessarily follow the most logical course of action."

"Particularly a callow pair acting out a mime put together from their own delusions."

"More a tragedy than a mime, Anatolius. At any rate, I decided if I allowed myself to be hooked and pulled in, eventually I could grasp the line and use it to haul out those responsible for the death of Zoe, as I thought of her."

Anatolius stared at his friend. "The fish capturing the fishers! I never saw you as a fish before!"

John chuckled.

"But wasn't it a strange coincidence that the man who was chasing poor Vigilia turned out to be Felix?" Anatolius demanded.

"Not at all. It was the two of them arriving at the theater at different times that suggested the plan to the conspirators. Felix tells me he is tormented by the thought had Vigilia not had that remarkable tattoo she would not have died so her corpse could be presented as that of Zoe. Agnes' tattoo of course was merely a copy drawn on her flesh, probably with henna."

"Is he also tormented by the thought that if it weren't for you he would have lost his head, thanks to his treasonable actions?"

"He insists his intent was always to keep an eye on the plotters by staying close to them, in order to make arrests at the appropriate time."

"And you believe him?"

"Felix has said very little about his role in the matter. It may be right up to the last he wavered between treason and his duty. After all, he's indicated more than once he considers his work at the palace an insult to a military man and that he would prefer to be fighting for the empire."

"From what you were telling me earlier," Anatolius said, "Felix seems to have spent a lot of time following you around at the behest of the conspirators. I suppose that he must have been protecting you as well. I would advise him to curb his restlessness in future, John."

"Felix may harbor ambitions, but he is not a fool. Even so, I do wonder if his discontent will eventually be his downfall."

"Affairs of the heart coupled with over-indulgence in wine, as is often the case, can turn anyone into a fool, and Felix has a weakness for both. Luckily he tipped the scales of justice the right way when he learned of Vigilia's murder."

"I had deduced the identity of the murdered girl by then, although I didn't know her name, and I realized Felix must have been unaware of her fate. In connection with this substitution of one woman for another, as I reminded you, Dedi's trick with the vanishing skull worked because it wasn't really a skull. Then there was the stylite who was made of metal."

Anatolius frowned. "But why didn't this Stephen, the acolyte you mentioned, realize something was wrong when the stylite he served didn't appear in public for a few days?"

John explained he had learnt from Stephen that the stylite was in the habit of withdrawing into the rough shelter on his platform for lengthy periods of time, and since the food offerings sent up were eaten, by Troilus as it turned out, there was no reason to think further about the matter.

"Thus," he continued, "this allowed the boy to remain hidden until the men left on guard in the square finally returned to the palace, at which point Menander was able to investigate the supposed miracle and having heard his remarkable story rescue Troilus. At the same time, he substituted one of his automatons for the dead stylite, who in a grisly jest against the official religion became part of the centaur in his shop. Presumably the rest of the body is hidden somewhere in the subterranean warren."

Anatolius said this seemed to fit the circumstances.

"And once I deduced how Troilus had been saved from discovery, it made me see how easily everything fit together, provided the dyed corpse in the cistern and the prostitute who fled from Theodora's convent were indeed the same person—but not Agnes."

"You might call it fitting everything together easily, John. Others might regard it as more of a leap in logic. And what about the dye?"

"Purchased or stolen from Jabesh, whose shop is close to the theater. It was probably its proximity that suggested that part of the plan. When Agnes was leading me back to Troilus' shop we ran past what I thought was a fountain basin filled with rust-coloured water, but in fact it must have been the red dye used when they were busy preparing the unfortunate Vigilia's body for its appearance in the cistern."

"And then there's Menander," Anatolius mused. "Now, I do have a notion how that was worked. With artisans repairing your bath mosaic coming and going and only Peter to keep an eye on them, Menander's body must have been smuggled into your house in a barrel. Doubtless it would be taken to be full of tesserae or plaster like the others, if indeed anyone had seen it brought in. That would be toward evening, like as not, so Menander could be tipped into the bath just after Figulus and his workers had left for the day."

"Indeed. Figulus wasn't a party to the plot. As a matter of fact he only agreed to finish work on the bath after I convinced him he would not be stumbling upon any bodies in it."

"I can see Figulus wasn't necessarily involved, but what about Petronia? Could she really have known as little as she claimed? She was once a member of court, after all, or so she said."

"That's a puzzle I haven't solved, nor do I intend to pursue it further. It makes no difference now."

John stared at the dark window, seeing only reflections of the lamplight. He took a sip of wine and continued his explanation.

"As for the matter of Helias, the sundial maker reported there was a body in the sack he saw Troilus dragging past, although not the corpse we suspected. Of course, when I saw the sack later its contents had been replaced by that enormous leather phallus. I suspect he chose that particular artifact to taunt both myself and Helias."

Anatolius inquired about the chamberlain Kyrillos.

"He's still in Theodora's service," John replied. "I promised Kyrillos a reward in return for his cooperation, by the way, and I've just sent him a small satyr for his collection."

Anatolius observed Kyrillos probably assumed John was offering his protection should Theodora hear of what he had revealed.

"Nobody can offer safety from the wrath of the empress. Not even the emperor," John replied. "I doubt Kyrillos will remain very long in Theodora's service, or for that matter in this world, if the aid he provided for my investigation becomes known."

A shadow passed over Anatolius' face. "Perhaps I shouldn't have mentioned...."

"We are both aware such information tends to be easily extracted by Justinian's torturers."

"Yes, I don't like to think about that. And speaking of information, how is Justinian reacting to the revelation that Theodora has an illegitimate child?"

"You mean a self-styled illegitimate child? How many of them do you suppose the imperial couple has encountered over the years? I gather the emperor was as chagrined as Theodora that this particular imposter hadn't been disposed of properly in the first place."

Anatolius nodded. "Of course, now that I think about it there wouldn't have been any reason for her not to tell Justinian about the boy after he first showed up. Only Theodora knows whether his story is true and Troilus had no real proof to offer. Is that malignant dwarf who failed in his duty still among the living?"

"He is still alive. He is after all one of Theodora's playthings and the emperor indulges her whims."

Anatolius stood. "I should be off home. It's very late." The wailing of the gusty wind rose into a shriek. "It sounds as if numerous shades are trying to force their way into your study."

"They are already here," John replied.

Anatolius hesitated in the doorway. Finally he asked "Is there any word about the fate of Troilus or Agnes?"

"Troilus was executed within an hour of arriving at the palace. As for Agnes, I suggested to Justinian he should spare the girl, exile her, or send her to a convent. She was, after all, more or less an innocent, if a deluded innocent."

"You surely did not mean it?"

John replied he did.

"And did he take your rash advice?"

"I understand Theodora interceded. When Agnes revealed she was pregnant with Troilus' child, she ordered the girl be cared for until the birth, which will take place without opiates or assistance of any kind. Should it survive, the baby will be murdered in Agnes' presence as soon as born. At that point Agnes is to be blinded, and then sent to the Repentance convent for the rest of her life, the better to reflect upon her sins, not to mention Theodora's charity in persuading Justinian to allow her to live."

Anatolius shuddered. "Theodora's charity is far worse than Justinian's rage! I wager it won't be long before Agnes finds her way to a window and throws herself out of it." With that, Anatolius took his leave.

Once alone John turned his attention, as so often in the past, to the mosaic girl Zoe.

Or was she Agnes now?

Would the mosaic girl's almond-shaped eyes change when Agnes' terrible punishment was carried out several months hence?

Would Zoe be aware?

Of course not.

The notion was absurd.

John lifted his wine cup to his lips.

Zoe stared back at him with familiar dark, haunted eyes.

Was her gaze colder than before?

Perhaps that was only John's imagination.

"Why, Zoe?" he asked.

But only silence was his answer.

Afterword

Seven For A Secret was inspired by certain events related by Procopius in his *Secret History*.

Glossary

All dates are CE unless otherwise indicated

AGAMEMNON
In Greek mythology, leader of the Greeks during the Trojan War. To obtain favorable winds for the voyage to Troy, he sacrificed one of his children, an act leading to his murder by his wife Clytemnestra and her lover after Agamemnon returned from Troy, followed by Clytemnestra's death at the hands of her two remaining children.

ARIAN
Adherent to Arianism, a Christian heresy. Propounded by Arius (c 256-?336) it held that Christ was not divine but rather the first and highest created being.

ARISTOPHANES (c448-c388 BC}
One of the greatest Greek playwrights, his comedies were written in a broad and often satirical style. Eleven of his works survive, including LYSISTRATA (411 BC), in which the women of Sparta and Athens refuse their husbands' conjugal rights in order to end the war between the two.

ATRIUM
Central area of a Roman house, open to the sky. An atrium not only provided light to rooms opening from it, but also held a shallow pool under the opening in its roof in order to catch rain water both for household use and decorative purposes.

AUGUSTAION
Square between the GREAT PALACE and the GREAT CHURCH.

AVERNUS
Lake in Campania, Italy. Regarded as an entrance to Hades, its name in proverbial use meant going down into the infernal regions was easy, but returning from them was much more difficult.

BATHS OF ZEUXIPPOS

Public baths in Constantinople, named after ZEUXIPPOS. Erected by order of Septimius Severus (146-211, r 193-211}, the baths were a casualty of the NIKA RIOTS (532). They were rebuilt by JUSTINIAN I. Situated near the HIPPODROME, they were generally considered the most luxurious of the city's baths and were famous for their statues of mythological figures and Greek and Roman notables.

BELISARIUS (c505-565)

Distinguished general who was instrumental in putting down the NIKA RIOTS. His exploits included retaking North Africa and later military action against the Persians and the Bulgarians. Belisarius led the campaign to reconquer Italy, which was ultimately successful after he was replaced by NARSES, upon recall to Constantinople as a result of palace intrigue. Accused of treachery, Belisarius was stripped of power, but later restored to favor.

BERYTUS

Prominent law school in what is now Beirut.

BLUES

See FACTIONS.

CENOBITE

Member of a religious community.

CHALKE

One of many structures destroyed during the NIKA RIOTS and rebuilt by JUSTINIAN I. The main entrance to the GREAT PALACE, its roof was tiled in bronze. Its interior had a domed ceiling, and was decorated with mosaics of JUSTINIAN I and THEODORA, as well as military triumphs, including those of BELISARIUS.

CISTERNS

Constantinople had difficulty supplying sufficient water to its populace, especially when under siege. To this end, a number of cisterns were built in various parts of the city, some above ground and others underground, often below buildings. These cisterns stored rainwater as well as water brought in by aqueducts.

CITY PREFECT

High ranking urban official.

CODEX

A bound book.

CONCRETE

Roman concrete, consisting of wet lime, volcanic ash, and pieces of rock, was used for a wide range of applications. One of the oldest remaining Roman concrete buildings is the Temple of Vesta at Tivoli, Italy, built during the first century BC.

DALMATIC

Loose over-garment worn by the Byzantine upper classes.

DEMOSTHENES (?384-322 BC)

Considered by many to be the foremost Greek orator. Having spoken out against the growing danger posed by the Macedonians, after the triumph of their general Antipater (?398-319 BC) he committed suicide rather than fall into enemy hands.

DIGEST

Part of the definitive codification of Roman law ordered by JUSTINIAN I. The Corpus Juris Civilis (Body of the Law) as it is now known was issued between 529 and 535. It consisted of The Institutes, a basic introduction to the law; the Digest, which included selections from classical jurists; and the Codex, dealing with legislation dating from the reign of Hadrian (76-138, r 117-138) onward. The Novels, a collection of legislation issued by JUSTINIAN I, were added between 535 and 565. This codification served as the foundation for present day civil law in most European countries and those whose legal systems are based thereon.

ELISABETH THE WONDERWORKER (fl 5th century)

Born in Thrace, Elisabeth distributed the wealth she inherited from her parents to the poor and entered a convent in Constantinople. Credited with numerous miracles, she is buried in the same city.

EUTROPIUS

See JOHN CHRYSOSTOM.

EUNUCH

Eunuchs played an important role in the military, ecclesiastical, and civil administrations of the Byzantine Empire. Many high offices were held by eunuchs.

EXCUBITORS

GREAT PALACE guards.

FACTIONS

Supporters of either the BLUES or the GREENS, taking their names from the racing colors of the faction they supported. Great rivalry existed between them, and they had their own seating sections at the HIPPODROME. Brawls between these factions were not uncommon. and occasionally escalated into city-wide riots.

GREAT CHURCH

Colloquial name for the Church of the Holy Wisdom (Hagia Sophia). One of the world's great architectural achievements, the Hagia Sophia was completed in 537, replacing the church burnt down during the NIKA RIOTS (532).

GREAT PALACE

Situated in the southeastern part of Constantinople, it was not one building but rather many, set amidst trees and gardens. Its grounds included barracks for the EXCUBITORS, ceremonial rooms, meeting halls, the imperial family's living quarters, churches, and housing provided for court officials, ambassadors, and various other dignitaries.

HERO OF ALEXANDRIA (fl 1st century AD)

Egyptian mathematician and inventor, also known as Heron of Alexandria. His writings included works on surveying, water clocks, geometry, and engineering. His Pneumatics describes how to construct useful, unusual, or amusing devices such as musical instruments played by air or water, a solar-operated fountain, a self-trimming lamp, and automatic wine dispensers.

GREENS

See FACTIONS.

HIPPODROME

U-shaped race track near the GREAT PALACE. The Hippodrome had tiered seating accommodating up to a hundred thousand spectators. It was also used for public celebrations and other civic events.

HORMISDAS

Hormisdas Palace, home of JUSTINIAN I and THEODORA before he became emperor.

HYPOCAUST

Roman form of central heating, distributing hot air through flues under the flooring.

ICONOSTASIS

Screen decorated with icons, separating the sanctuary from the rest of the church.

JOHN CHRYSOSTOM (c347-407)

Born in Antioch, St John Chrysostom (Greek, golden-mouth, a tribute to his eloquent preaching and writings) became PATRIARCH of Constantinople in 398. His piety, condemnation of the immorality of those in positions of power, and numerous charitable works made him well loved by the populace. He also made an unsuccessful attempt to save the life of the corrupt official Eutropius, when the latter fell from favor. Enemies in the imperial court, civil administration, and the church itself brought false accusations against John Chrysostom and he was exiled to Armenia. After unrest in Constantinople he was recalled to the city, but was soon again banished. Eventually ordered moved to an even more isolated location, he died during the journey. In 438 his remains were brought to Constantinople and buried in the Church of the Holy Apostles.

JOSHUA

During a battle in which the Israelites overcame an opposing army, Joshua commanded both sun and moon to stay their courses, which plea was granted (Joshua 10:12-14).

JUSTIN I (c450-527, r 518-527)

Born in the province of Dardania in present day Macedonia, Justin and two friends journeyed to Constantinople to seek their fortunes. All three joined the EXCUBITORS and Justin eventually rose to command them. He was declared emperor upon the death of Anastasius I (c430-518, r 491-518).

JUSTINIAN I (483-565, r 527-565)

Adopted nephew of JUSTIN I. His ambition was to restore the Roman Empire to its former glory and he succeeded in regaining North Africa, Italy, and southeastern Spain. His accomplishments included codifying Roman law (see DIGEST) and an extensive building program in Constantinople. He was married to THEODORA.

KALAMOS

Reed pen.

KEEPER OF THE PLATE

In addition to ceremonial items, imperial plate included tableware such as spoons, platters, ewers, goblets, and various types of dishes. In wealthier households and the GREAT PALACE these items were made of richly-decorated precious metals as well as glass and other materials.

LORD CHAMBERLAIN

Typically a EUNUCH, the Lord (or Grand) Chamberlain was the chief attendant to the emperor and supervised most of those serving at the GREAT PALACE. He also took a leading role in court ceremonial, but his real power arose from his close working relationship with the emperor, which allowed him to wield great influence.

LUCANIAN SAUSAGES

Sausages were a popular dish and spicy Lucanian sausages were considered the best type. These sausages are said to have been introduced to Roman society by soldiers returning from service in Lucania in southern Italy.

LYSISTRATA

See ARISTOPHANES.

MARCUS AURELIUS (121-180; r 161-180)

Adopted by his uncle by marriage Antoninus Pius (86-161, r 138-161) and succeeding him as emperor, Marcus Aurelius sought to improve conditions for slaves, criminals, and the poorer classes. However, he also persecuted Christians, viewing them as a threat to the empire. His Meditations expound upon his Stoic philosophy and sense of moral duty.

MASTER OF THE OFFICES

Chief administrator of the GREAT PALACE.

MESE

Main thoroughfare of Constantinople. Its entire length was rich with columns, arches, and statuary depicting secular, military, imperial, and religious subjects as well as fountains, churches, workshops, monuments, public baths, and private dwellings, making it a perfect mirror of the heavily populated and densely built city it traversed.

MILION

Situated near the GREAT CHURCH, it was the official milestone from which all distances in the empire were measured.

MIME

After the second century CE mime supplanted classical Roman pantomime in popularity. Unlike performers of pantomime, mimes spoke and did not wear masks. Their presentations featured extreme violence and graphic licentiousness and were strongly condemned by the Christian church.

MITHRA

Sun god. Born in a cave or from a rock, he slew the Great Bull, from whose body all animal and vegetable life sprang. Mithra is usually depicted wearing a tunic and Phrygian cap, his cloak flying out behind him, and in the act of slaying the Great Bull. He was also known as Mithras. His worship was spread throughout the Roman empire via its followers in various branches of the military.

MONOPHYSITES

Adherents to Monophysitism, which held Christ had only one nature and that it was divine.

NARSES (c480-574)

Serving JUSTINIAN I at various times as chamberlain and general, Narses, a EUNUCH, aided and ultimately replaced BELISARIUS as leader of the campaign to reconquer Italy.

NIKA RIOTS

Much of Constantinople was burnt down during these riots in 532, which took their name from the mob's cry of Nika! (Greek, Victory!).

NUMMI (singular: nummus)

Smallest copper coin during the early Byzantine period.

PALACE OF LAUSOS

Named after its owner and destroyed by fire in 475, the palace is now known only from its appearance in literary works. It was famous for its collection of Hellenic sculpture, including works by PRAXITELES.

PATRIACH

Head of a diocese or patriarchate.

PLATO'S ACADEMY

Plato (?428-?347 BC) founded his academy in 387 BC. Situated on the north-western side of Athens, its curriculum included natural science, mathematics, and training for public service. Along with other pagan schools it was closed in 529 by order of JUSTINIAN I.

POLYCLITUS (fl 5th century BC)

Greek sculptor, also known as Polykleitos. He created a number of bronze works, notably of athletes, and was also responsible for a highly praised gold and ivory Hera. His statue of a spear-carrier illustrated his theories on the body's ideal proportions and the representation of balanced movement in sculpture. None of his works survive and they are now known only through references in literature, depictions on coins, or Roman copies.

POLYTHEMUS
In Greek mythology, the one-eyed giant blinded by Odysseus.

PRAXITELES (fl 4th century BC)
Considered one of greatest Greek sculptors, Praxiteles' subjects were often taken from mythology. Aphrodite of Cnidus was his most celebrated statue. However, as is the case of all but one of his works, only descriptions and copies of the Aphrodite remain. The only surviving marble known to have been created by Praxiteles is Hermes Carrying the Infant Dionysus.

PREFECT
See CITY PREFECT.

PROCOPIUS (d ?565)
Born in Caesarea in Palestine, he was BELISARIUS' secretary and advisor and accompanied him on his campaigns. Procopius' writings include De Bellis (552, supplemented in 554), an eight volume history of the military campaigns of JUSTINIAN I, and De Aedificiis (561), six books describing numerous buildings erected by order of JUSTINIAN I. His scurrilous Anecdota, also known as The Secret History, relates scandalous and libelous tales about the imperial couple, members of the court, and other high personages. The Anecdota, thought to have been written in the mid or late 550s, was published posthumously.

REPENTANCE
PROCOPIUS records THEODORA founded a convent refuge for former prostitutes. Situated on the Asian shore, it was known as Metanoia, from the Greek, a change of heart or mind, although in this application usually translated as meaning repentance.

RIOTS
See NIKA RIOTS.

SAMSUN'S HOSPICE
Founded by St Samsun (d 530), a physician and priest. Also known as Sampson or Samson the Hospitable, he is often referred to as the Father of the Poor because of his work among the destitute. The hospice was near the GREAT CHURCH.

SILENTIARY
Court official whose duties were similar to those of an usher, and included guarding the room in which an imperial audience or meeting was being held.

SIMEON THE STYLITE (?390-459)
Born in Syria, Saint Simeon first lived as a hermit and then spent over 35 years as a STYLITE.

SISYPHUS
In Greek mythology, because he was disrespectful to Zeus, Sisyphus, king of Corinth, was condemned to keep pushing a heavy rock up a steep hill forever, since as soon as it reached the top, it rolled down again.

SOPHOCLES (c496-?406 BC)

Greek dramatist, famous for his tragedies. He wrote over 120 plays, of which seven survive, along with numerous fragments of his other works.

STYLITES

Holy men who lived atop columns, they were also known as pillar saints, from the Greek stylos, pillar.

TESSERAE (Singular: tessera)

Small pieces of glass, stone, marble, etc, used to create mosaics.

THEODORA (c497-548)

Influential and powerful wife of JUSTINIAN I. It has been alleged she had formerly been an actress and a prostitute. A woman of strong character, when the NIKA RIOTS broke out in Constantinople in 532, Theodora is said to have urged JUSTINIAN I to remain in the city, thus saving the imperial throne.

TUNICA

Tunic-like undergarment.

ZEUXIPPOS

Thracian deity whose name combined Zeus and Hippos (Greek: horse).

To receive a free catalog of Poisoned Pen Press titles, please contact us in one of the following ways:

Phone: 1-800-421-3976
Facsimile: 1-480-949-1707
Email: info@poisonedpenpress.com
Website: www.poisonedpenpress.com

Poisoned Pen Press
6962 E. First Ave. Ste. 103
Scottsdale, AZ 85251